In
Praise Of The
Bees

KRISTIN GLEESON

An Tig Beag Press

Published by An Tig Beag Press

Text Copyright 2015 © Kristin Gleeson

Other works by Kristin Gleeson

CELTIC KNOT SERIES:

Selkie Dreams

Along the Far Shores

Raven Brought the Light

A Treasure Beyond Worth (novella)

RENAISSANCE SOJOURNER SERIES

(With Moonyeen Blakey)

A Trick of Fate (novella)

The Imp of Eye

NON FICTION

Anahareo, A Wilderness Spirit

ISBN: 978-0-9931567-6-2

"Be Thou My Vision" from *Early Irish Lyrics* by Gerard Murphy

Cover image St Gobnait by Harry Clarke Courtesy of Rakow Research Library, Corning Museum of Glass

In Praise of the

Cover design: JDSmith Dessign

To the people of Ballyvourney.

Irish Bee Law:
Fer in-étet saithe nadbi lais co finnathar maigin i suidigetar: trian do thír frisa suidigetar, trian do fiur doda-etet, trian do lestur oa n-élat bes bunadach doib.

The man who follows a swarm which is not his and who finds the place where they settle: a third [goes] to the holding where they settle, a third to the man who tracks them, a third to [the owner of] the hive from which they escape and which is their original home.
(Bechbretha: An Old Irish Law Tract on Beekeeping ed. by Fergus Kelly and Thomas Charles Edwards)

MUMU, IRELAND 590 A.D.
CHAPTER ONE

A body lies bleeding and beaten beyond all recognition, in the shadow of An Dhá Chích Danann, mountains that rise out of the earth full and engorged as any woman's paps, to provide comfort, succour and even hope.

A farmer and his son discover the body as they lumber along in their cart, the old capall that pulls it, snorting at the scent of blood. These two men are on the track that many follow to lay their prayers in the lap of the mountains, the heart of the mother goddess Anu. The two stop and the son climbs down from the cart. The father is no longer nimble enough for such a scramble among the stumpy trees, rocks and bog that mark this area. The son follows the blood that stains the rush and the golden furze flowers, and finally discovers the body partially submerged in a bog. He can tell only that it is a person and, on closer inspection, that the person lives, because a heart still beats and small breaths are expelled into the cool morning air.

The son braces himself on the firmer part of the ground. He reaches carefully and drags the body from the ditch and hoists it onto his back. Each movement elicits a deep groan of pain from the body and it echoes along the valley. The father calls out to him from the cart and the son answers with brief words of assurance. He moves forward slowly, the water from the soaked body streaming down his back. Eventually, he makes it to the cart, and with his father's assistance, lays the body inside the cart, taking care for the lolling head and the limbs that are so obviously broken. They can see now it is a woman, but beyond that they have no clear impression about her identity or status. The cloth of her dress, what is left untorn and clear of blood, is fine enough. Her hair, too tangled and matted with clots to detect any remarkable colour, has lost its covering, if there was one. There are no signs of shoes and her feet are filthy with peat mud, as if she'd walked the length of the province of Mumu.

They miss the forefinger with its carefully shaped nail in its perfect oval bed. If they hadn't missed it, would they have understood its meaning?

The farmer and son decide to take her to Máthair Gobnait, though they follow nothing of the new ways. They know that not only she is a healer; she can shape metal with fire. She is the holy woman of the bees and it is from her bees she gets the honey that provides her healing tool. Her bees are her mouthpiece to her God, humming His praises.

~

She first hears Máthair Gobnait's voice, low and melodious, instructing the farmer and his son. 'Lift her carefully, now. Siúr Feidelm, fetch hot water and cloths.'

She recalls little of being lifted from the cart and placed on the hastily created pallet, because the pain causes a blackness to engulf her from the moment they touch her limbs. It is a blackness she welcomes, a release from all that she doesn't want to understand or experience. When she wakes again, night has fallen, and the light of a tallow candle hovers over her and a cool, dry hand is on her head. There is comfort there and it quietens the fear that rises in her and makes her flail her arms to beat away her terror.

'*Máthair,*' she says, for who but her mother would lay a hand on her with such care?

'Hush, child, don't try to speak,' comes the reply.

The woman's tones are soothing, but she knows now this woman isn't her mother and she wants to cry. She needs to release this fear that builds inside her. She tries instead to think of a melody that would fit a voice that is like sunshine. The melody she hears dips low and then rises slowly to a soaring peak, like the mountains so dear to her, the warm mounds of her mother. Oh Mother, come to me now. Hear my pleas. The words echo over and over until it becomes many voices in her head.

When the music comes again it is a single voice, a voice unfamiliar, yet so pure. Tears come to her eyes and she convinces herself it is the voice's beauty that brings them. She has drifted into a different world. A world in which she is safe. But still her fears awake. A light, bright and luminous, shines above her, radiating outwards. She tries to raise her arm to reach out to it, but pain, white and searing, keeps it immobile.

'Rest,' the voice says. 'Don't stir yourself.'

She tries to envelop herself in the warmth and security of the voice and bathes in the light, but all too soon the darkness takes her again.

~

She can hear murmurs, like the hum of bees, their tones low, vibrant and repetitive. The fear is still there, but becomes quieter under the soothing sounds, so she opens her eyes. Sunlight greets her, canted rays that come through the doorway. Against its radiance she can pick out numerous shapes sitting at a table. There are eight of them, murmuring with their heads bowed, lips moving and hands clasped. Fragrant odours of seasoned food wend their way to her, and for a moment, she thinks she too can eat, until her eyes close under the weight of her lids.

A bell wakes her the next time; a steady ringing that falls silent when its count is finished. From a distance, she can hear the voice again. The notes soar high, and the voice opens up rich and full like a great eagle stretching its wings. She opens her eyes and sees only the timber beams above, each end marked with a cross. She turns her head and notes the benches and stools near the large centre hearth where a fire burns. A stout woman sits on one of the stools, stirring a pot hanging over the fire. The room is warm and comforting, but still the fear creeps up again.

When she opens her eyes again, a tall woman is standing over her. Alarm and fear take her all at once. A small moan escapes her.

'Máthair Ab, she stirs,' the woman says. The woman lays the back of her hand on her head for a moment. 'The fever, has abated, *buíochas le Dia*.' A woman draws up beside her, touches her fingers to her head, chest and to both shoulders.

'That's good news, Siúr Feidelm.' It is the woman with the low melodious voice. The woman turns and addresses her. 'I am Máthair Gobnait, abbess here. I bid you welcome to our house. We've feared for your recovery many days now.'

She bites her lip to stop its trembling and stares into Máthair Gobnait's kind face. The face is neither young nor old and the head is covered with a dark grey linen cloth which matches the colour of the belted wool gown.

'Many days?' she says, her voice barely a whisper. She keeps her eyes fixed on Máthair Gobnait's face, drawing assurance from the gentleness she sees there. 'I've been here that long?'

'You have. You were badly injured when you first came; your body broken in several places and weak from losing so much blood from stab wounds.'

She inhales sharply and fights the fear that is swallowing her voice and taking her breath. She moistens her lips countless times before she manages to get out the small phrase. 'Who did it?'

'We don't know. We were hoping you might shed light on that.'

She shuts her eyes but can only feel her heart beating faster than before. She cannot bear to think what she would find in the recesses of her mind and opens her eyes again quickly. Looking back into Máthair Gobnait's face she can quieten enough of her fear to breathe. She shakes her head. 'Nothing,' she utters hoarsely.

'May we know your name, then child?'

'My name?' She allows herself to think a moment. A name could be harmless and perhaps make her more secure, but her racing heart tells her differently. Her family, their allegiance and rank, could all be revealed in her name. She shakes her head again.

'Don't worry over that,' the tall woman says. Her face is exceedingly plain, but the eyes are full of compassion. She too wears a grey veil, leather belt and dark gown. 'You have had a severe blow to the head, and more than likely it causes your lack of memory.' She gives her arm a gentle pat. 'It will return in time, along with your health, I'm certain.'

'Until then, we must call you something,' says Máthair Gobnait. 'Áine, I think. May your radiance shine forth.'

'A name from the Bible?' A small gaunt woman comes up beside Máthair Gobnait. Her fingers, skeletal and long, are clasped at her breast, as if in prayer. The tone of her words carries a hint of criticism.

'This lost sheep has been brought into our fold, now. We must act as her shepherd and bring her back to her health and then to her flock.' Máthair Gobnait's tone carries no reprimand, but it is firm. 'Siúr Feidelm, maybe something nourishing would go down well?'

'Of course. And later I'll apply a poultice of *Lus na gCnámh mBriste* and a brew honey to knit her bones,' says the tall plain woman, who she now knows is Siúr Feidelm.

Máthair Gobnait smiles. 'Honey is always welcome. As for the rest of us, we can return to our tasks. The day is well under way.'

They depart and she closes her eyes, hearing only a swish of a hem brushing against a post and a sigh of a breath. She savours the solitude and, just for a moment, her tension and fear seep out of her.

What seems only moments later, Siúr Feidelm returns with a steaming bowl and wooden mug that she sets down on the ground. She draws up a small stool beside the pallet. Áine (for she must think of herself with some name) makes an effort to raise her head. The tension has returned and some of the fear, but still she makes herself speak.

'What is this place?'

'Careful with your head.' Siúr Feidelm pushes a small bolster filled with straw carefully behind her head and gently lays her back on it. 'You are in the *Tech Mor* of Máthair Gobnait's community of *cailech*. You must have heard tell of her.'

'No. I know nothing.' Her voice is a little stronger and she takes courage from its strength.

Siúr Feidelm holds the small wooden mug to her mouth and helps her take some sips. The pungent smell of garlic and celery coming from the bowl overpowers the odours in the mug. The taste is pleasant but she finds it difficult to take much.

'No, of course,' says Siúr Feidelm. 'You wouldn't have heard of Máthair Ab if you don't know your own self.' She sits back a little. 'She came from the north to Uisneach, the place of the deer, by Gort na Tiobratán, here in Boirneach, about five summers ago, looking for the right signs. And they were here, the nine white deer, and she knew then she'd found what she sought.'

'She saw nine white deer?'

'Yes.'

Áine looks around her again, seeking that unique quality that would draw nine white deer. Nine, it would have to be that number. It is a number she knows is sacred, though how she knows is a mystery. This woman, Máthair Gobnait, is another mystery and Áine isn't certain whether to be fearful or assured. 'Nine deer and all of them white?' she asks softly.

Siúr Feidelm nods. 'Precisely nine.'

'And what was she to do when she saw these nine white deer?'

'What she has done. Begin a community and go among the people offering her help and kindness, in the name of God.'

Áine nods though she cannot imagine what links nine deer and the urge to begin a community of women to help people of a *tuath*. 'Don't the nobles or even the local king look after the needs well enough?' She breathes heavily after speaking so long, as much from the tension that still grips her as the effort it takes to speak.

'The king and the lords do their share, but it's not always enough. The weather and the soil are unforgiving. Máthair Ab gives them food when they need it and offers counsel if asked when there is some dispute, but mostly she tends to the sick and dying. Many come to her with all manner of ailments. I help her with the healing.'

'And you've been with her since she came?'

'I came to her the summer following her arrival. I asked my father to let me, so that I might learn her healing arts and her holy ways.'

'Her holy ways?' Something compels Áine to follow this line of discussion, though she is almost afraid to hear the answers. She is just as likely to be in danger from a holy person as anyone else, she tells herself. That she can identify no specific danger does little to reassure the feelings that constantly grip her.

Siúr Feidelm looks at her in surprise. 'She's a *cailech*, a woman of God who's taken the veil. She is the abbess here, as she mentioned.'

'Taken a veil for a god? What god?'

'The Lord God. Are you not familiar with those who follow Christ?'

She tests the thought for a moment, feels nothing except the fear that simmers, ready to rise at the least cause. 'I have no idea,' she whispers.

Siúr Feidelm considers the statement while she continues to spoon the mixture into Áine's mouth. Áine can see now how young she is. Her skill with herbs is manifest in the strength and potency of the brew she sips, but her smooth trim cheeks show no sign of weather or age.

'Perhaps you are a Christian, perhaps not, but you'll find Máthair Ab is a good, compassionate woman.'

Áine's mind acknowledges this statement. 'She's shown me nothing but kindness and me a stranger with no memory of my origins. I could be her enemy.'

'She has no enemies.' The young woman's words are guileless and spoken with alarming sincerity.

Áine wonders at this statement but says nothing, so as not to offend her. She shifts the subject. 'Do you sing in your worship?'

'You heard us?' Siúr Feidelm's face brightens.

Áine smiles weakly and manages a calm answer. 'I did. There was one particular piece, sung so beautifully by a lone woman. Who composed it?'

'Siúr Sodelb, the one who sang it. She is wonderfully talented.'

'Siúr Sodelb?' She rolls the name around in her mind and likes the ring it has. 'She is talented.'

'You are a musician?'

Áine looks at her. 'You think I might be?' Her voice catches at the thought that a fragment of her identity might have so easily been uncovered. Was she ready to know this much even?

'Perhaps. The pleasure you just expressed might suggest it. Máthair Ab felt you had some love for music when she saw the only remaining nail on your fingers was curved. The mark of a harper.'

Áine glances down at her hand. It is swathed in bandages, no nail or finger in sight. She thinks again about how she came to be this way and the tension returns.

Siúr Feidelm places a hand over the bandages. 'No, she had to trim the nail in the end, for fear you might harm yourself. You were delirious.'

'Did I say anything in my delirium?' She tenses even more, wondering if Máthair Gobnait knows more about her than she indicated.

'You must ask Máthair Ab. She tended you. Set your bones, bathed and packed your wounds with honey and herbs. And she prayed.'

She suddenly becomes aware of the splints and bandages that envelop her legs, arms and torso. Is there any place uncovered? Any part of her that is whole, undamaged? A roaring erupts in her head.

~

The light still shines through the doorway though the angle has shifted. This time she examines the rafters above her, picks out the sturdy wooden beams that radiate from the centre pole. Their pungent odour speaks of their newness, as does the sweet freshness of the tightly bound thatch laid on them. The walls are stone, carefully laid and chinked against the biting winds that must come to a place named for its rocky hills, rather than the wattle that might be expected of a community of no wealth. But, she reminds herself, this is a holy community, one whose leader is undoubtedly of some consequence if she can command such a place. Her speech and manner reinforce this impression. It is another piece of knowledge for which she has no source or explanation. She sighs.

'You are with us again.' Máthair Gobnait appears at her side and gazes down at her. Áine can see her clearly this time. The soft grey eyes, the straight nose, almost too long, and the firm lips now pulled back in a smile. A small brown curl escaping the dark veil teases her forehead. But there is something more that draws her to this woman, something in her countenance that shines out. A knowing. That is all she can identify, when she considers it carefully, later. How or what it was she knows, Áine cannot say. She can only feel it reaching out to her, making her in turns comforted and uneasy.

Áine tries to smile. 'I am awake.'

'We mustn't rush the healing.'

Áine isn't certain that the words are directed at her or Máthair Gobnait herself.

She decides to venture a question. 'How long have I been here?'

'The moon has waxed and waned since the farmer brought you to us.'

'How can that be?' It terrifies her how ill she's been for such a length of time to have passed unnoticed.

'Yes, it's over halfway to midsummer and you were brought to us just after Bealtaine.'

Bealtaine. The celebrations for summer beginning and now summer is half over. She forces herself to ask more about her arrival. 'I was told a farmer and his son brought me here. They had no idea who I am?'

'I'm afraid not. Word has spread in Boirneach about your attack, but none have claimed any knowledge of you or who you might be. I am reluctant to make inquiries further afield among other tuath of the Érann and the Eóganacht just yet, until I can be more certain you are in no danger of further harm.'

The words both reassure and frighten her. That this woman had a care to her wellbeing is a comfort but the confirmation of the danger fights that assurance. 'You feel I am still in danger?' She is unable to keep the shake from her voice.

'There is no cause for worry.' Máthair Gobnait lays a hand on her cheek. It feels cool and dry against her and she closes her eyes a moment against its calming touch.

'I would only take a more cautious approach,' says Máthair Gobnait. 'There is no clear understanding of why you were so sorely injured. It might be nothing more than a random assault for your belongings.'

Something inside her denies that benign explanation, though she tries to accept it as the most probable. 'Whatever the cause might be it appears I am not from this tuath.'

'No.'

'And nowhere else reports a missing daughter or wife?'

'I am afraid not.' Her replies are very matter of fact, her voice firm. Is it the deep, rich quality of it that makes the dreadful answers much more bearable? 'You must not despair. It is early days yet and for now, you have a place here with us while you recover.'

Áine tests these words and is able to feel some calm. That this woman has taken her in and shown her nothing but kindness is some evidence that she is in a safe place. Her words are as sincere as she can make them. 'And I am so grateful for all you've done for me. I can only hope that someday I might repay all this kindness.'

'I do only what the Lord himself would do.' Máthair Gobnait gives a mischievous twinkle. 'Or any other person who has a stranger cross his threshold.'

'Despite what you say, you are a woman of true good nature and your lord is fortunate to have such person in his tuath.'

'My lord is Lord of all. The Christian Lord.'

'How many women are there here in this community?'

Máthair Gobnait tilts her head slightly. 'There are eight here living at the moment. Nine including you. Not all are cailecha.'

'Nine women here, the same number as the deer?'

She smiles at Áine, accepting it as a joke, though Áine isn't certain she means it as such. 'Yes, and just as beautiful in their own way. There are the servants too, and the bishop's client workers, like the wives of the ócaire and bothach, who help out from time to time and share with us their rents. We also have people who come for mass and for healing. Some of them help with tasks on occasion. At the moment we also have workmen constructing sheds and sleeping huts staying with us. They built this Tech Mor last summer and have returned to complete more sleeping quarters and another shed.'

Áine is taken aback at the number of people that are attached to this community in one way or another. Thinking about such numbers makes her shrink physically, as withdrawing into her sheepskin coverlet will allow her to disappear. That some of these people are men and they're working in close proximity creates further alarm. Her eyes sweep the room, looking for anything that might contradict this fear and this time she notes the newly fashioned wooden benches around the central hearth. Along the wall to the side, near the door are large water vats, and next to them leans the board that serves as a dining table. Her pallet is near enough to the fire to get some benefit from it, but not too much to feel uncomfortable. On the other side of the fire she can see Siúr Feidelm working quietly on a stool with a young girl, sorting and cutting vegetables that are then deposited in an iron pot, ready for the fire.

'You don't sleep in here?' The question pops out and for a moment she is glad to be distracted by a simple matter.

'We house guests here, if the need arises, but it serves all our other purposes, bar sleeping and worship. We have the oratory for the offices and weekly mass.'

She nods and thinks of the bells, the singing and the humming buzz that must have been praying. 'The bells?' She asks about them not because she doesn't realize they are used in their worship in some ways, but because she wants to hear more about them. There is something about their regularity and the orderly manner of their ringing that draws her, though she could not say why.

'We attend the oratory several times a day to offer our prayers and praise to God,' Máthair Gobnait says. 'The bell calls us there for each office.'

She thinks of the women's ritual, pictures them rising from their tasks or their beds at the sound of the bell, processing to the oratory to sing and pray in unison. She feels a connection to that idea and reaches out for it, tries to make it grow into a real memory, but does not succeed. Frustrated, she closes her eyes a moment. She thinks of a different tactic.

'How do you worship? What do you pray?'

'You have heard enough from me for now. There is no need to learn everything again all at once.' Máthair Gobnait pats her arm lightly. 'Rest now. I'll ask Siúr Feidelm to give you more broth. That will do you more good at this moment than any words.'

Áine watches Máthair Gobnait rise and make her way out the door, her strides efficient but unhurried. She speaks softly to Siúr Feidelm before she leaves and disappears into the light that pours through the opening. Áine lays back a moment and then lifts up her bandaged arms. She examines the cloth that is wrapped around her forearms, hands and fingers and holds varying splints in position. All of her right leg and the lower half of her right are also strapped to supports. She tries to ease herself on the pallet and the pain shoots from all directions, including her side and chest. At this moment the wretchedness of her condition becomes truly apparent. She is helpless. She can rely on neither her body nor her mind. There is nothing she can do to defend herself from anyone that might still want to cause her harm, here, wherever they might be. For the present she can only hope and trust that Máthair Gobnait and her community can keep her safe while she heals.

CHAPTER TWO

More days than Áine wishes pass before she is even able to sit up. In that time she hears the bell ring at regular intervals, a task she learns is the responsibility of thin, stern Siúr Ethne. After the bell finishes, Áine imagines herself a cailech looking up from her task, or if she is asleep, rubbing her eyes and gathering her thoughts. She hears the soft fall of sandaled feet upon the ground that changes to a slapping when they cross the stone threshold of the oratory and she sees herself among them as they file in. Inside the oratory, in the silence that follows, she pictures Máthair Gobnait lighting a special beeswax candle, for she is certain she can smell its pungent grease even lying on her pallet in the Tech Mor.

The candle is lit, and in her mind the *cailecha* take a moment to prepare their voices and wait for the signal to begin. It is then she closes her eyes and really feels that she is there. She loses herself in the soothing sounds of their prayer, the songs and even the silent contemplation that follows. Often there is a murmur of words. It is a single voice that tells the story from a holy work she learns only later is the Gospel, the sayings of the Christ they follow and an account of his life.

Siúr Sodelb's voice is easy to pick out from the others, it is so pure and rich. When Siúr Sodelb sings on her own, it seems as if Áine has left this world and entered another.

It lifts her up, so that she can almost feel her whole body lighten and rise upwards, following the music.

Rop tú mo baile, A Choimdiu cride:
Ní ní nech aile acht Rí secht nime.
Rop tú mo scrútain I llos 's I n-iadche;
Rop tú ad-chëar im chotlud caidche.
Rop tú mo labra, rop tú mo thuicsiu;
Rop tussu damsa, rob misse duitsiu.

Be thou my vision, beloved Lord:
None other is aught but the King of the seven heavens
Be thou my meditation by day and night;
May it be thou that I behold forever in my sleep.
Be thou my speech, be thou my understanding;
Be thou for me; may I be for thee.

The song invokes a union of spirit of the highest and most divine intensity. But the voice is what made its most perfect message clear. She loses herself in that voice, imagining the possessor as the most perfect of beings; a goddess come here for the privileged to bear witness to.

She sees Siúr Sodelb at her place with the other women around the large wooden board taken from against the wall for mealtimes to rest on the woven straw support placed there. There is no need for anyone to point her out, she knows Siúr Sodelb can only be the woman with the flawless nose, unblemished skin and polished golden hair.

The other women take on names and distinctive features, including Siúr Mugain's broad frame and interest in all things agricultural that mark her as the daughter of a *bóaire,* and the cheerful, round faced Siúr Sadhbh who takes great care over the girls who do the milking and churning. It is Máthair Gobnait and Siúr Feidelm, who tend her wounds, she comes to know most, since it is they who feed her and occasionally keep her company. About Máthair Gobnait's background she can discover little more than she already knows, and it is not clear what *tuath* she came from or who her kin are.

It is Siúr Feidelm who tells what is known when Áine finds it in her to ask one morning. 'When she arrived Epscop Ábán granted her the land and encouraged her in her work. He has a monastery not far from here.' Siúr Feidelm gestures around her. 'He had this built for her, to enable her to do even greater works here, among our people.'

'He must think well of her then, this holy man.' Something in her stirs. Is it admiration or something deeper that a woman could compel so much from men in authority without the backing of her family? She has no idea.

'He does, as do the other bishops. It isn't always the case, you know. But Máthair Ab is a pure woman and much respected by the people.'

Áine has no doubt that Siúr Feidelm speaks the truth. Her words are always exact and precise in meaning, but Áine has also learned Siúr Feidelm is a local woman, one of too many daughters of a minor noblemen. But Siúr Feidelm is more than content with her lot. In fact Áine can see she thrives here, where she is free to study and brew her herbs, in addition to the tasks of supervising the cooking and the vegetable garden. The vegetable garden especially seems to provide more opportunities for close study and observation, a fact that becomes evident a day or so after her conversation about Máthair Gobnait when Siúr Feidelm offers up a garden slug for her inspection. It is thick and striped.

'Have you ever seen such odd markings?'

Áine looks down at the dark slug. 'In truth I can't say that I have.'

Siúr Feidelm peers at it closely, poking it a little with her nail. In response it squirms and forms a tighter ball. She remarks on its colour and watches it, probing it curiously with her finger. Áine finds herself smiling at Siúr Feidelm's enthusiasm and for a moment feels lighter. Who else would notice variations in a creature that eats gardens and marvel at it?

Siúr Feidelm takes her leave. She says she will not kill the slug, only place it as far from the garden as possible. Such thoughtfulness warms Áine and she feels for the first time safe and secure.

~

When she is able to sit up with a plumped straw-filled bolster to support her, the pain it gives her side is little compared to the sense of satisfaction she feels at her progress. Though she must still submit to the indignity of Siúr Feidelm or Máthair Gobnait feeding, washing her and assisting her eliminations, as well as applying honey to her wounds, she is left unattended and is free to observe more of her surroundings.

It is then, too, that others are let loose upon her, or at least given more free access to the *Tech Mor*. Siúr Ethne, her work and personal vocation being clearly centred on keeping things clean and orderly, wields her mighty broom, cloth and bucket of water like an avenger as soon as Máthair Gobnait gives her permission.

Siúr Ethne's face and features defy any attempts to mark her age. Her sallow colouring, the skin stretched tight across the bones of her face, suggests someone who is not in her first youth. Her hair, what little pokes out from her covering, is limp and persuading itself to grey. She is not given to conversation and Áine is too intimidated at first to do anything more than hope she remains unnoticed.

Eventually Áine works up enough courage to ask a question that will not leave her mind. 'Have you been here with Gobnait long?'

For a moment Siúr Ethne stops her relentless scrubbing of the deal board propped against the wall. The grain on it is well risen under her effort and all the water she has lavished upon it. 'I was one of Máthair Ab's first true acolytes.' She lays great emphasis on the word 'mother' as if to chastise Áine for using only her given name.

Áine cannot help but note her choice of the word 'true' and makes herself remark upon it.

'I am here only for the service and glory of the Lord,' Siúr Ethne replies. She takes up her cloth and resumes her work, as if to demonstrate how she feels 'service' should be interpreted.

The set of Siúr Ethne's mouth and her posture make plain her refusal to say anything more, so Áine settles back and watches her work. Once Siúr Ethne finishes scrubbing the table and the long benches, she removes the rushes that are strewn on the floor and replaces them with fresh ones, then cleans away all trace of cobwebs with her broom from every rafter and beam, imaginary or otherwise. Áine is glad that Siúr Ethne's efforts raise little dust, since she can only guess what might happen if stray dirt should fall on Áine or make her cough. Despite that, Áine is still exhausted at the end of Siúr Ethne's cleaning spree, if only from watching her expend such a great amount of energy.

She sleeps again and does not wake until she feels something heavy pressing on her chest, taking her breath. She flails her arms in an attempt to remove her attacker and feels her bandaged hand make contact, though she refuses to open her eyes. A howl pierces the air and she dares to look but can see only the roof above her. She scans the room carefully, panting.

'Méone, be careful.' Máthair Gobnait draws alongside of Áine, a large bundle of ginger fur in her arms. 'I'm so sorry, Áine. He has discovered the *Tech Mor* is a good place for food, hunted or otherwise.' She glances across where Siúr Feidelm and others are preparing a meal. 'I've kept him from the *Tech Mor* up to now, in case he should disturb you or your dressings. But he is a wily old thing, and though he is large enough, he can be quick and agile when he wants and slip into the most unlikely places.'

Áine gives her a weak smile, and tries to bring her breathing back to an even pace. 'No, it is my mistake. I was dreaming and felt only his weight.'

Máthair Gobnait sets the cat down and strokes his back. A loud purring answers her actions. Áine holds out her bandaged hand and murmurs soothing words to the cat. Méone moves towards her, tentatively at first, and sniffs a moment until he decides he will permit further attention and collapses beside her in a large heap.

'His name is Méone? Surely such a sizeable cat cannot have a little meow.'

'He has certainly outgrown that name. There is nothing little about the way he meows.' She speaks with affection and it is obvious that she forgives any of his transgressions. Áine can understand why. Beside her, he purrs contently, his paws stuffed underneath him, his eyes slowly closing. She pets the cat again and the cat closes his eyes and pushes his head against her bandaged hand.

Máthair Gobnait smiles. 'He loves attention and will do anything for it.'

Áine attempts another pat of the cat. 'Is it possible for my bandages to be removed soon?' She looks up carefully under the curtain of her hair at Máthair Gobnait, her breath held.

'I discussed this with Siúr Feidelm and we thought we could take off the splints and rewrap the dressings to allow your fingers more freedom. They should be healed well enough by now, but you will find them stiff at first.'

Áine tries to move her fingers, testing each one for strength and agility. There is little pain, for which she's grateful, but the splints are too restrictive to get any clear sense of their condition.

'I would count it a great accomplishment if I could feed myself.'

'And it would be.' Máthair Gobnait pats her arm. 'Now that you're well on the road to recovery you will find patience your greatest challenge. We must give the healing all the time it needs.' She looks down at Méone. 'Meanwhile, we'll see that you aren't in want of company or amusement.' She rises and moves towards the door, turning once to give Áine a smile before she vanishes outside.

Áine glances down at Méone. His eyes are fully closed, his body heavy against her. It is a reassuring feeling and she tries to recall the last time she felt this secure and comforted. 'You are good to remain behind on such a summer's day,' she tells the cat. 'I'm sure there is much you would rather be doing outside.' Méone opens his eyes and looks up, his green eyes wide and unblinking. A moment later he closes them once again. After a while a gentle snore rises up.

~

Máthair Gobnait holds to her promise and Áine is able to cradle her bowl and spoon porridge into her mouth the next morning while the rest sit at the table to break their fast. Máthair Gobnait leads the blessing and the women reach for their share of porridge and bread. From her position propped on her pallet, Áine can see the women who have assembled. There are only a few now that aren't familiar. The *cailecha* wear their familiar grey garb over a linen *léine*, drawn in at the waist with a leather belt and the grey veil covering their hair. One of the workers has a small child in her lap. She can see even from her pallet the frayed edges of the woman's sleeves and the shabby quality *léine* that pokes out from under it that suggest she might even be a slave. Beside her, Siúr Mugain spoons more porridge from the large bowl placed in the table's centre into the poor woman's vessel. The woman nods her silent thanks, dips in her spoon and attempts to feed her child, but the child will have none of it.

Siúr Mugain opens her copious arms. 'Here, let me try. My own little brothers were fussy when eating first thing in the morning.' The child smiles at Siúr Mugain and moves over to her waiting lap.

'How are the wheat and oat fields, Siúr Mugain?' asks Máthair Gobnait. 'I haven't had the time to walk them lately. The bees have kept me so busy.'

'The grain is swelling nicely and is nearly as tall as my waist already,' Siúr Mugain answers. 'Please God we'll get only a little rain this month coming.'

'Please God we'll only get a little the next month after. The cattle have nearly grazed the top field, and in a few days I'll need to move them to the field by the river. It's only now, after drying up, enough to bear the cattle.' It is Siúr Sadhbh who has spoken, the sister who tends the livestock. Throughout this exchange Siúr Ethne casts disdainful looks at the two women while she stirs her spoon around her porridge, never once bringing it to her mouth.

'Would you like some honey for that?' Máthair Gobnait asks Siúr Ethne. Her back is to Áine but the soft note of pleading is distinct.

Siúr Ethne looks over at her, startled. 'No, thank you, Máthair Ab. I prefer not to adorn my food in any way.'

'Honey is from the bees, that the Lord has seen fit to bless us with. It has many gifts and it would do the Lord a disservice if we didn't honour these gifts by making use of them.'

Siúr Ethne gives a weak smile. 'I'm sorry. It's not that I wouldn't honour the gift, but that I'm unworthy of it.'

The sigh Máthair Gobnait emits is barely detectable. Siúr Mugain shakes her head and Siúr Sadhbh frowns. It is then Áine sees Siúr Sodelb's golden head, the covering slipped back. Siúr Sodelb reaches out and places her slim white hand over Siúr Ethne's, but Siúr Ethne withdraws her own hand and places it in her lap.

Unobserved, and from the safety of her pallet, Áine contemplates these women, each distinct in their approach to the community, but each believing something good, something holy is at work here. She cannot dispute Máthair Gobnait's otherworldly qualities, or the sacred air that permeates this place. Some would ascribe this quality to the nearby ancient holy well that has drawn countless through the ages.

It's a question that begins to occupy her while she sits alone on her pallet and the women are busy serving the community, Máthair Gobnait and God. It becomes increasingly clear to her that each one has a place, an idea of themselves in this sheltered community that provides welcome to likeminded souls. How does she, injured, with no name, no memory of who she is, figure in such a place? Though her body is knitting slowly, her mind is still a blank. Her memory, if restored, might give her a place, but is it one that is no longer safe? It's a question she can only answer with her instinct and the answer is not comforting.

'You look troubled.'

She looks up and sees Máthair Gobnait standing before her holding a spindle whorl and a sack.

'I think it's time you had a taste of fresh air and sunshine.'

She feels a sense of alarm. 'I-I'm not sure I'm ready for that.'

'Nonsense. You are, of course.'

Áine bites her lip. 'I don't know. Moving me too far or too soon may ruin all your efforts.'

Máthair Gobnait kneels down beside her. The copper cross that she has fashioned hangs from a leather thong down her chest and glints in the firelight. 'You will be fine, I assure you. We will take every care moving you.' She takes Áine's right hand. 'All will be well. I will be there to look out for you.'

Áine looks into Máthair Gobnait's face and can see nothing but kindness there. It's a face to trust, though Áine knows she hasn't the luxury of choosing otherwise. 'You've been so very kind to me. I'm grateful you took me in.'

'We are glad to have you here and you're welcome to stay with us until your health is recovered and you feel able to leave.'

Where she would go is not mentioned, nor is the thought that it might not be safe to leave with no notion of who she is, or where she is from. That she might never have anywhere to go. The idea makes her uneasy, but there is no fear attached to it, nothing so pungent and real that makes her heart race, as the notion of leaving here does.

'There is still no word of your identity, but you mustn't feel discouraged. These things take time. Soon enough we'll know who you are.' She gives Áine a piercing look. No words are needed. Áine shakes her head. She's recalled nothing more about her identity.

'What will I do?' she whispers to Máthair Gobnait. She is overcome with a sense of helplessness.

'For now you need to rest and recover.' Máthair Gobnait hands her the spindle whorl and the sack. 'But there's no harm in helping out in small ways. And it will keep your fingers occupied and perhaps a bit of your mind too.'

Áine takes the sack and spindle. Inside the sack she finds a large hank of wool.

'You know how to spin the wool?'

She looks at the wooden spindle for a moment, wondering. Was something as simple as this part of her memory? Had she spun wool? 'I don't know. I'll try.'

'I'm sure you do. It's not difficult.' Máthair Gobnait reaches over, takes the spindle and a clump of wool and gives a brief demonstration. It looks easy in her deft strong fingers. She hands it back to Áine and rises. 'When Siúr Mugain and Siúr Sadhbh are done with the morning chores, I'll get them to carry you outside. You'll see better out there.'

Áine watches Máthair Gobnait leave, the spindle and hank of wool in her lap. She looks down. Somehow, without Máthair Gobnait by her side, spinning wool seems an impossible task, one that would test too much of what she feels unprepared to examine. She closes her eyes. Her fingers, still stiff and awkward, enfold the spindle. Touching its surface, polished smooth from years of use, somehow offers comfort. Her other hand reaches for the soft dark wool. Even now, she can smell faint traces of lanolin.

Her eyes still closed, she takes up the thread of wool in the hank, twisting and twirling it in her hand, shaping the clump into a soft long thread. She sighs, opens her eyes and takes up the spindle and lets it dangle as she'd seen Máthair Gobnait do. After a few moments it's all a tangle, the spindle whirling too quickly, the spokes catching on the wool that soon becomes lumpy. She drops it back onto her lap and resists the urge to hurl it all across the room. Was it her fingers, still too stiff to handle spinning, or was it something deeper, that even the most basic of women's tasks was lost to her with everything else? She looks at the spindle, the hank of wool, searching for something familiar. There is nothing.

CHAPTER THREE

The hives are everywhere. Each *beachair,* lovingly formed from sedge grass and bound by long ropes of split briar to form a cone shape, sits on a wooden platform that faces south. They line the western part of the wall that encloses the *faithche,* the buildings and yard that comprise the religious community. There must have been twenty *beachair* in all. Sitting in the propped farm cart, the sun shining strongly on her, Áine finds a small bit of contentment watching the bees fly off and return, drunken on fruits like some wayward alemaker. Around her, she can see the women at their tasks and men at their construction, busy like the bees at their own husbandry. She feels safe. The safety is hard won. She has expelled much effort to remain calm enough to accept their ministrations as they moved her to this cart, out in the open, exposed. It is only now, with the sun nearly above her, that she is able to breathe evenly and let herself take in the benign activity around her.

Áine sees Máthair Gobnait among the *beachair,* talking to the bees and checking that they are feeding. Through these actions Máthair Gobnait manifests her love of these creatures. Méone sits near her, bathing in the warm sun, studiously cleaning his paws. Máthair Gobnait wears an extra linen veil around her head and draped loosely over her back. Her hands are clad in leather gloves. At this moment her work absorbs her entirely and Áine can feel some envy for her, and even perhaps for the bees that they receive such attention. She reminds herself how much she's benefitted from their work and to be grateful for it. She isn't the only one that receives their bounty. The bees also provide the wax for the candles at mass and special feast days. The wax is shaped into tablets on which Máthair Gobnait records the communities' produce. Their honey is used too for healing brews and balms on wounds, as well as food that is vital not only to the sisters but to the community at large. With all of that weighing in their favour Áine really cannot begrudge them their share of Máthair Gobnait's attention.

She closes her eyes and listens to the hum that fills the air, finding a certain joy in the sound that seems so energetic and happy. She allows the hum to resonate inside her and shape itself into something more. She finds that she's humming too, a bee filling herself with the nectar of music. It's only a small phrase, an idea, but it won't let her go and she can only hum it louder, with a little more definition, so it will bloom.

'That's lovely.'

The voice tells her it's Siúr Sodelb before she turns in the cart and sees her standing there. Áine had observed her in the garden earlier, helping Siúr Feidelm, her bright hair nearly white in the strong sun. She looks no more earthly outside, in the full light, than she does inside the *Tech Mor*.

Áine reddens, nervous that Siúr Sodelb has noticed her. 'Ah, no, no. It's only something that came in my head as I watched the bees.'

Perhaps it's because her eyes are so transparently blue they nearly reflect the sky that Áine is flustered. She finds she has to take a deep breath, shift her gaze to the field beyond to reclaim some calm. Siúr Sodelb comes around the cart to her side. Her movements are slow, hampered by the awkward gait made necessary by the left foot that is shorter and turned in slightly. Áine is overwhelmed by her disappointment. It doesn't seem possible or fair that such perfection could be marred in this manner.

'Your foot,' she says. 'It's damaged.' The words leap out of her like some frogs springing for freedom.

Tears glisten in Siúr Sodelb eyes and she glances downward. 'Yes. I was born this way.'

'I'm sorry. That was thoughtless of me. I imagine you have enough comments from others without my own unthinking words.'

Her eyes are clear now, but distant. 'It used to be so. Here, the women are familiar with the way I look. And there is little need for me to walk far.'

'I'm sorry.' The apology doesn't seem enough, especially since she cannot banish the thought that, if not for the deformity, someone so beautiful, of obviously good family, would have won many a heart, married well and attained great status. She says nothing but the words are there, hanging between them.

Siúr Sodelb chooses to address the thought nonetheless. 'I am content here, I assure you,' she says. 'These women are my family now, my home is here. I need nothing more.'

Áine is anxious to reassure her. 'I am certain of it. The beauty of your music shows the truth of your words.'

Siúr Sodelb smiles and it lights her face and eyes with a radiance that spills out from her. 'Music is my joy, my service to God. That's what Máthair Gobnait says.'

'Your singing, your compositions are truly a wonder. I've never heard anything like it before.'

'It's not mine in particular, it's what I've taken from others.'

'But surely such phrasing is unique.'

'Unique, no, but different from the old ways.'

'You know of the old ways of composition?'

'My father allowed me to study with a *file*. And then a *manach* at Epscop Ábán's monastery gave me some instruction when he came to say mass on occasion.'

Her words speak volumes about her background, her family and status. 'Your gift shines through nonetheless.'

'You seem to have some familiarity with the finer points too. You must have studied with someone, that piece you just hummed was lovely.'

Áine realizes the truth of her words. For some reason it hasn't occurred to her until now. It lay hidden inside her, rising to the surface only when Siúr Sodelb sang and now, with the bees inspiring her. She stops a moment, waiting for the panic to come, but it doesn't. She looks over at Máthair Gobnait bending down to one of the *beachair*, her lips moving.

'*An beacha.*'

'*An beacha?*'

'Yes, the bees, they gave me the piece. Just now.'

Siúr Sodelb nods. 'Ah, you're like Máthair Ab.'

'She composes music too?'

'No, she hears the bees speak to her. She sees God's love in them and all they give to us.'

Áine shakes her head. 'I'm nothing like Máthair Gobnait. I could never be like her.' She can't bring herself to call her 'Máthair Ab' yet. It seems too forward, too much like she belongs here.

Siúr Sodelb smiles. 'You've yet to know the extent of your goodness and kindness. The joy you find in music and our blessed bees is a firm beginning.'

Áine frowns a little at the reminder of her lack of memory. No, she has no idea what kind of person she is. She knows only that something in the music has captured her interest.

'I meant that this was a new opportunity for you, a blessing.' Though her manner is shy, her words are wise. 'You can choose the person you are, without anyone to think or remember differently. And music is a good starting point for that person you will be.'

'But I think it's always been a part of me.'

'I'm certain it has. And now you can shape it into something truly marvellous before God.'

The sentiment is reassuring but the last few words make her uneasy. What would that mean? 'I don't think I could do that.'

'There is nothing that can compare to it, I assure you.' Siúr Sodelb's voice takes on an energy and brilliance Áine remembers from her singing. 'The sounds, they fill you, take over your whole body and lift you up to the heavens. It's as though you are floating with the angels.'

Áine nods, though she can only remember the soothing sense of calm it gave her when she was so ill. And later, whenever she recalled it, she thought of the beauty. Still, these words stir something inside her. 'I think I would like to learn such a thing,' she says shyly.

Siúr Sodelb shines all her radiance on Áine. 'Would you hum that piece the bees inspired again, now?'

Áine repeats it and the next moment Siúr Sodelb gives voice to it, creating long full sounds to Áine's hummed phrase, her high voice containing a clarity any bell would envy. She sings it again and this time Áine joins her, her own voice's dark richness surprising her. They are well matched, her deeper tones adding an extra depth to Siúr Sodelb's. Siúr Sodelb laughs her pleasure and repeats the phrase, though this time she adds a variation. Áine follows it with· ease, its direction so natural it's as if the song hangs in the air waiting for them to voice it. The ease nearly frightens her for it's as though something else might be at work.

'The bees appreciate your music as much as I do.' Máthair Gobnait stands there beside them, the cat ambling up behind her. She takes off the gloves, works loose the woven linen veil and pulls it up from her face to halo her head. Rimmed in light, she looks ethereal. At the sound of Máthair Gobnait's voice Áine halts her singing, immediately self-conscious.

Siúr Sodelb eventually falls silent too and greets Máthair Gobnait. 'It's only right they should appreciate it since Áine took her inspiration from them.'

'Ah, I see. The bees give in so many ways and this is only one more. How marvellous.' She gives Áine a direct look. 'And how marvellous that you should manifest such inspiration in this way. You've made a work of beauty.'

Áine feels the warm praise suffuse her body and fill her spirit. It is like bathing in a pure light, a blessing shone upon her. She wants more.

'I wasn't alone in this creation. Siúr Sodelb has some part in shaping the piece. And it has yet to be finished. I would willingly do that if Siúr Sodelb would help.'

'Ah, no. I only added one bit of shine to it, but I would gladly help in any way you wish.'

'If Siúr Sodelb judges your music worthy then its quality cannot be denied. I would love to hear this piece completed, as I'm sure the other sisters would.'

'You must name it after the bees,' Siúr Sodelb says.

Máthair Gobnait nods. 'Yes. I agree. Perhaps *Um Mholadh Beacha.*'

33

It seems right to think that it would be named as a praise piece for the bees. Áine feels a rush of emotion, something stirring inside her. She tries to force it, but it remains just out of her reach. She shakes her head slightly, trying to clear it.

Máthair Gobnait lays a hand on her arm. 'I'm sorry. We've been carried away with our enthusiasm and it's too much for you.'

'No, no. It was only at that moment I felt something, some thread of memory perhaps, but it was so brief and now it's gone.' The panic that seemed to disappear comes back in full. Darkness threatens to swallow her for a moment. She closes her eyes, but there is no improvement. She utters a small wail and grabs the side of the cart.

'Shhh. Calm yourself,' says Máthair Gobnait. She brushes her hand across Áine's forehead and along her cheek. 'No need to worry. Things like this take soft handling. Let the memories come to you, however little, and one day it will all bear fruit.' She gestures to the row of hives. 'My bees. The bees build their store of honey slowly, each worker bee seeking out the flower dew to bring back to the hive to make into honey to feed the others. Not just one bee, but many many bees together. We're like those bees here. We help each other, we work and toil for this community and for God. We don't do it alone. And it's not for you to carry this burden by yourself. We are here to help you, to give you shelter, to give you comfort and to help you find the gift of joy in the precious life you have from God.'

Áine initially hears only her voice, the soothing rhythms and melodious tones that slowly wrap themselves around her, so warm and comforting, a sanctuary for her wounded spirit. The words come later, their meaning a balm like honey, seeking those deep hurts to begin a healing. She opens her eyes and looks at Máthair Gobnait and allows a little of the light that shines from her to warm her, as her words and voice had done.

'Thank you, Máthair Gobnait.'

Máthair Gobnait nods, squeezes her hand and lets it rest there a moment. No words are exchanged, but the healing continues, her heart slows, her mind feels at rest. Siúr Sodelb stands in silence behind them, a witness and support.

CHAPTER FOUR

Máthair Gobnait's community, is on the hillside of Gort na Tiobratán, among the Érainn people. And these people are part of the Eóganacht kingdom of Múscraige Mitine. This community is more than just a place for women to come to praise their God. The farm that supports them requires that the *cailecha* shoulder tasks and responsibilities that absorb many hours out of their day. The tasks and responsibilities change sometimes with the demands of the season and are supported by the client farmers and handful of slaves and servants attached to a holy community. They enjoy this bounty through the grace of Epscop Ábán and the Eóganacht ruler in Munster who owns the land in the name of the church, though the Érainn people who have lived here much longer might dispute that.

The farm itself could be seen as small. Rocks of all sizes jut from the earth nearly everywhere convenient and inconvenient, with rush and furze squeezed in between wherever they can find purchase. Small patches of green wrested from this parsimonious land are given over to the necessary cultivation of grain crops and grazing of animals. Despite the seeming resistance of such discommodious land, the farm is sufficiently large and productive to provide for the needs of the women, with some to share with those less successful.

Siúr Mugain ensures that the fields are ploughed with the oxen and hoed where necessary and then directs the sowing of barley, wheat and oats. When the August sun has ripened the grains to their fullest and September has stuck its nose in she organizes the reaping, marshalling the client worker, servants and slaves, men and women, into the fields with their sickles and gathers in the harvest. She coordinates the threshing, her strong arms setting the pace for the others as she flails the wheat, barley or oats to detach the grain. She is not of noble birth and willingly does the work.

With the harvest in, it is time to light the kiln fire to dry those grains so laboriously harvested, while ensuring no grain is scorched and all ash scrapings are removed to give to the poor. The winnowing takes Siúr Mugain next, fighting fatigue with the others, while she tosses the grain to separate the useless chaff. The grains amassed, the bags filled and stored in the shed, and her harvest is complete, one year's cycle finished.

The livestock falls to Siúr Sadhbh to oversee. Her love of animals and her status as a wealthy farmer's widow makes her a clear choice to ensure the sheep don't stray, the cows are milked twice daily, the calves remain healthy, the bull behaves, the hens are fed, the oxen are maintained and Máthair Gobnait's horse is loved. The horse is especially important, for she is no common *capall*, a work pony that any low class farmer would have on the land, but an *each,* used only for riding and fit for a noblewoman.

In early spring, Siúr Sadhbh supervises the lambing and the calving, making certain each newborn *úan* and *loég* is delivered safely from its mother and tended in its first few days by the children of servants and workers. The calves are eventually separated from their mother, except only at milking time, and by early summer the males are ready for castration, along with the male lambs. At midsummer, it's Siúr Sadhbh who leads the shearing, bending over the sheep, clipping the wool endlessly, though her muscles ache. Come late summer, she lets loose the bulls to service the cows, except the ones kept back for winter milk. She selects the animals for slaughtering, the lambs, sheep, cows or calves that fit the need of the time and watches carefully the client farmer's knife skills. She scrutinizes each tribute from the client farmers, the various cuts of meat or live animals they send to the community each year.

It's Siúr Feidelm who takes over when the slaughtering is finished. She oversees the meat preparation: its hanging, salting and curing, and deals with the kidney, liver and heart. Meat is only ever served on Sundays and feast days and rarely during the holy fasting periods of summer and winter Lent, and never in spring Lent. Siúr Feidelm also extracts the marrow from the bones, used in soup along with the wild garlic, onions, and celery from the garden, which is also her preserve. As *lubhghorteóir*, she grows leek and cabbage alongside of the celery.

In her kitchen, Siúr Feidelm supervises the churning to make the butter used on Sundays and feast days and ensures sufficient grain is ground in the *cern* to make the flour for the daily bread. Come early summer, with the fresh spring grass sweetening the milk, she sets out the soured milk to form the curds to make the cheese, leaving the whey for watering down the soured drink, *medcuisec,* for fasting days of penance.

Like any other farm, Máthair Gobnait's farm is governed by the seasons, the crops, the animals and their requirements, but it is also a community of women whose main desire is to worship, honour and celebrate God.

This they do primarily inside the oratory, situated in the confines of the *termann*, the sacred area. Each Sunday, those that believe can cross that threshold and gather around the oratory to hear the mass Epscop Ábán celebrates from his place behind the altar inside.

For these women honouring and celebrating God also means offering a sanctuary and sustenance to the sick, weary and hungry that come to the entrance of the *faithche*. Máthair Gobnait and the women are there, arms open, hands at the ready to present food, to tend wounds or offer comfort. If it's required, Máthair Gobnait leaves the community, taking one of the sisters with her, and ministers to the sick and holds vigil. Healing is Máthair Gobnait's biggest concern, a cause for which she has a natural desire with her connection to bees. There is also the community's placement by the ancient healing well. The place itself, Gort na Tiobratán, field of the well, marks the area's ancient reputation as a holy place.

Down through ages, countless desperate petitioners have come there, seeking healing, blessing and solace from this most sacred of places. They scoop up the water, drink its goodness, touch their foreheads and their lips with it. They tie bits of cloth to the branches of the overhanging tree, while the wealthy cast bracelets, rings and even coins of gold and silver into the water itself. There is so much power here, so much holiness. Where else would Máthair Gobnait see nine white deer but at Uisneach in Gort na Tiobratán?

It's unsurprising then that such a woman in a place as holy as this would soon garner a reputation. Epscop Ábán is there to offer his blessing and approve her work, and interferes only on occasion, when events demand it. He, or one of his own community in Sean Chluain, offer mass and act as *anam cara* to those who desire it.

Áine comes to know all these aspects of the community as the summer ripens past its fullness and her body heals at a slow but steady pace, like the sleeping huts and new sheds that are emerging under the careful hands of the builders. She has watched the builders fashion and weave the branches into close fitting wattle that shapes the walls and has marvelled at the smoothness of the daub they plaster over it. She's seen them make the wooden support beams with their mallets and saws and heave them into place ready to under pin the thatch for the roofs. When all is complete, they will have quarters for guests and any future *cailech* who might wish to join this community of women.

The three builders are skilled enough at their work. Findbar and Brendán are brothers who both possess the strong hands and fine eye required for such a job, but Cenél, the youngest of the three and no relation, is good only when they supervise him closely. On the rare times they join the sisters at the main meal, they keep their heads bowed, with only an occasional embarrassed glance upwards, and hastily swallow their food, their discomfort plain to see.

~

When Áine is well enough, they help her at night to one of the sleeping huts. She shares this small round dorm with Máthair Gobnait, Siúr Sodelb and Siúr Ethne while the others sleep in the bigger hut just beside theirs. It's only natural they should place her with Máthair Gobnait, where the holy woman can attend any medical need Áine might have in the night. She still feels fortunate and a little in awe that she should be placed in such company, to be near these women in the hours of darkness where their holy aspirations could shine out on her and give her some peace. And it gives her great comfort to know that

Máthair Gobnait is only a breath away, or that Siúr Sodelb, who lies in the cot next to her, could easily lay a hand in comfort should bad dreams overtake her.

She doesn't mind that twice in the night they rise to Siúr Ethne's bell ringing, don dark wool gowns over a *léine,* fasten the leather belts, place the linen veil over neatly bound hair and slide into their sandals to go to worship. From her place in the cot she can still hear the slap of sandals on the oratory threshold and waits to hear the opening phrases of the office. These are moments of peace for her, moments when she's not haunted by terrible dreams or the nagging fear that there is some hidden danger that her damaged mind no longer remembers.

The sisters require little in return for all this comfort, this nurture. What can she give them, after all? Not her name, for that still remains undiscovered. Not her full body's strength, for she is still mending slowly. She can barely join them at their meals, hobbling on two sticks like an old woman, with arms aching and sore at the effort. She doesn't go far, only to the small stool in the *Tech Mor,* or outside on the bench by the oratory when the weather is fine and on a bench inside when it is not. In either place she attempts mending, spinning or any small task she might turn her hand to now they are healed enough. She has learned these tasks like a child would and is clumsy enough. But as she works at the tasks, or sits quietly on a bench, she gives the community what she does possess: her music. She works with joy and diligence in her mind on the piece that came to her first when she watched Máthair Gobnait with the bees.

It's not only gratitude that brings her back time and again to compose this piece, but the feeling it gives her. When the music takes hold of her, the sense of loss, the incompleteness vanishes, and only the sounds are real. While she sits outside, the sun warming her face, watching the bees, the sisters, the builders and everyone else busy at their work, somehow the music finds words that slide next to each other with great ease to form phrases. Eventually, the words and the music follow her from her bench outside to the table. It is beside her when she eats her meals, and remains as she hobbles back to the sleeping hut for bed.

On occasion, if Siúr Sodelb hears her hum, she sits down beside Áine and joins in, first with the music, and then the words Áine shares with her. '*Um mholadh Beacha*. It's a poem praising bees,' says Siúr Sodelb, when it feels complete.

'A praise poem,' says Áine and she knows Siúr Sodelb is right. The two sit on the bench gazing down along the sloping ground where Siúr Sadhbh and the herd dog usher the calves into their pen for the night against any preying wolves. Behind her, the mallet lands with a thud against one of the timber roof poles of the nearly complete guest house.

'We must sing it now for Máthair Gobnait,' Siúr Sodelb says. 'She will love it.'

Áine isn't so certain. Máthair Gobnait has heard some early parts of the music, when it was only sounds in the air, but now it seems presumptuous to present a piece before her, especially one that praises bees.

'I don't know if it's yet ready for such a step.'

'It needs nothing more, it's perfect.'

Siúr Sodelb, so shy and meek in all her work and speech, finds confidence in things concerning music and it's that fact which encourages Áine to finally nod her head and softly utter a yes.

As if summoned, Máthair Gobnait appears at the doorway of the *Tech Mor* in conversation with Siúr Feidelm, her back to them. When she turns, Siúr Sodelb raises her hand in greeting and Máthair Gobnait moves over to them. A moment later Siúr Sodelb explains their desire to share the piece.

Máthair Gobnait is delighted and asks to hear it from Áine at that moment. She takes a seat beside the two of them.

'Siúr Sodelb must sing it, her voice is so beautiful.'

Siúr Sodelb will have none of that. 'It's your piece, you must give it first.'

'You had a part in it,' says Áine. Her request has nothing to do with modesty. She's certain that Siúr Sodelb has never felt the nerves that now make it difficult for Áine to open her mouth and sing.

Máthair Gobnait raises her hand. 'We'll give it over to God, and it will be His piece, in praise of the bees, His creation. For now, though, Áine, sing it as you choose.'

'Please, I would rather Siúr Sodelb sang with me.'

Siúr Sodelb nods and they begin, singing the words that seem so closely knit to the music it's impossible to believe they might not have emerged together, permanently entwined. Siúr Sodelb, clasping Áine's hand in hers, seems to match each of Áine's words to hers, and marry each note and tone to her deeper tones.

Over at the hives some bees emerge, circle and then fly off, rising higher as the notes of the piece climb. Áine loses herself in the notes, forgetting that Máthair Gobnait is listening attentively, that Siúr Sodelb still holds her hand, her face radiant. It's when the piece ends, the final notes lingering in the air, that she realizes she's been singing on her own. Her breath catches at the thought of it until Máthair Gobnait places a hand on her arm.

'It was a gift to hear that. Thank you.'

She blushes at the compliment. 'There's no need for any gratitude.' She gestures around her. 'It's this place, the bees, the women. They have brought this piece to me.' She gives her a bashful look. 'And you.'

'Máthair Gobnait is right, though. It is a gift. Such a gift deserves to be offered up to God.' Siúr Sodelb turns to her, her gaze intent. 'Would you consider such a thing? To sing this while we worship?'

Áine reddens at the thought. Is she ready to sing it anywhere, let alone during an observance they consider sacred? But perhaps it is just as sacred to her, and at that moment she wishes it were so. The ritual, the voices, the chanting, and most especially the music, all seem familiar to her, as if they were a part of her life. That she had at one time knelt, intoned chants and offered up prayers. She looks over at Siúr Sodelb, sees the earnest pleading, her large innocent eyes, the soft full mouth and golden hair that make any refusal impossible.

'I'll sing it,' says Áine. 'If Máthair Gobnait permits it.'

'I will, of course,' says Máthair Gobnait. 'There is no question of permission. We will make a special occasion of it. Save it for the Sunday mass when others join us and Epscop Ábán is here.'

'Epscop Ábán?' asks Áine.

'Yes, he'll be here. So you see, it's perfect.'

Áine nods and swallows, uncertain if she is able for such an occasion. Perhaps she'd be better off singing it first just among the women, the sisters. She speaks of her concerns.

'It will be fine,' says Máthair Gobnait when she's done. 'And there can be no better occasion.'

Áine sighs and hopes that Máthair Gobnait is right.

~

They let her sit on a bench at the back while the rest of them in turn stand and kneel, facing the grizzled countenance of Epscop Ábán as he says the mass. He wears a simple dark robe underneath a white linen alb embroidered with holy symbols, and stands behind the wooden altar that holds a cross made by Máthair Gobnait. The cross is two pieces of copper twisted together in a tight embrace upwards and then another two braced across it. Beeswax candles are on either side of the cross, their flickering light casting changing shadows on his nose and chin that make his face appear as though a thousand souls are passing through him.

The experience is unnerving for Áine and she sits silently listening to the others, her hands clasped tightly on her lap. These rituals hold no familiarity and she has no idea if it's the implied agony of the twisted cross or the suggestion of possession on Epscop Ábán's face that compels her to draw closer to this ritual that's unfolding before her.

She glances over at Máthair Gobnait and then Siúr Sodelb, her golden hair head caught in the angled light that shines through the oratory door. She acknowledges to herself that in this place she feels safe. The nagging fear that makes her voice a little more than a whisper, holds her back from singing in company, and venturing beyond the *faithche,* feels less at this moment.

Epscop Ábán holds up a chalice filled with wine, another work of Máthair Gobnait, this time fashioned not with copper, but with gold. It belongs to Epscop Ábán's monastery, but he brings it with him to celebrate the mass, a concession to Máthair Gobnait's part in its making. The wine, he tells them, is Christ's blood shed for them all in forgiveness of their sins. He says more, too, but it is the idea of shedding blood for someone else's sins that has caught her mind, and she contemplates that as the other women share in the blessing of Christ's body.

Máthair Gobnait gestures to her from her place across the room. It is time. Áine takes up the two sticks that help her walk and makes her way slowly to Máthair Gobnait's side as the *cailecha* part for Siúr Sodelb to come to the front. Her own awkward progress makes Siúr Sodelb's seem graceful in comparison. Áine is glad for it, that they share something more than this deep rooted love of music, at least for now.

Siúr Sodelb takes her hand and smiles. Áine focusses on that smile and the large transparent eyes that at this moment hold only warmth. After a slight nod from Siúr Sodelb, the two begin their piece. Áine closes her eyes. Her voice is a thread at the start, but she finds her way into the music and it fills out to become rich and strong, matching as much as possible the purity of Siúr Sodelb's voice. It is a joining at that moment, her voice blending, entwining with Siúr Sodelb's like the cross that sits firmly on the wooden altar. She loses herself for a brief time, so closely bound up there is no need to think, Siúr Sodelb's hand clasped in hers and their souls locked in the pure heights of the song.

It finishes and she finds there is no breath left in her. Siúr Sodelb squeezes her hand. She opens her eyes and looks at the radiant face beside her and smiles. It had been an experience like no other, one so unique, so special it could only be holy. Sacred. She bows her head and gives thanks for it, though she has no idea who she is giving thanks to.

A small nod and gesture from Máthair Gobnait signals she is free to return to her bench. But for some reason she can't contemplate the hobble back and feels instead the need to hold on to this moment with Siúr Sodelb and the completeness she has just felt. She gives a small shake of her head and moves closer to Siúr Sodelb, still grasping her hand.

~

Siúr Feidelm places the laden platter on the table beside the bowls of cooked celery and onion and the bread loaves. The haunch of beef, roasted the day before on the spit in the cooking pit in honour of Epscop Ábán's visit, is ready for carving on its wooden platter. All the *cailecha*, except perhaps Siúr Ethne, have looked forward to this celebratory feast and now gather around the table, their faces full of anticipation. It is seldom that Siúr Feidelm puts her culinary skills to such use, liberally sprinkling herbs in among the celery and onions set to cook slowly in milk, and the beef, under Siúr Feidelm's watchful eye, turned so carefully on its spit by the young widow's boy so that nary a drop of fat falls into the fire. There is even butter for the bread, a luxury that each *cailech* savours first, after ripping a bread portion apart and spreading a generous daub of it on with her knife.

The bishop has no less anticipation than the *cailecha*. He has removed his alb from his thin frame to preserve it against possible stains and attacks his share of bread with energy. After the first few mouthfuls are enjoyed he looks up. A slight twinkle comes into his eyes. '*Aon scéal agat?*'

It is common enough to ask a person if they have any news or stories to share when meeting. Such news or stories might relieve the tedium of the daily tasks. Everyone knows that in this case, the question posed humorously is part of the routine exchange Epscop Ábán has with Máthair Gobnait. That Máthair Gobnait always responds she has no stories to tell, no news of any worth, is her way of saying that she and the other women live quietly among the people here.

This time is no different. 'No news, *a thiarna Epscop*,' she says. In her view it is Epscop Ábán who must have the stories to tell, a man who was an *Episcopus Vagans*, travelling for many years all over Mumu, Connacht and Laigin, founding churches and monasteries. A man with so much experience and years can't fail to have something to tell. 'What stories will you share with us today?'

'I have more of a request than a story. But first I must insist that you do have news.' He looks over at Áine, who lowers her eyes under his sharp, discerning gaze. She has never been this close to him. Before, on the few visits since her arrival, she saw him only in the distance, mounting his horse, or blessing the new calves and lambs in their pens. Now she feels uneasy. Its cause might be the palpable tension and energy he barely manages to contain, but she is cautious nonetheless. She only knows that eyes such as his miss nothing, and at this moment they pin her to her seat.

'Ah, you mean the beautiful praise piece, *Um la Mholadh Beacha,* Siúr Sodelb and Áine sang today,' says Máthair Gobnait. 'Yes, you're right. That's news indeed.'

'*Um la Mholadh Beacha.* Yes, and how fitting that someone from your community should sing something so named. I'm not familiar with it. Who was it gave it to you? Is it one of Siúr Sodelb's?'

'Its creator is one of the singers, but not Siúr Sodelb.'

Epscop Ábán looks over at Áine again. 'Ah, one of your newcomers.' He takes in her grey gown that matches the gowns worn by the women, his eyes moving over the worn edges of the wool sleeves and that of the *léine* beneath. He notes too her hair, the dark curls fully revealed and tumbling in all their glory along her back. 'Not yet a *cailech*?' he asks.

'But welcome here nevertheless,' says Máthair Gobnait. 'She came to us in need of care and she has repaid us in many ways.'

'I have no doubt she's welcome here, as I am certain that your healing knows no bounds.' He reaches over and slices off the thinnest of pieces from the roasted haunch.

The meat is tender and juicy and the *cailecha*, glad that the bishop has finally taken the first slice, feel able to take their own pieces. Siúr Mugain is especially generous with her knife, whether it's her strong, well muscled arms that bring more force to her carving skills, or that her labours in the field give her an irrepressible appetite. It gives Siúr Ethne pause though, and with a raise of her brow and meatless fare on her own plate, her disapproval rings out. Despite Máthair Gobnait's protests, Siúr Ethne refuses all meat and drinks no beer, confining herself to water and the soured whey, like some of the penitential *manach*. Máthair Gobnait will allow Siúr Ethne some of her ascetic choices, but tries to rein in the most extreme.

Áine glances at Siúr Ethne's plate. It is filled only with a spoonful of celery and onion and some unbuttered bread. Áine is certain that she could never limit herself to such an extent. Her own plate contains a generous helping of the celery and onion, the meat and liberally buttered bread. With Epscop Ábán's scrutiny directed elsewhere, she can relax and eat with enjoyment.

'The healing is my calling from God and I must go where it takes me,' says Máthair Gobnait in response to the bishop's comment.

'And that's where my story comes in today,' says the bishop. 'I've lately travelled from the dún of Uí Blathnaic at Raithlinn. His favourite son is ill with a wasting disease.

He sought my advice, to my surprise. It shows his desperation. I told him of you and now he would like you to visit his son and perform a cure.'

'Uí Blathnaic. Illness can humble even a king, it seems.'

'I know he's not kindred to the Érainn people here and some may not take it kindly, but it would be a good opportunity for the church if you were to heal his son.'

Máthair Gobnait smiles at him, her eyes laughing. 'I will go, of course, *a thiarna Epscop*. He is a person in need. As for the people, they know my love and care for them and they will understand that by such an action I am putting Uí Blathnaic in my debt as well as the Church's.' She gazes warmly around at the other *cailech*, some of whom are the very people she speaks about. Siúr Mugain and Siúr Sadhbh nod as if to emphasize her point. 'I will gather together what I need tomorrow and go then. I'll take one of you to assist me, as I may be gone a good few days.' Her glance rests on Áine.

CHAPTER FIVE

She has rehearsed the words in her mind often while she lay in her pallet next to Siúr Sodelb's, and now, standing in front of Máthair Gobnait, she begins to doubt her decision. They are standing among the *beachair*, Máthair Gobnait collecting honey in preparation for her journey. On the grass nearby, Méone is curled up in a ball, basking in the early morning light. Áine knows that the unease that follows her around like some anxious lapdog has driven her in part to this decision and brings her here now, but there is also something more. It stems from that feeling she had when she sang with Siúr Sodelb. She wants more of that. She needs more of that.

She hesitates a fraction and stares at the wrought copper cross that hangs round Máthair Gobnait's neck, trying to remember the thoughts and words she's composed. Máthair Gobnait looks at her expectantly. She draws a breath. 'I've been thinking. That is to say, I've given this much thought. About the community. I would like to … the women here, the community…the sisters, they've been very supportive. I've found great comfort here.'

Máthair Gobnait regards her patiently. She removes the veil from her face and slips off the protective gloves. 'I'm glad that you've found comfort here.'

Emboldened by these words, Áine carries on, her words assembling in a more coherent pattern. 'I would like to become a part of the community. I feel more at home here among the sisters than I would in any other place. Here, my lack of memory causes myself and no one else any ill. In return, I would be happy to contribute to the community in any manner you wish.' She gestures to the bees. 'I've watched you with the hives, seen how much care you give the bees. It's something I would enjoy helping you with, if you need it.'

Máthair Gobnait scans her face slowly, missing nothing. 'I have no doubt of your sincerity, or the strength of your desire,' she says finally. 'I do wonder, though, at its source. You say you find great comfort here, and I'm glad, but that's not a reason to become a *cailech*.' She gives her a warm smile, her eyes full of understanding.

Perhaps it is that last statement that prompts Áine to protest; that gives her the certainty and focus that she found so elusive moments before. 'I'm sorry, I phrased my request very poorly. What I mean to say is that I have watched all of you very carefully over these past months, I see great faith and dedication in the manner in which you work and worship, and it touches me deeply. I feel during these times something more, something greater than myself is at work. It wasn't until today, when I heard mass with all of you in the presence of Epscop Ábán, that I realized that something was God. In that moment I sang with Siúr Sodelb, it seemed as though He was present. I felt such wonder and love. Surely that's a sign God is calling me to become a member of this community?'

Gobnait studies her. 'You felt that during mass?'

Áine nods. Tears gather in her eyes for a moment.

'I see.' She puts her hands in her sleeves, pensive. 'I think there is no doubt God is at work here in some way. And I would welcome you, my dear, without hesitation, if I knew it was with an open heart and spirit. My concern is that with your lack of memory I can't be certain your heart and spirit are open and desire this step.' She withdraws her hands from the sleeves and rests them on Áine's shoulders. 'What I will do is consult with the bishop and Uí Blathnaic further. Perhaps with more digging, they might determine who you are. In view of that, I would ask you to accompany me to see Uí Blathnaic.'

'Me?' Her heart races. The fear is present now, strong and unmistakeable. 'Siúr Sodelb would seem the better choice,' she says.

Gobnait gazes at her calmly and gives a gentle smile. 'I'm asking you,' she says. 'Siúr Sodelb seldom ventures outside of the *faithche*, let alone as far as Raithlinn.'

'I don't think I'm ready for such a step either,' she says. The very thought of riding or walking a track or across an open field nearly steals all the breath from her. She doesn't know who it is she fears, or even what, only that she can't leave the safety of this place.

It is as though Máthair Gobnait knows her thoughts. 'You mustn't feel frightened. Cadoc will be with us. I wouldn't have proposed it if I thought it was unsafe.'

Áine looks at Máthair Gobnait, notes her calm expression, the kind eyes and tries to take comfort. Perhaps her fears are unreasonable. Máthair Gobnait seems to think so. She gives a nod. 'I will go, of course.'

Máthair Gobnait pats her hand. 'Good. Now there are things to arrange. If you would go to Siúr Feidelm and collect the herbs, salves and honey she's prepared, I'll tell Siúr Sadhbh to get the horse ready.'

She pulls the sheer veil from her head and adjusts the thicker veil underneath. Áine can see the fine threads of grey in among the dark locks that betray her age and for a moment it shocks her to think this precious person would succumb to time. It is her spirit that has no age, Áine thinks before she takes up her sticks to complete her errand. She stops and turns back to Máthair Gobnait. 'May I call you *máthair*?'

'Of course. 'If it feels right to you.'

'They all call you Mother. Even those from Boirneach and further afar.'

'They do. It is an honour.'

'I would see you as *máthair* without that.'

Máthair Gobnait smiles and it reaches her eyes. 'I'm glad you do.'

~

The horse's pace is easy enough, limited by the simple cart that carries them and the roughness of the track. For now Cadoc, Máthair Gobnait's servant, leads the horse. For speed's sake it is Fionn who pulls the cart and not the small *capall* they normally use. He is left behind for others to use if needed.

The journey will take at least two days and a night and that in itself is enough to cause Áine's anxiety to rise. She looks at Cadoc's broad back and knotted muscles and tries to draw comfort from them. Her left leg and hip ache already with the jolting ride, but that she can bear. Beside her, Máthair Gobnait bumps against her periodically as the cart bounces along, a reminder that this holy woman has substance.

It's some time before Áine can relax enough to take notice of her surroundings. She finds they have descended from the hill, passed countless rocks and clumps of furze and rush. The morning is still young and she can smell the golden furze flowers, a scent that's strong for this time of the year. It's not long before the air is filled with the damp woody scents of the forest that threads its way along the banks of the Sullane River. The smell is welcome, because it promises some cool shade after the sun, surprisingly strong at this time of day. Or perhaps she feels the heat because of the anxiety and strain of being out in the open, vulnerable to any peering eyes. She wipes her brow with her sleeve and longs for the trees' shelter.

'The day will be hot,' says Máthair Gobnait. 'And the river looks inviting. Shall we stop for a drink in a while?'

'If you don't mind. Just a small one.'

Perhaps it's out of pity for Áine's flushed looks, because their journey is long, but before the sun reaches its apex, they pull up beside the river. Máthair Gobnait climbs down from the cart with Cadoc's aid and the two in turn help Áine. Cadoc leads the mare to the river's edge so she can drink. Máthair Gobnait follows them and strokes Fionn, murmuring endearments.

'You've had the horse a while?' Áine asks.

'I have. Fionn brought me here with Cadoc.' She smiles at Cadoc, and he nods silently, his weathered face lighting up for a moment. His hair, more grey than brown, shows his years, but he still stands firmly and his stride is long. A distant kinsman of Máthair Gobnait's, Cadoc is never intrusive; he is calm waters, soothing and full of reassurance in his silence. Áine feels no threat.

'Fionn came with me from my father's place.' She pats the horse and laughs. 'She was young then. We both were.'

'Do you miss your home?'

Máthair Gobnait turns to regard Áine. 'This is my home now. I do of course miss my father, but my life is full. I have many blessings to count.'

'And your mother?'

Máthair Gobnait shakes her head. 'She died when I was young.'

'And you had no desire to marry and become a mother yourself?'

'I have wed. God is my husband, my father, my guide all in one. Who could find a more fortunate situation?'

'And the women are your family.'

'I see you understand.'

'It's that I would wish to share.'

'It is a precious thing to share, but it is not for everyone. And you might already have a family that are searching for you, missing you.'

'I've thought about that and I don't think my mind would change.'

Máthair Gobnait sighs and reaches up to push aside a stray lock from Áine's face. 'I am glad to hear you say that, but we must give you more time. And first you must be baptized as a Christian.'

'Baptism?'

'Water poured over you. You will be cleansed of all sin and reborn into the Christian Church.'

Áine falls silent, captured by the idea of rebirth. She has made a new beginning, a rebirth of sorts, and this baptism would only confirm it. There can be no doubt now that she is on the right course. She asks Máthair Gobnait the particulars of the ritual, knowing that her questions indicate more about her past beliefs than she cares to show.

Their journey resumes and they continue to follow the track beside the river that slowly takes them down from the rocky bog land that marks Boirneach and its surroundings, to a more flat open area that has been cleared for farming. They meet a few other travellers on their journey. Each time they encounter anyone, they stop and speak a while, gleaning news and, in the pedlar's case, offering to share what food they have.

An *ócaire* hauling wood halts only briefly, remaining in his cart. He seems no more a threat than the few men who'd come on occasion to help on the farm, keeping a respectful distance from all the women. Still, Áine can do nothing to stop the fierce beating of her heart or the sweat that gathers in her clenched hands. She forces deep breaths as the *ócaire* speaks of the good weather and the hope that it might continue, adding the thought that a drop of rain now and again would not go amiss. A few moments later he is on his way, whistling a tune in a carefree manner.

When a pedlar approaches with his goods laden on his back, she can barely sit upright with the fear that seizes her. His manner is genial, but there is something more, some underlying menace that the open manner in which he regards her seems to emphasize. When Máthair Gobnait gives him greeting and offers to share some of their bread and cheese with the man, she grips Máthair Gobnait's arm in protest. Máthair Gobnait only pats her hand away and asks the pedlar to take the top sack from the cart.

The pedlar moves to oblige and his hand brushes against Áine's. She gasps at his contact, alarm ringing through her body. The man grins and removes the sack with a swift graceful movement and places it on the spot Cadoc indicates. Fionn seems unperturbed and busies herself with her own meal, the loud munch of her teeth as she tears at the grass filling the air.

Cadoc helps Máthair Gobnait to climb down from the cart, and before the two can assist Áine, the pedlar is there, his hands around her waist, lifting her through the air. She hangs weightless for a moment, her feet dangling and his face grinning up at her. It's all she can do to keep from screaming. Her feet find the ground and she stumbles a moment, her stick still in the cart. His hand is on her again immediately, steadying her. She gulps for air and hears herself hiccup.

Cadoc and Máthair Gobnait are busy laying out the food on the small blanket. Glimpsing Áine's face Máthair Gobnait, sends the pedlar to fill the leather flagon at the river. He lopes off, happy to oblige.

'There is no need to fear the man. I know him well enough.'

Áine looks at her and tears prick her eyes. 'I'm sorry. I can't help it.'

Máthair Gobnait sighs. 'Be calm. All will be well.'

The pedlar returns and they begin to eat, sharing his news and stories of his travels at Máthair Gobnait's prompting. He gives Áine an occasional glance and she can only be thankful that when Máthair Gobnait introduces her, she says nothing of her background.

'Have you heard anything of a woman gone missing from her family?' Máthair Gobnait asks.

The pedlar flicks his eyes over Áine for a moment, then shakes his head. 'I've been east, though, and have only lately come from Raithlinn.'

'How does Uí Blathnaic's son? We're on our way now to him.'

The pedlar shakes his head. 'Not well. Lately, he's become worse.'

Máthair Gobnait frowns. 'I'm sorry to hear that. I hope there's something I can do for him.' She exchanges a few more words with him and then explains that they must depart. They all rise and Áine can only feel relief that the ordeal is over.

The journey resumes, though this time it's with an urgent purpose that means the cart shakes harder under the horse's faster pace. Cadoc no longer walks leading Fionn, but stands in the cart with the reins while Máthair Gobnait and Áine sit behind and try to cushion themselves among the sacks against the bone-rattling ride. Áine has no objection to this arrangement, because tucked among the baggage she feels less noticeable, and for a silly moment hopes that she can remain in the cart during the visit to Raithlinn.

When they pull up into a small farmyard near dusk, Áine shrinks down between the sacks, searching the three figures that emerge from the round house. The thatch is still fresh, crisply cut and the pens are well maintained. She hears the bleat of a lamb and the mother ewe's comforting answer. The man steps forward, one of the client farmers of some connection to Epscop Ábán, a Christian man who treats Máthair Gobnait as if she were otherworldly. The introductions are made and Áine is so tense she hears nothing of the names that are said or the words of welcome that accompany them.

The night passes slowly as she sits as small as possible by the fire, barely touching the plate of food that is placed before her. She refuses a seat at the table, preferring to remain tucked behind the centre pole that supports the house, by the fire, away from the notice of the household. She knows they look at her curiously, but she keeps her head bowed, and uses the curtain of her hair to block her face from the others.

Máthair Gobnait appears to take no notice of her behaviour and converses calmly with them, exchanging minor bits of news and sharing their admiration for Epscop Ábán. She is given a place of honour and the man attends her enthusiastically, providing her with the choicest portions. Cadoc is in the shed, minding Fionn and taking his ease with his own share of porridge and a heel of bread, baked on the hearthstone of this Christian home.

Áine notices that there is a small copper cross nailed to the post she clings to. She wonders if Máthair Gobnait's hands have fashioned this piece too, though its shape is cruder and there are no fine etchings on it.

At the table, Máthair Gobnait asks them if they have heard news of a missing woman and Áine's heart sinks. Though she knows she must recover her memory, she would rather do it on her own, when she is ready and feels there is no fear that a person wishing her ill might discover her location. There is no doubt in her mind that some kind of danger exists for her, but at the moment she would rather just spend time in Máthair Gobnait's community where few would notice her. But Máthair Gobnait ploughs on, pressing the question.

'Is this missing woman from your community?' the man asks. His head is bowed, his tone respectful.

'No, not really,' says Máthair Gobnait.

'But she is a noblewoman, or you wouldn't ask after her,' says the wife. She preens braided hair, careful to tuck in a stray lock.

Máthair Gobnait pulls herself up and narrows her eyes. 'I would care for any woman who is missing.'

'It matters not, of course. She is a Christian,' the man says.

'She is a woman in distress,' says Máthair Gobnait.

'What is her name? What does she look like?' asks the man.

'I don't know her name, I'm sorry. I ask after her as a favour to others.'

'We have heard nothing of a missing woman,' says the man. There is regret in his voice. He is desperate to be helpful. 'But if we hear news of her we'll let you know. In the meantime, we'll pray that you will find her.'

'Thank you.'

There are no glances in Áine's direction and so she relaxes somewhat, and by the time they are all ready to take their beds she can follow Máthair Gobnait to the sleeping cubicle with more attention to her walking than to hiding her face behind her hair. When the morning comes, and she has not been killed in the night, and no one has appeared to take her away, she can even manage a small smile of thanks when they take their leave.

~

It is nearly dusk again when they approach the *dún* that is Uí Blathnaic's. They have passed many of the holdings of Uí Blathnaic's client farmers, the prosperous *bóaire* and less prosperous *ócaire*, and even that of a few *aire déso*, the vassal lords, that surround this *dún*, and so she is not surprised that the *dún* is so large. Stone and wood buildings dot the yard of the large *ráth* that surrounds it. A sniff of the air tells her the pens and sheds are filled with pigs, sheep and calves, shut in for the night against wolves and other predators. The cattle low in the distance, still out in the field under watchful guard. She lifts her head, too curious to fear anyone in this failing light. She sees a few women still out in the field and others in the yard bent over spitted meats cooking slowly over a large pit. Near them, children run around, chasing the yard dog. The cart rolls by a vegetable garden where a woman kneels, pulling weeds. She looks up as they stop.

Máthair Gobnait greets her. '*Dé'd Bheatha-sa.*'

The woman is caught off guard by a noble woman greeting her and in a peculiarly Christian manner. She stares back, uncertain how to respond.

'The gods be with you,' the woman says finally, modifying the greeting to suit her own view.

'You are well, I hope? The weather has been so fine, one could only feel well.'

This exchange is more familiar to the woman and she answers more openly, though a thread of uncertainty is still present for someone unused to regular conversation with nobles. 'I'm grand altogether. I hope you are well yourself?'

'I am, and my companion, Áine, too. I'm called Gobnait and I'm looking for Uí Blathnaic.'

The woman nodded. 'He's here alright,' She indicates the large building. 'Up there you'll find him.'

Máthair Gobnait thanks her and Cadoc urges the horse on again, through the gap in the earthwork and stone wall that mark the *dún's* boundary, towards the large round building at its centre. She can hear a dog bark. A sizeable wolfhound and a young man emerge from the house. The man wears dark trews and a length of brightly coloured plaid tossed over his tunic and pinned with a gold brooch. The quality of all these items is unmistakeable. His green eyes study the two women a moment before he moves forward and catches Fionn's bridle. Áine tenses and ducks down among the sacks.

'You are the *cailech*, Gobnait?' he asks. Behind him, the dog jumps once and then sits when the man points his finger at him.

'I am,' says Máthair Gobnait. 'This is my servant Cadoc and behind me is my companion, Áine.'

Áine raises her head a little but takes care that her hair hides much of her face. The man gives her a brief nod, but even in that short space of time she has no doubt he misses no detail. She thinks he must be the *rectaire*, and realizes this household is very important and noble to have a steward dressed in such a manner.

'Good,' he says. 'We've been waiting for you. Your skills are needed now.' He offers his hand to help Máthair Gobnait down.

'And you are?'

He blinks a moment and then raises a brow. 'Excuse me. I thought you knew. I am Colmán, Uí Blathnaic's other son.'

Áine blushes at her mistake, but Máthair Gobnait nods and takes the offered hand. 'I didn't know you were Uí Blathnaic's son. I've had little cause to come here before this.'

'If it pleases the gods you will have no further cause to come here after this,' he says. There is no malice in his words, but they are firm enough. It doesn't make Áine's fear any less. When she presses her hand in his, it's trembling and it's not only her healing injuries that make her stumble when he helps her down. This time there are no hands gripping her waist and arms swinging her in the air. He allows her to lift her leg over the side and use the wheel to balance and climb down. It is only when her leg collapses under the effort that he supports her and gently eases her to the ground. She looks at him quickly and all the fear she has suppressed over the past two days jumps into her throat. She lowers her eyes and hopes he hasn't seen the terror in her face.

Máthair Gobnait motions for Cadoc to unload the sacks. 'I will do my best to help your brother.' She points to one sack. 'If you could bring that one with us I can go to him immediately.'

Colmán gives her an astonished look. He says something to a small group of well dressed men and they in turn look at each other. He gives an impatient snort and takes up the sack himself, brushing by the others who gape at the sight. Cadoc hides a smile just in time and pretends to fuss with Fionn's bridle. After a moment, Cadoc takes her off to one of the buildings beyond. Áine looks after Cadoc with longing. Her only wish at this moment is to follow him to the obscurity of the horse shed.

Instead, she turns and follows Máthair Gobnait through the passage doorway and into the house. The men follow her and she can feel their curious eyes scanning every bit of her hair and dress.

Áine blinks her eyes against the change of light, aware only that there are many people here, women and men. She smells the turf burning in the hearth and from its glow and the small shaft of light from above, she gradually makes out the size and grandeur of the room. Every item is in its proper place. There is the cauldron, with a spit, the vat for brewing beer, the mugs, the kneading trough. The floor is strewn with rushes and she feels them even now as she moves carefully across the floor, her stick providing support that is more than physical.

People are milling about, mostly men chatting in small groups or sitting on benches, periodically lifting mugs of beer and mead to their mouths. In the back, she can see the real *rectaire* and wonders how she could have mistaken Colmán's authoritative bearing for this man who lazes against the wall instead of checking that the servants fulfil their tasks. It's clear this group are waiting for something, while one lone woman struggles to fill mugs and press a chunk of bread on them. Colmán strides past them, barely sparing them a glance, and heads toward the back of the room where connecting passageways lead to the many sleeping cubicles. It's at one of the larger sleeping cubicles that he stops and ushers the pair inside.

She can smell the sickness even before she enters the room. Once in, she sees immediately the emaciated figure that lies in the wooden bed that takes up much of the room. Beside him, a woman sits on a stool, stroking his forehead. Her dark hair is heavily laced with grey and her gown, of a bright soft material, hangs loosely on her gaunt frame. She turns to them when they enter and the dark rings under her eyes are noticeable.

'You have come to help Domnall?' she says. Her eyes are almost feverish.

A man steps forward from the other side of the bed, his broad chest and muscular arms still evident, despite the white in his hair and his gnarled beard. A torc of twisted copper and gold circles his neck and a gold brooch fastens the blue and red plaid *brat* at his left shoulder.

'You are the Christian woman I've heard about? The one who heals?'

Máthair Gobnait nods. 'I am.'

He acknowledges her nod with a curt one of his own and frowns. 'It's at my wife Rónnat's insistence that you're here. I must make that clear. But she is determined that we try all possibilities to heal my son.' He looks across at his wife and for a moment his expression softens. 'Well, if you do succeed, then I will say no more ill against your people, I can assure you that much. Let your god do his work.'

'I can make no promises in that way for myself, nor for God. I am not privy to his counsel. I can only do my best with my knowledge and pray and hold vigil for your son's recovery. That I promise you I will do.'

Uí Blathnaic sighs and gives a small wave of his hand. 'As you will. You must accept our hospitality for as long as it takes. One of the women will see to you. My wife prefers to stay at Domnall's side.'

He looks over again at his son, his face etched in worry. Colmán draws up beside him and puts a hand on his arm. 'There are many matters to attend to *a t'áthair*.'

Uí Blathnaic nods and the two leave Máthair Gobnait and Áine alone with the patient and his mother. The patient's skin is sallow, except for the bright spots of colour on his cheek and his eyes are dark rimmed and sunken. The outline of his skull is clear under the tightly stretched skin. He opens his eyes a moment as if sensing a new turn of events and tries to speak, but a terrible coughing fit overtakes him. His mother holds him tenderly for its duration, stroking his head and then, once it subsides, gently lays him back against the pillow that supports his head. Sweat beads his forehead and pastes his damp curls against his head.

Máthair Gobnait approaches the bed on the other side and lays her hand along his brow. It rests there for a few moments before she withdraws it.

Rónnat reaches across the bed and clutches Máthair Gobnait's arm. 'You'll help my son, won't you?' Her face is intent, willing a positive answer.

'I'm sure you know the serious nature of his illness. I will do all I can to help him, but there are no guarantees. But I can most certainly ease that cough.'

Rónnat nods and releases Máthair Gobnait's arm. Máthair Gobnait looks over at Áine and then the mother. 'I'll go now and make up the medicinal drink, if you could show me where I might mix it.'

'I'll call one of the women.'

'It will be quicker if you show me now.'

Rónnat glances over at her son. 'But I can't leave Domnall.'

'Áine can remain with him for the time. It won't take long.'

Rónnat looks down at her son again, anguish written on her face and then turns to study Áine. Áine tries not to shrink from her gaze, but when she sees the desperation in Rónnat's eyes her fear evaporates. She gives a tentative smile. There is no question now that she will do what she can to nurse and comfort this sick young man.

After a moment's further hesitation Rónnat nods slightly and rises, gathering up the *brat* that drapes her shoulders even on this warm summer day. In the brief moment before the woman quickly wraps her *brat* tighter Áine can see that her dress is soiled and stained.

Once the pair are gone, bearing the bundle of Máthair Gobnait's medicines, Áine settles herself on Rónnat's stool next to the patient. Gazing at him, she feels none of the unease that has dominated her since entering this place. Domnall opens his eyes and looks at her. The eyes are glazed and feverish, but she can still make out their hazel colour. They're not quite the bright compelling green of his brother's, but there's a kindness about them she finds appealing. She takes up the cloth his mother has placed in the wooden bowl beside the bed, squeezes it of excess water and places it on his brow. He gives a little smile.

'It's nice to see such a fair face as yours,' he says. His voice is weak, but there's no trace of malice. She returns the smile and continues dabbing the cloth along his brow. His hand seems to come from nowhere and grabs her wrist. 'You're not a spirit, a *ban sídh,* are you?'

She jumps at his touch and for a moment she wonders if what he asks her might be true, that she is the harbinger of death.

CHAPTER SIX

'I thank you for persuading my mother to take some rest.'

Áine jumps and all the fear returns at the sound of his voice. Her hands shake as she finishes emptying the pot into the tub. She has stepped outside the house for only a moment, passing through the throng of men, the chatting women and ambling servants, to make her way behind one of the sheds where the tubs of urine are kept. She wrinkles her nose at the sour smell that rises up as she keeps pouring, letting its unpleasant odour fill her nostrils and mute her nerves. The urine is used in the processes of tanning hides and fulling and dyeing cloth, and she tries to imagine the depth of colour such potency can create. Finally, she takes a deep breath and turns to Colmán, knowing she must be polite to members of this king's household, even though she would rather be back in Gort na Tiobratán, in the sparely furnished room that holds her cot.

'It's to Máthair Gobnait you owe your thanks,' she says, her head lowered.

'How do you come to be with her? You're not a Christian.'

She tenses even more at the directness of his question. 'How do you know I'm not a Christian?' she asks softly.

'Unlike her, you're not wearing a cross and you don't cover your hair.' He reaches over, fingers a lock of her hair and she flinches. 'Though it is of such quality it should never be covered.'

She holds herself completely still, her head remaining lowered, enduring his touch. Eventually, he drops the lock of hair and studies her intently. 'I notice you limp. What happened? Did you go to her for healing?' His voice is kind, sympathetic.

His gentle tone startles her into a confession. 'I-I did. My leg was broken.' Her voice shakes and she raises her head a moment and looks beyond him for a means of escape. She feels his eyes on her, penetrating her wool dress, her *léine,* to the scars that mark her chest and sides. 'I'm sorry, I must go,' she says after a moment, desperate. She moves away from him and he catches her arm.

'I meant no harm by my questions,' he says.

She extricates her arm and gives a little nod before scurrying off to the safety of the sleeping cubicle that holds Domnall.

When she enters the room she sees that Rónnat and Máthair Gobnait have returned and Rónnat has resumed her seat by Domnall's side. The servant who had stayed with Domnall has gone and Domnall lies on the bed, pale, but awake. At the foot of the bed a harp rests, its dark wood polished smooth. The intricate carving, the grace of its construction testifies to its quality, even without the accompanying sound. It is sound that is foremost for Áine—no, music—she corrects herself, and without thinking, she leans over and plucks a string. Her nails are short and uncurved, so the string hasn't the clarity it would normally if she could pluck it correctly, but nevertheless, she sighs to hear its beauty.

'You play the harp?' asks Rónnat. Her voice holds a hopeful note.

'I-I... Yes,' Áine says. She looks down at her hand which rests against the strings and she can see the harp is different. It's a harp of the same kind that once sat on her lap and tucked itself against her shoulder, as natural a placement as a mother suckling a child. She takes a deep breath, overwhelmed by the image for a moment. She looks up, bewildered. It is a small piece of herself, but it is genuine and she has no idea what to do with it.

'Would you play for my son? Senán, our revered bard, had hardly begun before he was called away.'

'It would please me greatly, if you would,' Domnall says. He smiles and this time it lights his eyes. There is kindness of such depth there she can hardly refuse.

Áine glances over at Máthair Gobnait who nods. She runs her hand along the harp a moment, uncertain. 'I'll try.'

'Just some bit of music. Anything to soothe Domnall.'

She takes up the harp and sits on the edge of the bed, settling the instrument on her lap, leaning it against her left shoulder and apologizes that her lack of nails will make for a poor sound. She runs her fingers lightly along the strings, dampening them slightly with the other hand, testing their tension and glorying in the ringing tones that answer. Closing her eyes for only a moment, she lets her hands and fingers find their place. She plucks the strings slowly at first, working her way into a tune that suddenly fills her head only after it does her fingers. They are stiff, her fingers, but not so stiff that it causes her to stumble over the tune. She plays the tune slowly, dreamlike. The tune consumes her, makes her smile, so soft and lilting, it echoes back on itself in the string's vibrato, and she finds herself humming along quietly. The hum forms words and the words melt with the music, a lullaby wave, soft and rolling. A voice sings with her in her mind, the voice of her *máthair*. For a moment she can see her, the fine bones of her cheeks, the smiling mouth and light eyes. But only for a moment, and then her mother vanishes into the world of dreams.

She looks up from the harp, suddenly aware of the three pairs of eyes fixed on her. She feels another pair behind her and turns only in time to see a familiar flash of colour disappearing. Colmán. Suddenly, she is afraid again and puts the harp back on the bed carefully. She folds her hands firmly in her lap. There are all sorts of self-betrayal, but for her, the love of music must be the worst. 'I'm sorry. I don't play well. Your bard would be sorry his instrument found its way into such inexpert hands.'

'On the contrary. That was beautiful. My thanks for playing,' Rónnat says. 'It was so kind of you.'

'I think Senán would agree there is some competition here,' Domnall says.

'Oh, no. I'm sure not. I am not a bard of any degree at all. That would mean years of training.'

'Your skill and voice speak differently,' Domnall says.

'You are a very accomplished musician, Áine.' Máthair Gobnait's voice is firm. She does not approve of false modesty.

Áine examines the hands in her lap. After so many months it is difficult to find the traces of a harper. All she knows is that her fingers found their places on the strings with such ease, the music poured out without thinking and the songs came from a place she can't enter at will. For now, she has these scant random memories. But even as she treasures these pieces of herself, she can't deny the panic that accompanies them, and the thought that others know as much, and perhaps more. She looks at Domnall and Rónnat and for a brief moment wonders if they are hiding any knowledge of her identity to act upon later. She discards the thought almost immediately, until she remembers Colmán, and the unease returns.

~

The evening meal is everything she dreaded. Máthair Gobnait insists she accept the hospitality, at least on this first night, rather than sit with Domnall as she had offered to do. There is no hiding, no obscure seat she can take and hope to remain unnoticed throughout the meal, because the two women are guided to designated places amid the cluster of men and women who gather around the table. She looks through the smoke that drifts about the room and sees the numerous spears, shields and other bits of war that hang on its walls. There are some feminine touches too, in the curtain of finely woven fabrics hanging discreetly in a few areas and the piece stretched on the small loom at the back.

She notes with relief that the bard Senán has taken the place beside her, and that it's on Máthair Gobnait's other side that Uí Blathnaic has chosen to sit. When she dares to look around the rest of the table from under the protection of her loosely draped hair, she realizes that many of the people gathered earlier when they arrived have left, and all that remain are only the household members and guests that have most likely travelled far to see the king on some matter. It calms her somewhat, until her eyes light on Colmán, who returns her look with a curious stare. She forces a smile and wills her eyes to look away, and it is then she sees the woman seated next to him. There is something that tells her this woman is his wife, though nothing outward in their manner supports this realization. For a moment she is shocked, since his married state never occurred to her during their few encounters. He would of course be married, she tells herself and she examines the woman carefully, if only to get a deeper impression of the man. She is small, this woman. Her hair, tied back loosely, is a nondescript brown, and the nails on her fidgeting hands are bitten to the quick. Áine stares at the bitten nails for a moment, wondering what they tell her about the man. It's only later, when Uí Blathnaic introduces the woman as Bruinech, that her relationship to Colmán is confirmed. Áine doesn't know what to make of her astute insight and whether she should take comfort in it.

The conversation flows loudly around her and there is no shortage of food on the table. Still, though the food's quality is better than anything she has eaten at Gort na Tiobratán, something tells her that this is a lesser king, ruling only a *tuath,* and he is not as prosperous as some, and has no real influential connections. She thinks again to what Epscop Ábán had said about the family, but can really find no clue there. She knows that kingship is a fleeting thing, passing to those who can provide the strength, wealth and prosperity to the *tuath,* and has little to do with directness of descent. She knows it with a firm conviction, but has no source of this knowledge. Another piece of herself, it seems at first, but the knowledge isn't personal, it's common to all.

She sees Colmán taste the beer and frown. It's sour, she knows from her own earlier sip of it. He glances at his wife and then across at the *rectaire,* who at this moment has found his voice and orders a servant to bring a plate of meat more quickly. Though Áine can't hear Colmán sigh, she knows he's given one and there is a touch of frustration in it. His eyes rest on hers for a moment and she sees the despair in them, and it makes her breath catch. Hurriedly, she finds something else to study, the rich red of his father's *brat* that hangs over one shoulder. Beside him, Rónnat pushes her food around on the plate and gives a feeble smile to the man across from her who utters some reassuring words. She realizes now that with Rónnat spending all her time with Domnall, the household supervision has fallen to Bruinech and the steward has taken advantage.

Bruinech picks up a small bit of bread on her platter then puts it down. Even from her place across from her, Áine can see the bottom is burnt. An angry flush creeps up Bruinech's face. She glances at Áine and then shifts her gaze to Máthair Gobnait.

'How does Domnall fare?' she asks. Her voice is overloud and there is a slight tremor in it.

'I've been able to ease his cough and make him more comfortable, I think,' Máthair Gobnait says in a calm tone.

'I'm sure Rónnat is grateful for even the slightest of improvements.' There is no warmth in her expression or her tone. Colmán glances at her and narrows his eyes.

'I make no promises about what I might achieve with Domnall,' Máthair Gobnait says, 'but I will do my best to help him in any way that I can, and I will pray for him. God's love is infinite.'

'Infinite love won't cure Domnall,' Colmán mutters.

Bruinech frowns. 'My mother-in-law must be made to feel she's doing all she can for her son.'

'Have you any children of your own?' Máthair Gobnait asks.

Bruinech stiffens and raises eyes glittering with tears. 'I have no children.'

Áine can see the tiny lines around her eyes, that on a poor woman might signify long days in harsh weather, but in this case she knows it means that this woman has few enough years left for childbearing.

'There is time yet,' says Máthair Gobnait. 'The Bible tells us the story of Sarah, Abraham's wife, who thought she was long past bearing children. Eventually she gave birth to a healthy son.'

A glimmer of hope lights her face, creating a momentary youthful beauty, but it disappears, leaving her face sullen. 'As you say, it is only a story.'

'You have no fosterlings?' Áine asks. The question pops out before she realizes and she wishes to retrieve it immediately when Bruinech and Colmán turn to look at her.

Bruinech casts a glance at Colmán. 'My mother-in-law has lately fostered a girl. She's gone back to her parents to prepare for her marriage.' The tears are there again for a moment. She looks at Máthair Gobnait. 'But you've no children yourself, have you? You women remain unwed, virginal. Don't you wish for the protection of a husband, a family?'

'Some of us have wed and borne children. As for me, the church is my family, the Lord is my husband.'

'You don't wish for children? Even a fosterling?'

'A distant kinsman of one of the sisters is bringing his daughter come the autumn. We hope that eventually she'll want to join us.'

'She will bring a dowry with her?' asks Colmán. His face is curious but there is a hint of scepticism in his voice.

'Yes, a small parcel of farmland to add to our own. She's a kinswoman to one of the sisters in the *tuath*.'

'And you,' Bruinech says, looking at Áine, 'you have no children, no wish to have them, or a husband?'

76

Áine hesitates, pushing down the unease. 'I have no children, no. And I'm not wed.'

'Yet, you're not one of the community.'

'Áine has met with some misfortune,' says Máthair Gobnait. She gives a brief account of the circumstances that brought her to Gort na Tiobratán and the nunnery. Áine wails inside at each word that reveals more of herself to these people. To this man. Her heart is beating wildly and it's all she can do to remain seated.

'And you have no recollection of what happened?' asks Colmán. He gives her a hard stare, but there is no menace there. Clever men can be dangerous, though. 'Nor any clue to your identity?'

Áine shakes her head and reminds herself that her ignorance is her protection. Her heart slows, but still she reaches for Máthair Gobnait's hand under the table.

'What is the first thing you recall after your accident?' His tone has turned curt.

'You must forgive my husband his manner,' Bruinech says, her voice a wobble. 'He is in the law profession and has the rank of *aigne*. Searching questions are second nature to him.'

'You act for the law courts?' asks Máthair Gobnait. She nods thoughtfully. 'That's better than I hoped. One reason I requested Áine to accompany me here is to enlist your father's help to discover who her family might be. If it's possible.'

'She's not from this *tuath,*' says Colmán. 'Nor anyone just east of here. I travel much fulfilling my duties and I've heard nothing of this tale. But as you say, she was found west of you.' He examines Áine closely, his profession and Máthair Gobnait's request giving him free rein. 'Do you recall anything of your former life?'

Áine lowers her eyes, feeling the heat of his scrutiny that seems to lift her hair and peer into her soul. What should she say to him? 'Just today, I found I have played the harp.'

Senán takes this moment to join the conversation. 'I understand you play well.' His tall wiry frame sits awkwardly at the table, a paradox of the grace his hands and fingers suggest. 'Domnall praised you and that means much. He thinks you're a bard, or some sort of harper of some experience and learning.'

'He knows music?' asks Áine. It's a question she knows the answer to before she asks it, but it changes the direction of the conversation as she hopes, though only for a moment.

'He does, under my tutelage.'

'If you have no memory, how is it that you're called Áine?'

Colmán's abrupt question unbalances her for a moment and she pauses to collect herself. 'Máthair Gobnait gave me the name.'

'You call her "Mother?"'

'I'm called that because I'm a *banóircindeach*, an honour Epscop Ábán conferred on me. I'm mother to the women and girls in my care.'

'Mother to grown women.' Colmán looks at her thoughtfully.

'Everyone has a mother, whether they are grown or still a child. These women look to me, those whose kin are dead and gone.'

'You are like their *Muimme*,' says Bruinech, a small smile appearing on her face. 'You've not given birth to these women but you nurture and instruct them, isn't that right?'

Máthair Gobnait turns the full force of her warmth on Bruinech. 'That expresses it very well and so beautifully.'

Colmán frowns and looks at Áine. 'And you would become one of these women should you not find your kin?'

'I would hope to, no matter the outcome.'

Máthair Gobnait pats her hand. 'There's time enough to decide all that. For now, we must hope that Colmán's investigations provide some answers.'

Áine resists looking at Colmán though she can feel his gaze once again, taking in her hair, her face, lingering overlong on her mouth, to travel down along her shoulders, studying the length of her fingers, the smallest one now somewhat crooked from her injuries. His intensity unnerves her, fuels the anxiety that he evokes so easily when he's near. Beside her Máthair Gobnait squeezes her hand.

～

Áine's days at Raithlinn beside Máthair Gobnait are filled with activity that give her little time to contemplate her fears, though some of that is of her own choosing. She finds she misses Siúr Sodelb, though, and she allows her thoughts to dwindle on memories of their time together. She does all she can to avoid Colmán's company the first few days. On the fourth day he leaves to attend to some legal matter on the far end of the *tuath* and she feels relief when she hears he will be gone a while.

Much of her time is taken up helping Máthair Gobnait tend Domnall, mixing tinctures, fetching broth and fresh water for him to sip. She also assists in washing his body and freshening the bedclothes and spending time by his side to allow Rónnat periods of rest. She finds Domnall an uncomplaining patient, grateful for the small kindnesses she can manage, but still too weak to say more than a few words each time she sees him. His love of music is evident, though, and his large sunken eyes light up when she first offers to play the harp again. She curses herself for such foolishness, but reasons that Domnall is hardly going to jump out of his sickbed and tell others that she plays.

It's Rónnat's reaction that starts her worries anew when she asks her quietly if she might borrow the harp once more. Rónnat is overjoyed and fusses about, calling a servant to fetch Senán with his harp, and when the servant takes overlong, she leaves the room to search him out herself. Áine can almost hear her telling all and sundry that she wants Senán to bring his harp to Domnall's room so Áine can play for him.

Domnall gives her a rueful look and mouths the words, 'I'm sorry.' That he understands her reluctance makes it worse in a way, and she chides herself for being so fanciful.

'I think it will give you just as much pleasure to play as it will Domnall to listen,' says Máthair Gobnait.

Áine only nods because she is afraid of what she might say if she speaks.

By the time the harp is in her lap, there is a small group gathered at the doorway. She is flushed and trembling, anxious for so many reasons, the least of which is whether she will be able to play again at all. She starts out slowly and soon her fingers are finding their way, this time with greater ease. The tune is the same, she won't risk anything else, not only for the sake of her fragile memory, but because she isn't certain what such display of skill would mean for her.

When the tune is completed, this time without any accompanying humming, she turns slightly and sees that Bruinech is at the front of the small group and she watches Áine with such intensity, Áine can't help but feel a twinge of fear. Has she seen something, recognized some gesture of Áine's that marks her for who she is? She tries to shake off the feeling as she hands the harp back to Senán and says she can remember no other tune. Senán takes the harp and sits on her vacated stool and plies his craft. The group at the doorway lingers, all except Bruinech, who has vanished.

~

Not all of her time is spent tending Domnall. There are points in the day when she and Máthair Gobnait are free to do as they will. Máthair Gobnait makes it clear from the first that she will still observe the offices throughout the day. For this purpose she goes to their sleeping cubicle and kneels among the rushes on the beaten earth. Holding the cross that hangs around her neck, she prays, recites the psalms, sings the *Beati* and other hymns, makes counted genuflections and repeats some words of the Gospel. With a mixture of feelings, Áine asks to join her and Máthair Gobnait welcomes her to sit and listen as she says each prayer, psalm and hymn aloud and makes her genuflections. It's in these moments too that Áine can feel closer to Siúr Sodelb and sometimes picture her kneeling beside Máthair Gobnait.

Áine finds it soothing to attend the offices. It also allows her to remain in the cubicle out of sight of anyone else. But as the offices take shape and *Terce* becomes distinct from *Prime* and *Sext,* and all the others distinguish themselves, she begins to look forward to the recitation, to even long for the assurance of each one's pattern. The words take shape in her own mind before she hears Máthair Gobnait give voice to them, and she mouths some of the prayers almost in full, taking pleasure in the beauty of the words, the cadences of the rhythms.

It's when she is sitting on the bed and Máthair Gobnait is kneeling on the floor, in the early hours one morning, with only a shaft of light coming from the passageway that leads to the back entrance of this section of sleeping cubicles, that she becomes conscious of someone hovering at their doorway. Máthair Gobnait's eyes are closed and she is positioned away from the entrance, but Áine is facing forward and can see the movement of a shadow. She clutches the bedclothes and casts her eyes wildly around for something to fend off the person should they enter. The figure moves further into view, a head leans over, tentative. Áine starts to rise and sees that it is Bruinech, still clad only in her *léine*. Bruinech stands there, only half visible, her eyes fixed on Máthair Gobnait, who continues with her recitation.

'The Lord is my Shepherd,' she says, 'I shall not want…'

In the pale light Áine can see that, though Bruinech's eyes are expressionless, silent tears are making their way down her cheeks. Áine releases the breath she didn't know she was holding. It comes out with a soft sigh and Bruinech looks up at Áine and her face hardens. A moment later she is gone.

~

Domnall's health makes no marked improvement, though it's evident that his breathing has eased, and his bouts of painful coughing have lessened considerably. Rónnat holds on to these signs as an indication of hope and Máthair Gobnait tries to gently point out the truth. The truth is undeniable in the hollowed eyes, the blood that spatters the linen when he does cough, the little broth he sips and the thin frame that continues to lose its flesh. Still, even Áine finds it difficult not to support Rónnat's hopeful observations and pray that some miracle might heal Domnall.

'You must not give them false hope,' Máthair Gobnait tells her one afternoon as they sit for a moment in the afternoon sunshine. 'Nor yourself. The outcome is certain. At this point we can only ease his passing.'

'But surely when God hears our prayers he won't let such a man as Domnall die so needlessly. I will fast to prove the sincerity of my prayers.'

'God will hear the prayers and have no doubt of their sincerity, but you cannot bargain with Him.'

Áine sighs and asks nothing more, leaving unspoken the question that has plagued her. Would prayers from an unbaptized woman reach God's ears, and even more troubling, what would happen to Domnall, once he died? If the Lord was the one and only God, was there a place for Domnall in the heaven they speak about? Or will he go to the Otherworld, just as surely as all his ancestors had before him? But these are questions that she can't bring herself to ask, not because she has no courage to ask them, but because she has no courage to hear the answers.

~

They stay for ten days, though in some ways it seems more than that to Áine, if only that the person she feels she was when she entered the *dún* is different to the one who leaves. Perhaps Colmán's absence makes her more at ease, so she can take pleasure in the ritual of the daily offices, as well as concentrate on assisting Domnall.

Whatever the cause, she eventually moves through the day without jumping like some wild hare whenever someone unfamiliar approaches her. Bruinech aside, the rest of the household take little notice of her movements, especially since she refuses any further requests to play the harp.

All her calm evaporates with Máthair Gobnait's last words when they take their leave. Máthair Gobnait, having shown Rónnat and a serving girl in detail all that they must do to mix the broths and tinctures to continue Domnall's care, speaks words of encouragement to Rónnat and Uí Blathnaic before climbing up onto the cart.

'You will send me word when he passes. I will pray for him and come if you would like. It will be a little while yet, though.'

Rónnat wrings her hands and looks at her husband. Her hair hangs in hanks and her clothes are dishevelled. They are clean, though, with no trace of a stain. Áine and Máthair Gobnait have seen to that and impressed the importance of such acts to help Domnall feel better.

Uí Blathnaic gives her a hard stare. 'We appreciate all that you've done for my son, make no mistake. But there is no need to attend us then, nor say the prayers you mention.'

Máthair Gobnait nods. 'And your other son, Colmán, I had hoped to speak to him before I left about the matter of Áine. Would you have him send word to me if he discovers anything?'

Uí Blathnaic agrees and spares a glance for Áine. She is paralysed by the thought Colmán might uncover information that would be shared around like an old mug and can only stare back wide-eyed. She is convinced this will not end well.

CHAPTER SEVEN

The measure of relief Áine feels when the cart enters the *faithche* is almost tangible. The air is pungent with the smell of ripening fields and she can nearly taste the bread that is baking. Siúr Sodelb emerges from the *Tech Mor*, her arms circling an empty basket. Áine raises her hand for a wave, her heart lifting more because she feels that she is home.

'*Failte arais*,' says Siúr Sodelb, moving toward them. Her gait is still awkward, but Áine finds that reassuring somehow, a sign that some things are unchanged, expected.

'Thank you. It is good to be back.' Máthair Gobnait returns her greeting and Cadoc moves toward her to help her down. 'Any news? The sisters are well? And the bees?'

Siúr Sodelb smiles and once again Áine marvels at her unearthly beauty. 'All is well, including the bees, though I'm sure they've missed you.'

Máthair Gobnait nods in satisfaction. She turns to instruct Cadoc to give Fionn an extra ration and gives her a loving pat before Cadoc leads her away. 'She's a good beast, still. She took us far.'

'She'll be glad of the ration, Mistress,' says Cadoc. 'Things were slack enough in some ways at Raithlinn. I kept my eye out to see that she was led out to grass each day, but there were other horses too, and I don't know their pastures the way I do here.'

'I know you did what you could, Cadoc.' She nods briefly and Cadoc moves away. It's obvious Cadoc knows he has said enough.

~

Áine greets the other sisters later, just after the office of *Vespers*. When she hears the bell ringing this time, she rises from her seat on the bench just outside the *Tech Mor* where she is resting after her journey and makes her way to the oratory. After a quick nod from Máthair Gobnait she stands at the back. She sings the *Beati* softly, recites the psalms barely above a whisper and dares to join in with the *Pater Noster,* though she keeps the tone evenly blended with the others. The genuflections are made over and over and by the tenth, she has them perfected and in harmony with the others.

Siúr Ethne stands to recite the designated section of the Gospel and her eyes fix on Áine. There's no doubt of her opinion of Áine's decision to come. Her eyes are narrowed and her mouth still manages a frown, though it forms the holy words of the Apostle Luke. Áine lowers her head under such overt disapproval and edges towards the door, until she feels Siúr Sodelb's warm hand slip into hers. With Siúr Sodelb's support she can look at the twisted cross on the altar and listen to St Luke describing Jesus' escape into Egypt.

She studies the small figure of Jesus affixed to the twisted cross, a working in copper that shows arms stretched wide, legs hanging down. Siúr Ethne described this event to her in great detail before she left for Raithlinn. She told her of the soldiers scourging his back as He carried the cross past onlookers and up the hill, the nails driven through His palms to secure Him to the cross, the thorns piercing the flesh and his head, and the wounds at His side that weep blood. Áine thinks of the pain of such wounds, the arms disjointed by the weight of the body, a body already broken and beaten. She closes her eyes, rubs her palm with her thumb and imagines a nail there, just as Siúr Ethne has told her to. The pain comes as she said it would, just as if the nail had pierced her flesh. She feels hands restrain her, despite her desperate struggles and blows rain down upon her and knives slash her, until the sweet darkness takes over. She opens her eyes and finds herself lying on the floor, the sisters and Máthair Gobnait gathered around her.

'What happened?' she asks.

'You moaned and then fainted,' Máthair Gobnait says. Her eyes are filled with concern.

'She's not fully prepared to undertake the offices. She shouldn't have participated, she is not baptized,' says Siúr Ethne.

'She will be baptized soon.' Máthair Gobnait's voice is firm. 'Though I'm certain that had nothing to do with it.'

Máthair Gobnait requests Siúr Feidelm to bring water and kneels beside her. She places a hand on her head. 'You're not feverish, *buíochas le Dia*.'

'I'm sorry to have caused such a stir. It's nothing, I assure you. A fragment of memory from my beating came upon me suddenly.'

Máthair Gobnait frowns. 'I'm sorry. Those memories would be very painful, I'm sure.'

Siúr Sodelb kneels on her other side and without a word takes her hand. Áine is grateful for the gesture, feeling more able to explain something of the experience a few moments before. She takes a deep breath. 'There were men, some restraining me and others beating me.'

Siúr Feidelm returns and hands Máthair Gobnait a cup of water. 'Did you know these men?' she asks.

Áine's mind conjures up one of the images briefly before she pushes it away. 'I don't know. I didn't see them.'

'You didn't see them?' asks Siúr Ethne. Her tone is sceptical.

'Did you recognize any of the voices?' asks Siúr Feidelm. 'You said you heard them shouting.'

Máthair Gobnait holds up her hand. 'I think it's best that we defer the questions for now. We must give Áine some time to recover. And then it's for her to decide what she can tell us, or if she needs help to understand what she's remembered.'

At Máthair Gobnait's insistence, Siúr Feidelm and Siúr Mugain help her to rise and sit on a bench. Áine assures them she is fine and well able to eat the small meal of bread and cheese waiting for them at the *Tech Mor*. After a few moments, they help her there and seat her next to Máthair Gobnait. Once the blessing is given, she even manages a few sips of beer and bites of bread. Around her, chatter about the weather and the new calves breaks out in small spurts.

Máthair Gobnait brings her own news to the fore after a while and begins recounting their time spent at Raithlinn. It is a tale with purpose, showing the others how their duty is shaped by the needs of the sick and how the holy vigil is given to those who are dying. She explains what she was allowed to do, and what she had to do and would wish to do to ease the physical and spiritual passing of one not Christian. She makes it clear that there is never a point where a person is no longer able to come to the faith, and so it's important to treat everyone as a child of Christ. Siúr Ethne tears angrily at her bread and says nothing.

'I feel that Uí Blathnaic will now look more kindly on our community and perhaps Boirneach too,' Máthair Gobnait adds to emphasize her point.

'Perhaps if Uí Blathnaic became a Christian, his son would get well.' It's Siúr Mugain who makes the remark. There's no malice in her tone, but Siúr Ethne raises a brow and waits for Máthair Gobnait's response, her mouth prim.

'Did you really mean to say that, Siúr Mugain?'

Siúr Mugain flushes. 'Doesn't the Lord work miracles for his flock?'

Máthair Gobnait sighs and looks around at the others, her face clearly expressing dismay and speculation over how many others failed to understand what she'd been explaining moments before. Áine holds her gaze, sorry for the frustration, though she has her own doubts about Máthair Gobnait's sentiments.

Siúr Sadhbh decides a change of subject is in order. 'Epscop Ábán comes next Sunday for mass and to collect the finished wool robes, Máthair Ab. Should I slaughter that lame calf?'

There is only a moment's pause before Máthair Gobnait decides to accept this new direction in the end. 'No, we'll save that for the harvesting, when we have the extra workers on the farm. Epscop Ábán won't mind.'

'It'll be Lughnasadh soon. Time for the annual *Oenach*. Will we give some meat to Epscop Ábán to take to the fair? There's a lamb that that would suit, if you need it.'

'Ah yes, the fair. Good. And perhaps this year we might give some cheese, too. Epscop Ábán had his share at Whitsun so there should be some to spare now.'

Máthair Gobnait looks at Siúr Sodelb. 'Are the robes finished?'

'Yes. They just need folding and wrapping in readiness. There are six in all.'

'Well done. That should see the bishop and the *manaigh* through the winter. *Buíochas le Dia* they require no fancy vestments. When he comes he'll be presiding over a baptism as well.' She nods to Áine.

Áine is too startled to say a word. A jumbled mixture of feelings surge inside. There is pleasure and joy, but also fear and, more disturbing, reluctance. This an emotion she tries to push aside to allow a positive expression that signals her thanks to this woman next to her who has taken her under her wing.

Siúr Ethne has no such conflicting feelings. Her view is clear from the grim line of her mouth and the darkening eyes. 'You will have her baptized so soon? Do you really feel she's ready after what happened only a little while ago?'

'Of course. What better way to help and protect her than to invoke the Lord's blessing and acceptance into his fold?'

Eyes narrowed, Siúr Ethne studies Máthair Gobnait a moment and gives a barely detectable snort. There are no more words, but in that small expression much is conveyed about such a step. There is no need for her to physically move away, it is clear that Siúr Ethne is distancing herself from this decision and Máthair Gobnait's role in it.

Máthair Gobnait gazes around the group seeking out other points of discussion, but there is only silence. A few manage to give Áine tentative smiles.

~

Áine rises the second hour past midnight, when Siúr Ethne sounds the bell for the office of *Matins*. She pulls her plain wool gown over her *léine,* ties her leather belt around her waist and slips on her sandals to follow Máthair Gobnait and Siúr Sodelb out of the sleeping hut over to the oratory. She ignores Siúr Ethne's pursed mouth when she assembles with the other women, some suppressing yawns and others rubbing their eyes. She joins them in the *Beati* and notices a few of the voices are rusty from sleep. None of it takes from the simple beauty of the singing that breaks the silence of the night.

On her way back to the sleeping hut, following Siúr Sodelb, she can feel the dewy grass that sweeps the tops of her sandals and brushes her toes. The moisture is cold and chills her feet in the cool night air. Once inside the hut, she slips into her bed quickly, searching for the vestiges of warmth that remain. Máthair Gobnait and Siúr Ethne have lingered in the oratory, Máthair Gobnait taking an opportunity for a private discussion with Siúr Ethne.

'I'm glad you're back,' whispers Siúr Sodelb from her cot next to Áine. She reaches over and grasps her hand. 'I missed your company.' It's the first time they have had an opportunity to exchange any words out of range of other listeners.

'And I yours.' Áine is shy about expressing how much she missed Siúr Sodelb and can only squeeze her hand to emphasize the depth of her feelings for her.

'Your presence here has brought such joy,' says Siúr Sodelb. 'I find even more pleasure in the music we lay before God.'

'There was a bard, Senán, at Raithlinn. He had a vast amount of music.'

'My father had a bard. It's from him that I learned music.'

Áine takes this in, wondering if she too learned from a bard in her father's household. 'I played Senán's harp,' she says finally, uncertain if she should mention this small piece of herself, even to Siúr Sodelb.

But the information comes as no surprise and that thought calms her. 'So it's as we thought,' says Siúr Sodelb. 'You know music. That's a step forward.'

Áine murmurs words of agreement but there is no conviction behind them. 'Máthair Gobnait has asked Colmán, Domnall's brother, to find out what he can about me. He's a legal representative.' She thinks of Bruinech. 'Do you ever wish for a husband and children, Sodelb?'

Sodelb gives a little sigh. 'What I may wish for and what is possible are too different things. Besides, I'm more than content here.' She presses Áine's hand. 'And you've made me happier still.'

Máthair Gobnait enters at that moment. 'Sleep is what will make you happiest now. We'll be up again soon enough.'

'I'm sorry, Máthair Gobnait,' says Siúr Sodelb. 'You're right, of course.'

Áine murmurs her own apologies and turns to settle back to sleep. She is still awake when Siúr Ethne returns, sometime later, creeping to her small cot. From her own cot nearby, Máthair Gobnait speaks in a low voice, the words barely discernible.

'The Lord does not see sleep as a luxury, Siúr Ethne. You must get your rest the same as all the others.'

'I only sought to offer a few more prayers. Some of the brothers at Ard Maigh keep vigil all night.'

'That might be so, but it's not something the Lord or we require here.'

'If we're not here to worship and pray to God, what are we here for?'

'Being in the service of God can take many forms, but this is not the time or place to discuss it.'

Máthair Gobnait's voice is firm. Siúr Ethne offers no other comment, but Áine knows she isn't satisfied. Siúr Ethne clearly has her own vision of God's work, and the actions, words and thoughts such service entails. She is finding her own way to God.

~

The next morning when the sisters and Máthair Gobnait sit down to break their fast Siúr Ethne declines to take anything but water. The bowl of plain porridge Siúr Feidelm spoons up is pushed away, despite Máthair Gobnait's frown and Siúr Ethne passes the heel of bread to Siúr Mugain.

'I hope you feel well enough to eat later,' says Máthair Gobnait. 'You wouldn't want to faint during mass, especially in *an Thiarna Epscop's* presence.'

'I'm fine. I promise you I will not faint.'

'Well if you do feel unwell, you may go and take your rest.'

'I'm sure that won't be necessary.'

Silence falls on the group and hunches them over their bowls, none daring to look up and catch the eye of anyone else at this small challenge to Máthair Gobnait's rule.

Siúr Sodelb has told Áine about the group of Penitential *manaigh* scattered around the monasteries who believed following an extreme ascetic life made them closer to Christ's suffering and His grace, and that they, and all men, are so sinful by nature they must starve and beat themselves, and spend hours on their knees in atonement. Such views seem out of place here. God is love, God is forgiveness, God is protector and comforter and all are his children, here among this community of women.

~

Just as Máthair Gobnait said, Epscop Ábán baptizes Áine on the next Sunday. The thought that this rite might bring about changes gives rise to such fear in her that she nearly backs away when she is led forward to the small well just outside the oratory. She will be born anew, nestled firmly in the bosom of God, they tell her, but she can't imagine this. She can only picture all her memories flooding back in the wake of her cleansing, her mind clear, but most certainly not pure. Someone beaten near to death as she has been must have led the most impure life.

At the well, they ask her the questions and she mumbles the answers she was told to give, while Máthair Gobnait adds her own supportive statements. Áine trembles, looking around her as Epscop Ábán cups his hand and reaches down into the well and pours water over her. She closes her eyes, holds her breath and waits for the worst to happen.

Her eyes are still closed when she feels an arm around her. She opens them and sees Máthair Gobnait leaning in to kiss her forehead. She blinks a few times, still poised and waiting, testing herself to mark any changes when they arrive. There is nothing. She feels a glow of happiness spread through her, because she can now begin her life in truth as Áine. There are no memories of another woman to clamour for attention and push her into becoming something she no longer wants. What she does want is to join this community of women and become a *cailech*.

CHAPTER EIGHT

It is only when Fionn emerges out of the mist, galloping toward the *faithche,* a rider clinging to her mane, that the women realize she's been missing. It's Siúr Sadhbh who sees the horse first, as she carries buckets of milk taken from the cows in the field above. Two girls struggle after her, carrying a third bucket between them, but they drop the bucket at the sight of Fionn riding towards them, the mist swirling and gathering about the horse like something from a *seanachaí's* tale.

Áine sees them when she appears in the doorway of the sleeping hut, freshly dressed in her wool gown and a veil she's tentatively placed on her head after persuading a loan of it from Siúr Sodelb.

Fionn draws nearer, bouncing the perilously perched man with his leather satchel slung across his back. Though fear knits his brow and flattens his mouth in a near rictus pose, Áine recognizes him as Cenél, one of the builders. The sound of hooves draws Máthair Gobnait from the oratory and Siúr Feidelm from the kitchen, a spoon in her hand. Siúr Mugain steps from the larger sleeping hut, fastening her veil with small wooden hair pins.

'Siúr Mugain, will you fetch the other builders?' says Máthair Gobnait.

Siúr Mugain strides off, filled with righteous purpose, and disappears into the shed. Her voice can be heard, loud and firm, as she rustles the two men from their sleep.

Fionn slows to a trot as she approaches the entrance, and passing through, greets her beloved Máthair Gobnait with a whinny, the morning dew clinging to her mane. Cenél, terrified and exhausted, slides from her before Fionn even halts, and he collapses on the ground a small distance from Máthair Gobnait. Hands on hips, she surveys the miscreant. For what else could he be, taking a night's gallop with his mistress's horse; a horse that is not even a lowly *capall*, but an *each* that belonged only to a noble?

Behind Máthair Gobnait, Siúr Mugain pulls along the other two dishevelled builders, Findbar and Brendán, their eyes blinking hard against the sudden light, their faces both bewildered and resentful. Siúr Mugain takes Fionn and leads her away with the promise of food. Siúr Sadhbh and the two girls join the group that forms an assembly of a sort, an impromptu *juris consult* who immediately draw their own conclusions of the man that now lies shaking and fearful before them, damning himself with his pose, the satchel of tools still hanging along his back and the words of excuse that pour from his mouth.

'I didn't go far, I promise you. And I was going to return. It was that I had to go to my family, a sick brother.'

'A sick brother?' asks Findbar. 'What sick brother?'

Cenél pales. 'A cousin—distant.'

'A cousin? Where? Who? You've no sick cousin.'

'Why did you need tools to visit a sick cousin?' asks Brendán.

Máthair Gobnait holds up a hand. 'Why didn't you ask permission? If you needed to visit a sick relation, we would have been happy to help.'

'I only heard about it late at night, and I didn't want to wake you.'

'Late at night?' Findbar says. 'Who told you late at night? I heard no one.'

'It-it was a cousin, brother to the sick one. You were fast asleep when he came.'

Findbar snorts. 'This cousin told you to bring tools? What were you going to do with them, cut off a limb?'

Máthair Gobnait points to the satchel. 'Findbar, perhaps you should check which tools are in there.'

Cenél cowers as Findbar leans over and pulls the satchel from Cenél's shoulder, giving his head a smack in the process. 'Fool,' he mutters.

Cenél flushes. 'I would have been long gone if not for the horse. How much a fool then, eh?'

Findbar shakes his head and searches the satchel, squatting on the ground next to Cenél. A fine soft rain has begun to fall, forming droplets on his brown curls and thick beard.

'All of our tools are here,' he says. 'All of them.' He repeats the phrase, his voice hard. It's clear to him there is nothing innocent about Cenél's night ride.

'Do any belong to Cenél?' asks Áine. All eyes turn to her, but the veil she wears gives her courage and she returns their looks calmly.

'No,' Findbar says. 'They all belong to my brother and me.'

'Ah, now, he must be brought before the court for theft,' Siúr Sadhbh says. 'Sure, that's only right.'

'Perhaps,' says Máthair Gobnait. 'But I would like to confer with Epscop Ábán in this too.'

'Shouldn't we ask a representative of the law to come, Máthair Ab?' says Áine. The words slip out of her mouth before she realizes the law representative in this *tuath* unnerves her and is determined to discover her past.

'Colmán?' Máthair Gobnait pauses, as if considering her question. It might be that she stalls for time, confronted with a situation in which a horse and tools were stolen, yet returned before they were missed. The horse is not an ordinary *capall*, belonging only to an *ócaire*, and taken less than the distance of nine bridges that means only a small fine is paid. But the horse has returned and the tools back in the owner's possession, so there really is no permanent loss. Though it is clearly a matter for a wise law representative, the offence happened at Máthair Gobnait's community and is therefore against the church, and these days the church is increasingly interested in addressing its own matters. There is the further consideration that Colmán is not one of the Érainn people, he was Eóganacht, and though the people here are part of his *tuath*, the *dún* is in distant Raithlinn. Máthair Gobnait's decision now could affect the future of the community and should not to be taken lightly.

Áine sees this and also understands without question that in ordinary circumstances the *cáin* governing a crime like this would be specific and exacting, weighing out the subtle elements of a particular situation against past practice. The certainty of her knowledge startles her, for it is a fine point known usually to those nobly born. She glances around at the others, searching for signs that someone else possesses this information besides Máthair Gobnait, and finds no such indication. Áine holds her breath and awaits the decision.

Máthair Gobnait gives her a speculative look. 'Yes, you're right. It would be best if we ask Colmán to come.'

She turns and asks Siúr Mugain to take Cenél and put him under Cadoc's watchful eye until the matter is resolved. 'If you have no objection,' she says to Findbar and Brendán, 'and your tools are still fit to use, I would like you to continue with your work in the meantime.'

'They are and thanks, Máthair Ab,' says Findbar, bowing to her and unable to meet her eye. He gathers up the satchel. 'It's my thinking the horse is the one responsible for the recovery of all that was stolen. There's nothing favourable to be said about Cenél.'

His words are muttered, but Áine hears him and suppresses a smile at such an astute remark. Máthair Gobnait only nods. 'We'll consider everything when the time comes, rest assured.'

The group breaks up soon after, Findbar and Brendán retreating to the safety of the cowshed to restore their dignity and vent their spleen. Siúr Sadhbh and Siúr Feidelm usher the wide-eyed girls with the full pails of milk to Siúr Feidelm's kitchen to use for the morning meal, leaving only Áine and Máthair Gobnait to make their way together to the oratory in silence, Máthair Gobnait deep in thought.

~

By evening, the fine misty rain has cleared, leaving only a scattering of clouds blown by a gentle wind that dries the grass and rocks and gives the air a fresh scent. It is such a fine evening, that all who are able stretch their legs or sit outside, eager to enjoy the remaining sunlit hours, the chores finished for the day. Máthair Gobnait is one of those who takes advantage of the dry evening and climbs the hill to its summit, walks along the ridge, and finds her usual comfortable perch among the boulders that have flung themselves about the land so generously.

Áine accompanies Máthair Gobnait at her request, Áine's legs now strong enough to bear the complaints of her calf muscles as she mounts the hill. At the top, she settles herself on a dry spot next to Máthair Gobnait, her breath coming in bursts. While she recovers, she gazes beyond the immediate small fields, their downward slope meeting the trees that meander down to the river's edge and resume on the other side. A farmer from elsewhere would read this landscape with little envy and perhaps pity, but Áine knows now the valley and hillside with its rain-soaked soil and whose single most productive crop is rock, has its own value to the people of this area. Uisneach and the sacred well are only two manifestations of this value.

She shifts her gaze slightly and sees in the slopes of An Dhá Chích Danann rising up in the distance and she gives a small cry at the sight. It at once comforts her and unnerves her. She realizes she knows the place. These sacred mountains, the home of the mother goddess, are now witness to her presence here with Máthair Gobnait. Two mothers, protective of their own. She turns away quickly and looks at Máthair Gobnait. She has made her choice of protector.

Máthair Gobnait points, distracting Áine from her thoughts. 'Are my eyes failing, or is someone clearing that area there?'

Áine squints in the direction indicated. It does appear as though trees have been felled across the river, near the bank and some stones are piled on one another. 'I think you're right, Máthair Ab.'

Máthair Gobnait sits back and frowns. 'I wonder what that signifies. Uí Blathnaic spoke nothing of this to me when we were there. Did you hear of anything?'

Áine shakes her head. 'Nothing was said to me.'

Máthair Gobnait regards the area intently as if it might reveal more. Silence falls between them, heavy for only a moment, then slipping into something more benign.

'You have knowledge of the law?' Máthair Gobnait says, eventually.

Áine assembles her thoughts, tests the fear that is always lurking and finds no answers there. 'It seems I do,' she says in the end. Part of her would like to help, to offer the benefit of her understanding to enable Máthair Gobnait to make the best decisions for the community. 'I know nothing more than that.'

'So you wouldn't know what the law would decide in this case?'

Áine shakes her head. 'I'm sorry.'

Máthair Gobnait nods. There is little more to say on the subject and it's clear Máthair Gobnait understands that it's one more piece of Áine's former life come to light. Not every noble woman would have knowledge of any point of the law, Máthair Gobnait tells her. It's a revelation that Áine would rather not have, and she is uneasy about what it suggests.

Máthair Gobnait touches Áine's veil. 'I see you've covered your head.'

Áine lowers her eyes and blushes. 'I-I hope you don't mind. I borrowed one from Siúr Sodelb.'

'I don't mind, but others might find your commitment too sudden and hurried. Not everyone is suited to the path the women here follow. Haste, they might feel, does not indicate certainty and makes light of their own commitment.'

The delicate and charitable phrasing does nothing to disguise the person behind these sentiments. Áine feels a moment's anger and fear that Siúr Ethne might prevent her from becoming a *cailech*, a sister to the others.

'My intentions and heart are sincere, Máthair Ab.'

'I have no doubt of that, Daughter. But it's for you to convince God and Siúr Ethne that you have a true calling to the Lord's service.'

Áine stares out across the valley to the assembled stones that are starting to form the foundations of a small *dún*, until they dissolve under the weight of tears that fill her eyes.

CHAPTER NINE

Colmán appears the next morning, before midday, surprising everyone. When Áine sees him coming up the slope, his companions trailing after him, she thinks for a minute that he's been conjured out of the air, summoned from the Otherworld. She's sitting on the bench in front of the *Tech Mor,* mending a *léine,* and stabs her finger when she hears him hailing his arrival. Méone winds himself through her legs and meows softly. Áine tugs her veil forward, ensuring her hair is well covered, sets aside her sewing and picks up the cat. The rumble of his answering purr almost corresponds to the pace of her heart.

Colmán's men gather around him as he dismounts. She can see he is dressed for travelling, his *brat* pinned securely around him, his woollen trews dark. A small breeze ruffles his hair and he flings back a corner of his *brat* and glances around. She knows she is the only one in view. Máthair Gobnait is inside the oratory, deep in conversation with Siúr Ethne, and Siúr Sodelb is helping some of the women making butter under Siúr Feidelm's supervision. The rest of the sisters are scattered further afield.

She rises reluctantly, knowing that the required hospitality falls to her, though for a moment she contemplates hiding. But he has already spotted her and is moving quickly in her direction. The cat remains clutched in her arms. Soon Meone becomes uncomfortable and leaps out to the ground, leaving her arms hanging open. She greets Colmán and makes an effort to keep her voice even and firm.

She can see no suspicion or alarm in his eyes, or any indication that he might have information to impart. His manner appears more relaxed than her previous encounters with him at Raithlinn, as if he is more comfortable in his role as a legal representative than as son, brother, or husband.

He gives her a wide smile and his eye holds a hint of a twinkle.

'*Dé'd Bheatha-sa*,' she says.

'Is it your god now, too?' He cocks his head slightly and touches her veil.

She detects no malice in his voice. 'It is. I'm baptized.'

'But are you a *cailech*?'

She lowers her eyes. As much as she wishes to say she is, she can't lie. 'No, not yet.'

He nods, his look speculative. 'In time then. But you are well, otherwise?' He glances down at her legs. 'Bones fully knit?'

'Yes, I'm all but healed, now.'

'And your memory? Has it returned?'

'No.' She studies his face, looking again for any sign that might reveal more of his thoughts.

'You're still Áine, then.'

'I am baptized Áine and I'm a Christian and part of this community. This is where I belong now.' She makes the statement, knowing her tone is defensive, but she can't help herself. It's what she wants, it's what she needs, to be part of this community. She cannot contemplate anything else.

Though he doesn't challenge her statement, he still must ever rise to his legal rank of *aigne*. 'You're not worried that someone, a father, a husband might now be searching for you, worried for your safety, perhaps thinking you dead?'

This thought hasn't escaped her, but the fear that rises when she has contemplated it makes her feel that it is better pushed aside. She schools her expression to something approaching resolve. 'Perhaps, though I doubt it. I'm certain it would have come to light before this, if it was so.'

He gives a slight shrug. Cadoc emerges from the half built sleeping quarters, a mallet in his hand. Since the theft he's been assisting the builders, while keeping Cenél under close supervision. Áine calls to Cadoc and asks him to see to the horses and direct Colmán's men to the *Tech Mor* for refreshment. They have wandered closer and she can see that some of them are client lords of his father. It might be necessary to move all the sisters into one sleeping hut to make room for Colmán and those men, as well as erecting cots in the *Tech Mor*, especially if Epscop Ábán is coming.

The thought reminds her of the business at hand. 'You have arrived quickly. We only sent word yesterday.'

'I was already travelling in this direction and met your messenger. There were some legal matters that needed my attention.'

'I hope we have not delayed you, then.'

He gives her a slow smile. 'It is nothing that can't wait.'

Máthair Gobnait appears at the oratory door and makes her way over to him, giving him greeting. She is clearly surprised, but makes no remark on his early arrival. Áine knows she would have preferred to see Epscop

Ábán before Colmán arrived, if only to get a clear impression on the bishop's view on the proceedings. She is clear on her own direction for the community, and isn't easily bent to a path that isn't to her liking, but she is not foolish enough to alienate those who support her cause to the church officials in Cashel.

After Máthair Gobnait greets Colmán she asks after Domnall.

'He grows worse, I fear,' Colmán says.

'Is he in any pain?' asks Máthair Gobnait.

Colmán shakes his head. 'There's no pain, your remedies are still effective in that way, but he is noticeably weaker and his breathing more laboured.'

'I'll have Siúr Feidelm mix up something to take back with you.'

'I thank you, Máthair Ab.'

'And we will, of course, pray for him.'

Colmán gives a small smile. Áine is surprised to hear him use Máthair Gobnait's title. Perhaps their visit to Raithlinn has softened the attitudes towards this community, as Máthair Gobnait suggested.

~

Epscop Ábán arrives only after Colmán's men are seated around the table and given cold beer and bread. They are clearly uneasy around the women, who place the loaves before them and pour the beer in their mugs. Áine steers well clear of them and sits outside, her own unease rising high among so many people. Though she can place some of them from her time at Raithlinn, it doesn't stop her fear when any of them give her a curious glance.

With some relief, she sees Epscop Ábán enter the *faithche*. He travels in a small cart, a *manach* beside him holding the reins. Normally he would travel by horse or, if he was traveling to Cashel where there is a main road, he would use a chariot. Here, among the rock-filled rough tracks, a chariot is impractical. The cart does little to convey the dignity of a respected bishop, but Epscop Ábán's own solid authority dispels any contrary impression.

Once he is helped down from the cart, Áine moves forward for his blessing and feels a sense of calm descend on her after he gives it. Máthair Gobnait is behind her then, moving forward to give her own greeting and Áine retreats to her bench. It's there Colmán finds her a few moments later, while the others have gone inside the *Tech Mor.*

'You will come to the discussion about the case?' he asks her.

She searches his face carefully, too startled to reply. This is a request that she can only greet with suspicion, for there can be no practical reason for her presence. 'I don't understand why you would want me there.'

'Máthair Ab mentioned you seem to have some knowledge of the law. This is a tricky and complicated case, and another keen mind with some insight would be welcome.'

She considers his words and sees that there could be truth in them. She is still wary, though. 'I'm not sure how keen my mind is, and as you know, there is little memory there, so any knowledge of the law I might have had once, is most likely vanished.'

He takes a seat beside her and gives her a direct look. 'Áine,' he says softly. 'I have no direct information on your identity yet, but there is no doubt that you are wellborn, most likely a noblewoman of some kind. That in itself gives you some standing. Here we have a case of a theft committed by a servant against his master, who is ultimately a Christian nun and has connections to Epscop

Ábán. The bishop will influence the direction and handling of the case, but I have some obligation to my profession and to my king, that the law of the land carries weight in these proceedings, despite the fact they tell me they will follow only an abbreviated form of it. You've been here only a short time and have some bit of objectivity. Any voice, even a woman's, can add something to this.'

'But I am not a *cailech*, yet. I cannot testify or give opinions.'

He smiles at her. 'More knowledge of the law?'

She flushes and the fear rises again. There is too much here that is uncontrollable, and she worries about what she might unconsciously reveal. She swallows her objections when he tells her that he's already spoken to Máthair Gobnait about it, and she agrees. The unkind thought that comes to her is fleeting, but it leaves a bitter taste in her mouth.

~

They discuss the case in the *Tech Mor*, seated on benches that are pushed nearer the far wall, away from the blistering heat of the fire. Máthair Gobnait had suggested the oratory, but Colmán was keen to point out that, though they would be questioning all who were involved in the case, it was an informal discussion at this point, and best served in the semi-private *Tech Mor*.

Áine sits on a bench next to the *manach*, refusing the place Colmán had indicated at his side. He has one of his men there instead, a squat, surly looking noble who frowns across at them. Máthair Gobnait and Epscop Ábán are seated together, their expressions reflecting the solemn nature of the matters at hand. Méone lies curled up on Máthair Gobnait's lap. By the fire, Siúr Feidelm works quietly with her herbs, only one other woman at her side. These are comforting sights and Áine draws on them.

Colmán speaks the moment everyone is settled, establishing his position with his opening remarks. 'I think it is safe to say that we are in a situation that requires some delicacy of judgement. I want to state that I will weigh in the many elements.'

Máthair Gobnait takes advantage of his pause. 'As I mentioned briefly to *An Thiarna Epscop* Ábán I would like this matter to be treated as quickly and quietly as possible, with little fuss, rather than wait for Lughnasadh for the judgement. The bishop agrees.'

Colmán glances at the bishop who gives his assent. Colman remains silent for a moment, regrouping in the face of this new direction. 'Am I to understand you would prefer a judgement made here, in the next few days?'

Máthair Gobnait gives him a serene smile and nods.

'But who will act for the plaintiff, the defendant, and who will be judge?'

The bishop isn't deterred by this problem. 'There is no need for the formality of a court. We can accommodate this situation which occurred on church land, by one of its flock.'

'Once those concerned are questioned, surely you can present the case. Say tomorrow,' Máthair Gobnait says. 'I will give my evidence, without prejudice, and act for myself. As an arbitrator and lawyer, you can help the bishop give judgement on the case.'

Colmán's mouth forms a grim line. Even Áine is astonished to hear such a suggestion that challenges much of the long established procedure for a Brehon court. But times are changing, and what was once clear and unwavering, is now full of grey areas. Those nobles that filled the ranks of the law profession are now found weaving their blood connections in the church. The influence of the church is not to be trifled with, a fact those in Cashel are well aware of.

'As you wish,' he says finally.

Colmán works hard to recover his authority and directs them to start the questioning with Cadoc, so that the nature and quality of the horse can be established.

Cadoc appears soon after, his face grim and filled with the responsibility of tending to the prisoner over the past few days. He clears his throat and gives his response after Colmán explains what his question is.

'Fionn is a fine mare, so. I saw her birthed years ago back in Connacht. Her dam was special, brought from across the sea at the lord's request. Pure white. This one, she has only a little dappling, but she's got spirit. She's an *each* of the highest quality.'

'And what age is she now?'

Cormac thinks a moment. 'She is ten, I do believe.'

'And she belongs to Máthair Ab?'

'She does, so.'

'And you would say she's in good condition?'

Cadoc lifts his chin a fraction. 'She's in the best condition. I do be taking her to the field every morning, brush her in the evening and examine her for any soreness of joints or hooves.'

'I've no doubt that you do, Cadoc. I just want to establish formally how well you look after her.'

'She's in top condition alright, or she wouldn't have been able to gallop around all night with that *bastún* on her back.'

Áine smiles at his words and sees the glint of humour in Máthair Gobnait's eyes. Colmán maintains a neutral expression, though his mouth twitches slightly.

He thanks Cadoc. It is Siúr Sadhbh's turn next. She describes her journey down the hillside, buckets in both hands, in a fulsome manner, her own talent for *scéal* worthy of a *seanachaí*.

'It was out of the mist she appeared, galloping hard, like something from *Tír na n'og,* snorting, her breath coming heavy from her nostrils.'

'And the man on her back?'

'Ah, Cenél was clinging to her mane that tight he could have pulled the hairs off her, the *cráthur.*' Her face flushes, all her practical inclinations now supplanted for a *seanachaí,* a role seldom employed in a place where prayers to God require no well drawn description and cows find little interest in them.

'And you're certain it was Cenél that you saw?'

'It was indeed of course, for who could miss his gangly frame?' The desire to point out matters so obvious puts a note of impatience into her tone. 'He was the one who fell off Fionn when she came to a halt. Even Méone could testify to that.' She gives a quick glance at the cat. He lifts his head for a moment from his place on Máthair Gobnait's lap.

Siúr Sadhbh's account is complete and all the questions asked. For a brief moment, her face registers a disappointment that her narrative hasn't been given greater time to take flight, until Máthair Gobnait rewards her with a smile.

The questioning takes a serious turn when Findbar and Brendán come in to give their accounts. Áine leans forward slightly, listening to their words. In the time she has been here in the community she has avoided their company, and now she wonders at the nature of these men.

111

Findbar and Brendán stand before the small group, eyes cast down, feet shuffling uncomfortably under their scrutiny. When Colmán asks the questions, their answers are straightforward, with no embellishment or humour. Yes, the tools in the satchel belonged to them. Yes, Cenél took them all. They are builders only, seeing mallet, hammer, stone, wood and nails for what they are and nothing more is needed. The answers are directed at Colmán, with only a few glances over to Epscop Ábán and Máthair Gobnait.

'We've taught him all he knows of building,' Findbar adds. 'And this is the thanks we get.' He shakes his head, puzzlement clear.

'Can you tell us how Cenél came to work for you?' The question comes from Epscop Ábán. Findbar flushes, looks at the bishop and then back at Colmán, who nods.

'We asked him to learn the craft when his mam died and the work was slack on my father's farm,' says Brendán.

'Is he an *ócaire*, like yourselves?' asks Colmán

'No, he's a servant. His mother served ours.'

'And his father?' Epscop Ábán adds.

'A servant too, died long since,' says Findbar.

This time it is Epscop Ábán who thanks the two questioned and they make a hasty retreat. Colmán's face reveals nothing of this change in procedure and calmly asks for Cenél to be presented. Máthair Gobnait mentions that it might be best to wait. It is noon, and time for the next office. The bell for the next office sounds, as if on cue, and Epscop Ábán, Máthair Gobnait and the *manaigh* rise in unison. Áine comes to her feet a few moments later, surprised and unnerved that so much time has passed and that the summons from the bell is almost unwelcome.

~

By the time they assemble again to hear Cenél, the sun is already well past its apex. Áine can see that Colmán has passed the time deep in thought, though his men move restlessly outside the *Tech Mor*, making conversation and observing the workings of the community.

Cadoc brings Cenél into the *Tech Mor*, holding him firmly by the arm. Cenél appears nervous, his eyes darting from Máthair Gobnait to Colmán, clearly uncertain what to expect. It is this moment that will bring clarity to the matter, or so it is hoped. Some thieves, when questioned, might tell or invent a story, or create a reason for such an action to invoke the questioner's pity or compassion. They might even suggest that, given the circumstances, the questioner too might have chosen a similar path, had they been bold enough. For it was a bold act this man committed, or perhaps a desperate one, his mother and father gone, no wife in sight and few enough friends or companions to pass the day. What would he have done with the horse, an *each* of great value, and tools that so clearly were not his own? No *tuath* or *dún* would entertain him, without family to vouch for him.

'You took the horse and the tools,' says Colmán. His voice is firm, there is no sense of play or humour. 'Can you explain why? Have you anything to say to defend your actions?'

Cenél remains silent, his head bowed, his shoulders hunched. This is a man who is either sorry or upset that he was found out. He shakes his head after a moment.

'You have no explanation in your defence?'

Cenél shakes his head again.

'Have you nothing to say?'

'I'm sorry,' he whispers.

'You're sorry.'

Cenél nods.

Colmán gives a nearly inaudible sigh. There is little more to say and no other person to question. It's not the evidence that is in doubt here, but the nature of how to approach its presentation and the resulting judgement.

'You accept you'll be required to pay restitution for this deed?' Colmán says finally.

Epscop Ábán interrupts. 'You repent your actions?' His eyes narrow.

Cenél gives another nod, stealing a quick look at Epscop Ábán. The bishop shows no reaction to this acknowledgement. His hands are pushed up inside his robe, out of sight.

Máthair Gobnait gives a nod to Cadoc to usher Cenél back to the shed. Siúr Feidelm hasn't returned with her companion after the noon office, and Méone has left long ago on his own kind of hunt. The room is silent for a moment. Colmán's companion leans over and whispers into his ear. Colmán frowns and nods.

'I don't think there is any more information we can gather about this case,' he says finally. He glances for a moment at Áine before looking at Epscop Ábán. 'I assume you would have the formal presentation tomorrow?'

Epscop Ábán nods. 'I don't see why the judgement can't be given the following day. Cenél's guilt is apparent. He's committed the sin of theft and thieves should be punished. But he's confessed to the sin and the church can show a degree of mercy on that count.'

Colmán's eyes show a flash of anger, but he quickly conceals it. 'We can, of course, make the presentation tomorrow. My men will be attending, as I'm certain will be your community, so I suggest we hold it outside the *Tech Mor*. My men will help arrange things.'

Máthair Gobnait glances at Epscop Ábán and nods. 'Your offer of help is welcome,' she says. She rises. 'Now if you will excuse me, I have much to see to before this day ends. *A Thiarna Epscop,* if you would like to take your rest until *Nones* I will happily show you and Brother Cormac to your beds.'

With those words she dismisses everyone, scattering each person to their own thoughts, away from physical contact from the others. It is a pause in a battle of old and new, and the battle's winner could be either group, though the war is clearly won already.

CHAPTER TEN

He catches her as she emerges from the oratory, after *Nones*. She is the last one to leave, not because she has lingered to pray longer, but because she hopes to avoid the men that wander the *faithche*. In the sacred area of the *termann* that surrounds the oratory, she feels safe. She's certain that the looks the men give her as she passes are beyond the norm and their meaning is nothing good. These thoughts crowd her mind as she steps over the threshold back outside, her sandals giving their reassuring slap on the stone. She stops abruptly when Colmán puts a hand on her arm and asks for a word.

She panics for a moment, certain that one of his men has told him something about her. He leads her to the south side of the building, away from the *Tech Mor* and most of the other buildings contained in the *faithche*. She can hear the cows lowing in the distance, and quickly tells him she must go help Siúr Sadhbh with the milking. He gives her a soft smile and lifts her hand. The nails are now fully repaired, the skin soft around them.

'You help by watching?' he asks.

She flushes, the lie too obvious and silly. Colmán knows she would never be called upon to perform such a menial task, something he'd only pointed out to her as recently as that morning.

'What is it you want?' Her tone is curt, defensive.

'I mean you no criticism. In fact, it's your help I need.'

'Why would you need my help? I was of no use to you during the proceedings today, how would it be any different now?'

'On the contrary, you listened carefully to all the testimonies. Now I would ask your opinion.'

'My opinion?' She's astonished he would even think to ask her. His surly companion would have all the information she possessed and would know more than she about the workings of the court, and Colmán's method of handling matters in the course of his profession. 'I'm sure I'd be of little help to you there.'

'Just listen for a moment, Áine,' he says. He takes up her hand and gives her a pleading look. 'This is a new situation for me, and I need someone who understands to some degree the workings of the church, and most particularly this community.'

She stares down at his hand clasped over hers and can feel the sweat break out on her palm. What has she become entangled in? This man with his precise ways and knowledge of the law is the last person she should become familiar with. She withdraws her hand carefully.

'I have been remiss in asking after your wife,' she says a moment later.

A brief look of frustration crosses his face and he waves his hand a little as if to brush the matter aside. 'She is as well as before. There is no change in her situation, and that of course makes her unhappy.'

'I'm sorry to hear it.'

He sighs and the sadness is there, filling his eyes. 'This is nothing new, Áine. My wife has been unhappy, even bitter, for years. It's a situation that hasn't been easy for anyone. I find my time is better spent pursuing my obligations in the law.'

'You're running away.'

He gives her a piercing look. The irony of the statement is immediately clear to her and she lowers her eyes and changes the subject. 'What would you ask of me?'

His face clears. 'In my view it seems that Máthair Ab doesn't see the theft to be as serious as the bishop does. Am I right?'

She gives a little nod. 'I cannot say that I know *An Thiarna Epscop* Ábán particularly well, but I think your assessment is correct.'

He frowns a moment, deep in thought. 'I'm not sure she would agree to any sort of *smachta*.'

'But wouldn't that be impossible in any case to have a fine, since she would be the person paying it and the fine would be to her? That's if they will be guided by the Brehon law in this matter.'

He looks at her and frowns. 'You see my dilemma. I must find some compromise that honours all aspects.'

She raises her brow and wishes him a clear mind for this judgement.

'And this judgement, like all the judgements that are being given now, should it be written down in your view, to become a matter of record?'

This is the heart of his real problem, the one that keeps his feet shifting restlessly in the grass and his fingers toying with a thread on his sleeve. In the past, the judgements were memorized and passed down orally, to be cited in cases where the decisions pertained. Each process and step those seeking the rank of *aigne, brithen* or any other rank, learned meticulously in the *nemed* they attended for numerous years. Only lately had these judgements been written down, become part of the official record upon which future practices and decisions would be based. Colmán's reluctance to record this proceeding and enter his judgement into the record was because he had no clear sense of the outcome. The law that had provided his direction for years might be seriously affected by any precedence he established in the judgement.

She understands this and is careful in her response. 'In my view, you shouldn't enter it into the record.'

He nods slightly, looking distracted. He takes her hand again and presses it firmly. 'Thank you. I appreciate your thoughts.'

She looks down at his hand and studies the rings that encompass two of the fingers there. The stones are good quality and the gold that holds them catches the light. He rubs her palm with the tip of his thumb and she pulls away. She really can't trust this man, she thinks, and flees.

~

They assemble in the morning, just after *Terce,* for the presentation of the case on benches, just outside the *Tech Mor.* The sisters find places on the benches, while Colmán's men stand behind them, each bearing witness to the proceedings for their own respective community. The others in the household are present too, the servants, the few poor *bothach*, and some of the *ócaire* and *bóaire* who heard of this event and are near enough to attend. Some trickle in as the day advances, people Áine has never seen, and they cram themselves behind the benches, determined not to miss out on such *craic* as this.

The sun shines down on them, casting a strong halo of light on Máthair Gobnait, who sits in the front, between Epscop Ábán and Colmán. Áine squeezes out a place next to Siúr Sodelb, who is well hidden to the side. It's not Siúr Sodelb's wish to be present in front of so many strangers, but she won't disobey Máthair Gobnait's request. Áine can only sympathize and try her best to be inconspicuous too. All who were questioned are present. Brendán and Findbar are seated near the front and Cenél is on the opposite side, Cadoc standing behind him with a hand on his shoulder.

Epscop Ábán rises and addresses the group, pressing his hands together against the woven leather belt that ties the plain dark robe. The sisters and Máthair Gobnait follow suit and bow their heads, ready for the prayer. He beseeches the Lord to bless the proceedings, guide those called to judge and those called to speak to tell only the truth. This is no easy task asked of the Lord, or any of the gods to whom Colmán and the other non-Christians in this assembled group might pray. While this prayer is offered, Colmán's head remains unbowed and there is a determined set to his mouth.

The prayer done, Colmán opens the proceedings, a tactic that might have seemed well played on his part, except that Epscop Ábán gave him a small nod first. Colmán begins confidently and outlines the events. The onlookers' initial awe- inspired silence eventually gives way to a few suppressed laughs and low murmurs. Periodically they glance at Cadoc, Siúr Sadhbh, or the builders, as each testimony is described. It is another reason to endure sitting or standing close-packed in a space where the heat of the sun and their bodies causes the sweat to form. It becomes pure *craic*, stored for later telling on some winter night around their hearth at home, or for the sisters to recall when trying to stab a needle through the thick coarse cloth of the *manach's* robe, by the light of a sputtering tallow candle, while they embroider the truth with as much skill as the fabric they work on.

When they hear Cenél's role described in full, even given the sympathetic presentation Colmán's position as a legal representative requires, they all look at Cenél, seeking an explanation. They want some bit of understanding for his actions. What reason can they insert that would give spice to the tale of the horseman who galloped away on Máthair Gobnait's precious horse with the builders' tools in the dead of night?

Máthair Gobnait rises at this point and indicates her own view of this theft by a servant of her community that caused no loss. She bears no grudge, she assures everyone, and the sense of disappointment is palpable.

'It seems we have heard all there is to hear regarding the facts of this matter,' Epscop Ábán says when she is finished. 'We will discuss it further and a judgement will be agreed and announced tomorrow. ' He turns and thanks Colmán for the presentation of the case.

Colmán rises and addresses the assembled group. He thanks them for their patience and bids them return the next day. It's not perhaps the most authoritative word, but it is the last word. The crowd disperses slowly, knowing it has been dismissed by both the church and the law.

~

Colmán presents the facts in a measured tone, his eyes moving slowly between Máthair Gobnait and Epscop Ábán. They sit in the *Tech Mor*, on the benches placed once again over to the side, away from the fire. This time it's not the distance from the heat they seek, but the bit of privacy it affords. Áine perches uneasily next to Máthair Gobnait. It's not until she sat down on the bench that she realizes she's the only one besides the three judging that is present for the discussion, and she wishes she could leave. The tension is high and there is no place for her opinion in this matter.

'The law in this situation is tricky,' says Colmán. 'We have a theft of a horse and tools. A horse that's worth much, even given her age. The tools are part of two men's livelihood. Yet they're all returned before the absence was noticed, but not by the thief. In this instance it seems to me that to require Cenél to pay a fine of four horses for the theft is excessive, as well as impractical, given that he's only a servant. And since his *tuath* is responsible for payment, it becomes more complex, because some would argue that it would be Máthair Ab who would be responsible.'

Máthair Gobnait smiles, an appreciative light in her eyes. 'You could see it that way.'

'The Lord doesn't like a thief,' says Epscop Ábán. 'But the man has repented. He said as much. In view of the points made I think some penance, some kind of punishment is in order. Bread and water, the *Pater Noster* said often and on the knees for at least a year, would help his soul and his contrition.'

'The Lord also teaches us mercy,' says Máthair Gobnait. 'Do you think such a penance is too harsh?'

Epscop Ábán frowns. 'Your compassion does you credit, Máthair Ab, but the penance is about more than punishment, it's about atonement, cleansing the soul. No, I don't think it too harsh.'

A flicker of anger passes across Máthair Gobnait's face. 'But I must disagree with you there, *A Thiarna Espcop*.'

The bishop turns and looks at her, his eyes narrowing. 'I speak for the Church, Daughter.'

Her eyes remain mutinous but she lowers her head. His message is clear, though. Obedience is the cornerstone of a community of *cailecha* and of *manaigh*. It is a lesson that must be repeated on occasion. For

Máthair Gobnait those occasions are not pleasant when she feels her understanding is the better one.

'You would rather a penance than a judgement under the law?' asks Colmán.

'This penance is a judgement under the law,' replies Epscop Ábán. 'We've all agreed that a theft took place and punishment is required.'

'Restitution, not punishment,' Colmán says. He frowns slightly.

'The penance is all the restitution we seek,' says Epscop Ábán. He smiles benignly but his tone is firm.

'I could argue that he is of my *tuath*, and my father is responsible for his fine,' says Colmán.

'Ah, but Findbar and Brendán's family are client workers on monastery land and Cenél is their servant. That makes him our responsibility.'

Colmán pauses and for a moment casts a glance in Áine's direction, as if she might come to his aid in this legal wrangling. She lowers her eyes and stares at her hands. Colmán sighs eventually and nods. 'If that's what you wish, Máthair Ab, then consider the matter settled.'

~

The crowd shifts and shuffles in their places. Yesterday brought some welcome entertainment, and though this case is not being conducted in the manner they are used to in proceedings held at Lughnasadh, some of the same ingredients are still present. A judgement is to be given, today, and they can see if their predictions on the outcome are accurate.

Colmán stands and presents the case summary first and then gives the judgement. Bread and water for a year and the *Pater Noster* said on his knees thirty times, seven times a day. The crowd shuffles loudly. Mutters and whispers push and shove their way around the gathered group and reach Findbar and Brendán. With an admirable internal cue, perhaps from years at the mallet, the two rise and speak in unison.

'He's only to pray and eat bread and drink water? Where is the restitution? What of the injury done to us? The man is a thief.'

'And he will be known as a thief from now on,' Máthair Gobnait says, her voice calm. 'There will be little sympathy for him. Few, if any will want to keep his company. He has many years of service to give you, and I suggest you forgo any wages for that service.'

'Would you employ a thief, Máthair Ab?' asks Findbar. He shakes his head and steps back, pulling Brendán with him. The matter is closed, the protest registered, it's only for *ócaire* to do as their betters command.

Silence falls and the crowd looks on, hoping for something more. Epscop Ábán stands, assumes the pose for the *Bendictus*, right hand raised with two fingers erect. He issues the blessing on all. It becomes a dismissal as much as anything else. A sigh escapes from many, but the message is clear and they obey. People filter through the doorway, talking in low voices about what has transpired.

Áine leans over to Siúr Sodelb and whispers an offer to accompany her wherever she might want to go. The weather is fine enough and perhaps she can help pull weeds among the herbs. Such a calming task would be perfect until she can slip into the oratory for the next office. The two head towards the garden, each with their own particular limp, until Colmán calls Áine's name and asks her to wait for him a moment. Her heart sinks, but she nods anyway.

Áine promises Siúr Sodelb to join her in a moment and watches her make slow progress to the garden, past the people that still linger, ignoring the turned heads. She wishes people could hear the perfection of Siúr Sodelb's voice and see the golden hair under her veil that frames the unearthly beautiful face.

'I want to thank you for your help in this matter.'

Áine turns and faces Colmán. 'As I said before, there is nothing to thank me for.'

'It's for me to decide that.' He places a hand lightly on her shoulder, but she shrugs it away.

Siúr Feidelm comes up beside Colmán. 'I beg you excuse me. Máthair Gobnait requested that I prepare something to help your brother's breathing, but I must ask you a few questions first.'

'Of course,' says Colmán. His eyes cloud.

'Does he cough?'

'He does.'

'And is the cough dry or wet?'

'Wet, I suppose. He coughs blood.'

Siúr Feidelm frowns. 'He coughs blood? Often?'

Colmán nods.

'And his breathing is difficult only at that time?'

'His breathing is increasingly difficult all the time.' Colmán's voice is pained and it cracks at the end of his statement.

'I'm sorry. I don't mean to distress you with these questions. I know it's difficult enough to observe it when it does occur.'

'Sister, my brother's imminent departure from this world is something that causes my whole family much distress, and the *tuath*. He is the *Tánaiste*.'

'Your brother was to take over the kingship at your father's death?' asks Áine. She sees now how much Domnall's death would be a mighty blow for the family and for the Uí Blathnaic.

'Domnall was a worthy choice. He knew all the people, was fair in his handling, and was adept at politics.' Colmán gives a rueful smile. 'More so than I.'

'Thank you for your help,' says Siúr Feidelm. 'I'll mix up the ingredients and give them to you in time for your departure. '

She starts to move away and Áine quickly offers to help with the preparation, allowing a moment's regret that her time in the vegetable garden would have to wait until later. Siúr Feidelm accepts her help and Áine starts to follow her to the *Tech Mor* but Colmán grabs her arm.

'There's more I would discuss with you, when you have a moment,' he says.

She resisted the urge to refuse and after a pause gives a reluctant nod, her heart racing in its familiar pattern.

CHAPTER ELEVEN

'Siúr Sodelb,' Siúr Feidelm calls from the doorway of the *Tech Mor*. She repeats the summons.

Áine turns. The morning sun shines in her eyes and makes it difficult to see, but she can't mistake Siúr Feidelm's tall frame.

'Ah, it's you, Áine. I'm sorry, I thought you were Siúr Sodelb. With the veil covering your head and your limp...,' she pauses. 'You're still limping. The break should have healed well enough by now for the limp to have gone. Come to me later and I'll examine it to see if there's a problem.'

'Did you want me to fetch Siúr Sodelb?'

'No, no. You will do just as well, if not better.' She closes the short distance between them and holds out a small basket. 'Would you give this to Colmán? I have an infusion brewing and can't leave it.' She points to the contents. 'Tell Colmán the small pot is to be rubbed on his chest at night, before sleep, to ease his breathing. The small packet is an herb to place in a bowl of hot water. He's to lean over it, a cloth on his head, and inhale the steam.' She continues with the instructions, her words crisp and clear, each symptom covered and addressed with precision. How is Áine to convey the underlying message; that death is imminent and really there is little to be done?

But Siúr Feidelm has read her thoughts and charges her with its delivery. 'I leave that to you,' Áine. 'You're much better with words of that type.'

Áine gazes down at the basket and reads the messages it contains. She sees the care, the understanding that a mother and a family want to do as much for the son as they possibly can. She also sees that they aren't yet ready to accept his passing.

She walks slowly away, staring at the basket, and gathers her thoughts, reluctant to encounter Colmán for many reasons. Until this moment she's been adept at avoiding him since their encounter the day before. She's always ensured she sat some distance from him during the meals, and has remained in the sleeping hut between the offices.

'Ah, I have found you at last.'

Startled, Áine raises her head and stares up at Colmán. He stands close to her, in the shadow of the nearly finished hut in which he slept the night before. He carries a large leather satchel, clearly ready for departure.

'I was hoping to see you before I left,' he says.

She holds out the basket. 'Siúr Feidelm asked me to give this to you.' She points out the various contents and recounts Siúr Feidelm's instructions, conscious of his intent regard. When she finishes, she looks up at him and catches the brief flicker of distress on his face. 'I'm sorry. I know this isn't easy for you.'

He shakes his head, as if he would shake away the grief and all the other issues that hang between them. 'It's more difficult for him. He knows he's dying, yet will let my mother do all she might to prolong his life, however painful it might be.' He takes the basket and gestures to the bench outside the oratory. 'Will you sit with me a little?'

For a moment she considers refusing, but knows it is useless. He would press her until she consents or he might seek out Máthair Gobnait to ensure her cooperation. They walk the short distance to the seat while Áine tries to calm herself.

He allows her a moment's respite, a moment where they both sit and consider the view that takes in Máthair Gobnait's hives, her figure weaving among them. The bees are a close kin group of their own and Máthair Gobnait their *banríon*. Beyond her is the vegetable garden, where Siúr Sodelb oversees the women armed with their baskets, kneeling in the beds, picking the cabbages and onions that swell with the earth's goodness. Further down the hillside, cows dot the field on one side and on the other, a field of oats sway under the heavy weight of their ripened seeds. Áine takes this in, extracting its benevolent energy and calm.

'You know it was legal matters that brought me travelling in this direction when I received the request to come here,' Colmán says finally.

She nearly sighs when he breaks the silence, but then she realizes he's been gathering his own thoughts and seeking his own source of calm. This realization alarms her. 'Yes, I had heard that,' she manages.

'I was in fact on my way west to the Eóganacht of Irluochair, near Lough Leane.'

She makes a noise of polite interest, but she becomes uneasy, though the remark seems benign enough.

'I go primarily to ask about you. To discover, if possible, who you are. I know inquiries were made in this *tuath* and eastwards, but I thought I would try westwards.'

She clasps her hands tightly, fighting to control her voice. 'You choose to go in person, rather than send a message?' The words come out strangled.

'I would rather go myself. I can put questions to people as they arise, read expressions, tease out information that might not be immediately apparent in words carefully phrased on a page. So hopefully it can be resolved much sooner.'

'Why do you do this, what is the rush?'

'Don't you want to discover who you are?' There is a mixture of puzzlement, hurt and anger in his voice.

'No, I mean yes, of course.' She tries to keep the petulance from her voice, but there is nothing but petulance attached to her thoughts, where it has free rein. The thoughts, given such freedom, scream around her head in all their petulant foot-stamping glory. She doesn't want his help, doesn't need to know who she was in the past. What matters is now, and how dare he presume otherwise. 'But why are you so interested?' she says finally.

'You were beaten, assaulted. It's a matter for the law.' His voice falters a little. 'I- I would do this for you because it's important for you to know yourself fully, before things....' He raises his hand and touches her veil. She looks away. 'I care about you. Since you left Raithlinn, I've thought of you constantly. I can't help it.' He cups his hand on her chin and pulls it toward him. 'Do you know how beautiful you are? I admit, I'm no *file* who can compose great poems in praise of you, I can speak only facts.' He leans across and kisses her lips.

The world tilts and roars. She jerks away and wipes her mouth. 'No. What are you doing?'

'I mean you no disrespect, Áine. It's part of the reason I want to discover who you are, so I can come to an honourable agreement with your family.'

'An honourable agreement? You would divorce your wife and make me *cétmuinter?*'

He reddens. 'Well, no. I wouldn't be permitted to do that by her family or mine.'

'Then what? A second wife? Or your mistress? Is that what you hope for?'

'A second wife, of course, with the formal contract, everything legally agreed, so there would be no question of your status.'

She stares at him, the sensation of his mouth on hers still lingering, tingling so alarmingly her hands start to shake. With a great wail she rises and stumbles away, her leg aching, the limp so pronounced it's nearly impossible to make any speed at all.

She arrives at the sleeping hut and shuts the door against Colmán and the rest of the world on its other side.

~

Sometime later, when she deems it safe, she makes her way down to the vegetable garden, to Siúr Sodelb. On her approach Siúr Sodelb turns to her.

'You're ashen, is there something wrong? Are you ill?'

Áine moves closer, puts her arms around Siúr Sodelb. 'Hold me, Sodelb, please.'

She feels Siúr Sodelb's arms go round her waist, pull her in close. She nestles her head in Siúr Sodelb's neck.

'All will be well,' Siúr Sodelb whispers. 'You have God's love to keep you safe. And mine.'

She allows Áine to remain there until Áine's breathing slows and her heart finds a calmer pace. It is only then Siúr Sodelb pulls away and asks her gently if she's recalled a memory that upsets her.

The memory is only the reeling of her mind, the fear of a touch, the nausea in her stomach and the sense of tides she cannot hold back. She shakes her head. 'I-I don't know.'

The arms come around her again and hold her close for a time that seems too short when her only instinct is to stay there forever.

~

The weather has played its part this harvest year, swelling the grains with enough rain and sun, so they hang in abundant ripeness, dry unbent rather than mouldy from too much wet. The heifers, calves and sheep, with all the plentiful grass, have fattened and grown to a great size and the milk has flowed from the udders of all the cows that have borne calves. The cabbage blossoms out, its broad leaves curling round a thick centre and the engorged onions expand to sizes some call miraculous. Blackberries and all their attending cousins make startling promises with great clusters of flowers.

Such bounty means hectic days, with every available person turning their hand to some task or chore that will ensure its collection. Scything, stuking, gathering, threshing, digging, slaughtering all take time and people, in addition to the cooking, baking, churning, butter-making, spinning, weaving and washing tasks that fall all year round.

In such good weather the builders work on too, their numbers fewer by one. Cenél has been sent back to Findbar and Brendán's father's farm, shunned by day and made to work as hard as the lowest man there, with only a diet of bread and water. Each morning, early, he is made to say his penance on his knees, in the oratory, under Siúr Ethne's watchful eye. Findbar and Brendán show no satisfaction that their felonious assistant is reduced to a state that still preserves his ability to labour for the family's farm. Without a word they seek their own measure of compensation and show surprisingly adept skills at fashioning Cenél's face in stone, and placing it among the others in the wall of the hut they build. By such design they make their own statement that can also be seen as a warning. That it gives them gratification is evident in the prominent place they site it, above the door. When Máthair Gobnait sees it, walking in the company of Siúr Ethne and Áine, she merely shakes her head and says it will remind people that everyone is subject to temptation.

The frantic days often stretch well into the evening and sometimes the night, taking every bit of light available, for this grace, this miracle of good weather, is not to be wasted. The next year's harvest is unknown. So much energy, so much effort brings higher numbers to Máthair Gobnait's community, all of them seeking cures for ailments and injuries sustained during and after the harvest. Some visit the holy well before and on the return from their journey to Máthair Gobnait, toss in a bit of metal, tie a cloutie on the overlooking tree for those left behind with summer fever, or a deeper ailment, in the hope of taking in every possibility. All sorts of problems appear, including broken, sliced and cut limbs, fingers and toes, sore heads from bangs and too much celebration, and any number of other strange or confidential rashes, itches, burns and bites acquired when the hay proved too inviting, and the sweet girl or boy too tempting.

Máthair Gobnait and Siúr Feidelm are kept busy enough, listening, examining and providing the treatments, so that when Áine offers to help it's accepted gladly. She watches them work, hands things to them when asked, and fetches, until she knows when and how to clean simple wounds and apply firm bandages. The rhythm established, she becomes part of a threesome, all of them understanding the silent language of healers. By extension she becomes a worker of bees, following

Máthair Gobnait, an extra veil covering her face, gloves on her hands, and she holds the basket and the bundle of rush for smoking the bees, while Máthair Gobnait collects the honey and wax from the *beachair*.

As Máthair Gobnait's handmaid, Áine watches her work in silence, hears the bees humming and Máthair Gobnait's response, her own words spoken so low and in a voice so calm that it's as though she speaks in their buzzing language. And after a while, Áine hears the bees' varying tones herself, notes the subtle changes in sound that registers their mood and temperament, and how the weather, light, moisture all invoke reactions. Máthair Gobnait knows the bees like she knows herself and can read their moods as well as they read hers.

The language is private, but over the days Áine catches words and phrases, so that on occasion she just smiles when Máthair Gobnait lifts the top off one of the *beachair* and nods in understanding. One of these mornings, watching Máthair Gobnait open the top of the hive, lifting out the comb filled with honey and wax, Áine realizes Máthair Gobnait's bond allows her access with little penalty. She is rarely stung and when she is, she no longer feels it.

'These bees are restless,' Máthair Gobnait says on this day. She peers inside and studies the hive, listening to their hum. 'A new king? Such a fruitful year, so much honey.' In a quiet voice she begins to sing *Um la Mholadh Beacha*, Áine's praise piece.

Áine flushes with pleasure and after a moment she joins her, measuring her tone, until the wonder of it takes over and she closes her eyes and hears the answering hum that gives support to the song. The piece finishes and Áine opens her eyes and watches as Máthair Gobnait replaces the top of the hive, and smiles warmly.

'Thank you, Áine. That was a wonderful gift to them, and to me.'

~

Even in these times the offices structure each day. They provide a touchstone, moments when the mind can move upwards, focus on the spirit, rather than the physical exertions that tax their bodies. Áine observes these offices with a fervour that only a person intent on drawing as much as possible from each day in the community could manage. She commits to memory all the psalms she hears, finds the tune to accompany them and sings them in addition to the canticles and the *Beati*. She offers the prayers and the *Pater Noster* with growing confidence. She listens to the verses from the Gospel Máthair Gobnait and Siúr Ethne recite, and asks that she might learn them too. When she realizes the sisters regularly make confession of transgressions to Máthair Gobnait, their *anam cara*, she confesses too, while Máthair Gobnait nods impassively on the bench in the oratory. She confesses again only a short time after the previous confession, and this time Máthair Gobnait chides her gently.

'What is my penance?' she asks when she has finished.

Máthair Gobnait gives a small smile. 'It has hardly been three days since you came to me last, so there is not the time to accumulate much in the way of sinful transgressions, even for the most wayward of people.' She looks at Áine intently. 'Is there something you haven't said? Something deeper that worries your soul?'

Áine gives a small shake of her head and then lowers it to hide the flush that rises on her face. Has she judged it wrong? She thought she understood the nature and timing of these confessions. It felt so comforting to sit before Máthair Gobnait and itemize those actions and thoughts she felt were improper, to feel that by such action they are wiped away, so she can start fresh once again. To make Máthair Gobnait her *anam cara.*

Siúr Ethne enters, her eyes blinking against the darkened room. She halts when it becomes apparent she isn't alone. 'Máthair Gobnait, I'm sorry to disturb you. I didn't realize there was anyone in here. I sought some time alone to pray.'

Máthair Gobnait rises. 'No you're not disturbing us.' She looks down at Áine. 'Think about what I said, child. In the meantime a few *Pater Nosters* will suffice for what you've just told me.' She nods to Siúr Ethne and departs.

'Sometimes I wonder if Máthair Gobnait understands how much purifying the body can in turn cleanse the soul,' Siúr Ethne says. She looks down at Áine. 'You're welcome to join me in prayer. Though I shall be doing more than saying a few *Pater Nosters.*'

Áine stares at Siúr Ethne a moment, wondering if she's imagined the words. Siúr Ethne looks at her expectantly and with a small measure of disbelief Áine murmurs her thanks and joins Siúr Ethne on the floor in front of the altar bearing the copper crucifix. She says the prayers, her eyes fixed on the cross, and finds herself praying more. She prays for Domnall as she always does and for Siúr Sodelb; that her foot might someday cause her less pain in both the heart and body. This time though, she prays for Colmán. She thinks first of his searching eyes, the strong jaw and sensuous lips. May he be kept safe on his journey, she asks, a journey that, please God, will be fruitless.

CHAPTER TWELVE

Longer than anyone's memory, the fair has marked the change of seasons, figured as it was on the sun, the moon and all the fluctuations of the Earth. Its origins stretch back to tales of special fairs, on sites sacred and political, so no one can tell when the first fair was, or where it took place, or if it was at Lughnasadh. It's only important that it occurred. That its purpose isn't limited to any one thing also makes it difficult to place, yet no one can doubt that in times plentiful and sparse it is important to bring people together to share and trade wares, to settle matters in legal ways (and on occasion not so legal), to socialize, meet kith and kin in places too distant to see regularly, and to exchange tales and gossip for storage against the dark winter days.

Though the Church might frown, those pious groups of influential bishops in their monasteries in Ard Maigh, Clonmacnoise and even Cashel, it is at the local level that its practicalities can't be ignored, even in Boirneach, for all that Epscop Ábán might have answered it with an another fair at the time of Whitsun.

This year in Boirneach, it seems more necessary to go the fair, that everyone might trade such an abundant harvest with those that might have sustained a failure in some way: those that had calves that were stillborn, sheep with liver fluke, or perhaps faulty seed. Those whose sheep had flourished, producing wool so thick and of such quality it would nearly spin itself into yarn, will perhaps look to trade its excess for some cheese, or even the special honey that marks the Boirneach fair. It is a wife's dream, after all, an outing where she can meet with other women, compare the sweetness of her butter, the smoothness of her yarn and exchange stories of children with sore gums or chronic rashes. And if she is unmarried, eye a man who might one day become her husband.

Máthair Gobnait knows this and uses the fair to make her own observations and trades. This year with extra honey, cheese and butter that even Epscop Ábán's monastery can't consume in the next year, but lacking enough wool and flax to meet their needs now there were new members to think of, she makes arrangements for the goods to be made ready and the farm cart loaded. She announces it during their weekly meetings after the midday meal.

Siúr Ethne frowns. 'I cannot spare the time to go, Máthair Ab. Not this year.' 'I know, you've much to do with Siúr Feidelm, organizing the stores for winter. I'll arrange for someone else to go with Cadoc.'

It's later, after *Nocturns,* that Máthair Gobnait approaches Áine and asks her if she will go. Startled, she can only ask why.

'I would like someone with a fine eye for good wool and flax thread. Your deft handling with the needle shows you have experience with cloth. Cadoc will be there to ensure that any trade is fair. Besides, I thought you might enjoy it.'

She forces a smile and turns away so that Máthair Gobnait cannot read the fear in her face. It isn't the thought of being cheated in the trade that worries her.

Máthair Gobnait's description of her needlework is a blatant lie, though she has come a long way since she first sewed here some months ago with awkward fingers. 'I will, of course, go if you wish it, Máthair Ab.'

Traces of this worry linger on her face when she meets Siúr Sodelb a few moments later inside their sleeping hut as they slip off their gowns ready for bed. Siúr Sodelb reaches out and touches her arm. 'What is it, Áine? What's wrong?'

She looks into Siúr Sodelb's beautiful eyes that promise access to a different world, a higher, purer place. As much as she wishes to, she cannot utter the words that would deny her distress and confesses her fear instead. 'I can't go. I'm afraid, Sodelb. God, please help me, I'm afraid.'

'Afraid? Of what? Where can't you go?'

She worries at her lip with her teeth, trying to find words that will explain what upsets her. The crowds of strangers, the fear and danger of recognition, was that the source of her deep-seated unease? She cannot explain something for which she has no clear understanding.

'It's the fair. Máthair Gobnait wants me to go in Siúr Ethne's place and I would rather not.'

Siúr Sodelb takes her into an embrace. 'I know, I understand. You needn't justify any of it to me.'

Áine stands in the fold of Siúr Sodelb's arms, draws comfort from their warmth, their protection and drifts into her pure world. The two remain unmoving, while the light fades from the doorway.

'I'll go with you,' Sodelb whispers eventually. 'We'll face it together.'

Áine pulls away from her and looks at her in disbelief, tears in her eyes. 'Truly, you'd do that for me?'

Siúr Sodelb nods solemnly. 'I would, Áine, I would. What does it matter that my foot is misshapen and I cannot walk with ease? God loves us all. And we'll walk in His grace, though our own might be lacking.'

Áine kisses her cheek. 'My dearest sister.'

Later, she lies in the bed, lifts her *léine* and feels the scar that runs along her side. The ridge is barely discernible now. It has healed well, the new skin forming more smoothly than anyone expected, even under Máthair Gobnait's skilled care. It is now only a faint reminder that there has been a time when she hasn't lived under this roof.

~

Their pace is slow, but that is unremarkable when there are so many people. Some are in clusters, deep in conversation, and others lean over blankets or carts eager to inspect what is on offer. The cluck of a hen, the lowing of a cow, the bleat of a sheep; all of it can be heard among the voices that shout or speak behind cupped hands. Aromas of fresh bread, butter and onions fill the air and on occasion mix with the less sweet odours of animals out in the baking sun.

Áine and Siúr Sodelb take it all in, the flash of ribbon in a young woman's hair, the brilliant colour of a woman's newly woven shawl, a man wearing a highly polished brooch. It is too glorious a day to miss out the chance to show such finery. In the sky, the clouds billow high in the west, as if they are gathering their own fleeces or hanks of wool for trade.

Áine and Siúr Sodelb finger the wool yarn and exchange smiles, knowing that each agree that the even colour, the smooth texture, is the best they have seen yet. They barter with the woman, offering the honey Áine holds in her basket, in exchange for all the yarn she has.

It's a friendly transaction, simple and straightforward, and requires nothing of Cadoc's canny trading expertise.

'Cuimne.'

Why does she turn? It isn't the voice, though later she will convince herself that was the reason. Why doesn't she feel the dread then, the unease that has caused her such anguish under Máthair Gobnait's gaze and in Siúr Sodelb's arms? As it is, she drops her basket to the grass when she turns and sees Colmán standing before her, his face tentative and joyful.

'Why did you call me that?'

'You are Cuimne, I think.'

She refuses the name and trembles with the effort. 'Cuimne? I don't know anyone of that name.'

He bends down, picks up her basket and places it back into her hands, his own lingering. She pulls away.

'I've returned from Lough Leane and I believe I've discovered who you are.'

'Lough Leane? No, I don't think so.' She clasps the basket handle tightly.

'It's true. Cuimne, the daughter of a king of the Irluachoir Eóganacht. She has gone missing on her return to her foster family. Some spoke of it when I was north of here. Her father is not long dead, and when I met the new king he was unable to tell me more than the fact of her disappearance. He and his men are outside the father's *derbfine* and knew little of her since she left as a tiny child. I was summoned home to Domnall before I could discover more.'

'Your brother, how does he fare?' asks Siúr Sodelb. She moves forward and slips her hand inside Áine's.

Colmán's face clouds. 'He does not fare at all. He died the day I returned.'

Siúr Sodelb crosses herself and a moment later Áine follows suit. 'I am sorry for your loss. May his soul rest in peace.'

'I thank you.' He looks at Áine. She echoes Siúr Sodelb's words, her breath held. 'I will find out more of Cuimne when I can,' he adds. 'Are you certain that it means nothing to you?'

She shakes her head firmly. 'Nothing of it is familiar. In my mind I am Áine, soon to be Siúr Áine.' There is an edge to her voice that can leave him in no doubt about her meaning.

He narrows his eyes and for a moment she sees hurt and sadness there, and she regrets that she's spoken so sharply. He has, after all, just lost his brother. 'I'm sorry, but I don't think you have the right person.' She takes her leave then, though Siúr Sodelb pauses to add some more kind words to those she's already given. Cadoc and the two make their way towards the cart. Colmán follows silently behind, his face filled with speculation.

Áine sits in the cart next to Siúr Sodelb on the journey home, the ox lumbering slowly along, and tries to deflect Siúr Sodelb's quiet but persistent questions about Colmáns findings. All sense of enjoyment that has filled the day earlier vanishes like the clear skies and bright sun. The clouds hunch together now, large and menacing, like a band of soldiers ready for battle. Cadoc casts dark meaningful glances above him, as if he would keep them in check by his will alone.

'You're certain you don't recognize the name Cuimne?'

'Yes, I'm certain.'

'It stirs no sense of familiarity, not even the slightest twinge?'

'No, it stirs nothing in me.' In that she knows she lies. It stirs panic in her, makes the bile rise to her mouth and takes the breath from her. The hand that clasps Siúr Sodelb's sweats badly.

'Perhaps you might remember it later, when your mind is more at rest, maybe singing, or at prayers,' says Siúr Sodelb.

'Does it matter so much? Isn't it possible that I will never discover who I was? Will that stop me from becoming a *cailech*, to live permanently with you?'

'It does matter, in that you are in a sense missing a part of yourself, your connection to your family, and who you were born to. But it doesn't matter to God, and it doesn't matter to me. I wouldn't wish you to live anywhere else but in the community with us, under Máthair Gobnait's care.'

Áine raises Siúr Sodelb's clasped hand and kisses it. 'Thank you. I promise you, that no matter what is or isn't discovered, it will make no difference. I'll remain with you and the others.' She leans over and whispers in Siúr Sodelb's ear. 'I would never leave you.'

~

That night she goes to her bed with some semblance of peace. The office at Nocturns calms her mind even more than Siúr Sodelb's words, and the prayers and psalms she offers up with even more sincerity on that night. She settles down and reaches over to Siúr Sodelb, strokes her hand to bid her a silent goodnight and falls asleep. When the bell for Matins sounds, she rises with a yawn, feeling better than she had since the days before the fair. She draws on her gown and marvels that the loud pelt of heavy rain on the roof above hasn't wakened her before this.

She pauses at the door. Máthair Gobnait and Siúr Ethne have already gone before her, but Siúr Sodelb is still in her bed. She calls to her, but the only reply is a moan. Áine moves quickly to her side and sees her flushed face and feverish eyes. She places a hand on her forehead and feels the raging heat.

'Sodelb,' she wails. 'Oh, Sodelb.' The sheepskin blanket is tossed aside, the linen cover underneath soaked with sweat. It is no ordinary fever. She stumbles away and runs out into the wet dark night after Máthair Gobnait.

CHAPTER THIRTEEN

She bathes Siúr Sodelb's forehead, the back of her neck and along her wrists, constantly. She feeds her thin gruel, herbal mixtures and honey, and anything else she can persuade Siúr Feidelm to mix or cook that might be tempting enough to remain in Siúr Sodelb's stomach and not retched into a bowl moments after it passes her lips. The times that Siúr Sodelb doesn't stir restlessly in her bed, hot and feverish, Áine goes to pray. She prays so hard, kneeling on the floor beside Siúr Sodelb's bed, her voice insistent and pleading, that her hands hurt from clasping them so tight. When Siúr Sodelb's eyes are open and slightly less clouded, she sings to her, all the psalms and canticles she knows, all of Siúr Sodelb's pieces. She sings most often *Um la Mholadh Beacha,* their own piece praising the bees. The bees that provide the honey that heals the sick.

After three days at her bedside, it takes all of Máthair Gobnait's skills of persuasion to convince Áine to come away, to attend the office of *Matins* and offer her prayers to God with the other sisters, and afterwards to seek her rest. The notion that such prayers might be more effective if offered from the oratory among the force of the voices of the sisters is what allows Áine to relinquish her place at Siúr Sodelb's bedside to Siúr Feidelm.

Inside the oratory, she falls to her knees on the hard floor, in some part enjoying the pain of the impact, hopeful that such suffering might bring the reward she yearns for desperately. The thought of losing Siúr Sodelb is unbearable, and so she sets her mind to silent pleading and bargaining. If only she knew what He wanted. The prayers spoken aloud seem not enough, even Máthair Gobnait's eloquent pleas do not appear insistent enough to Áine's ears.

It is the psalms that give her mind some confidence; the beauty of the tones, the voices so unified and perfect, she can't doubt their efficacy. Surely God will hear them now. The thought gives her strength, and when the final psalm is sung she begins, *Um la Mholadh Beacha*. Her voice soars high and she's certain it joins the angels and sends her message, the plea, that she now knows will be answered. She is still kneeling in front of the altar when *Matins* is finished. Her head is bowed and she is sleeping, her mind filled with the notes of her praise song.

She wakes later, when the first notes of birdsong filter into the oratory and she finds herself prostrate on the floor. She rises slowly, her legs stiff from the awkward position, and makes her way through door. A damp mist hangs in the air, little droplets settling just above the grass, making slick the hardened surface of the path that leads to the sleeping huts. She slides only once in her passage, but it takes her breath for a moment. She rights herself and moves on, her eye firmly on the door of the hut.

She opens the door slowly, lest it squeak and awake those within. Peering inside, she sees Siúr Ethne's bed is empty, as it has often been in the last few nights she has tended Siúr Sodelb. Now Máthair Gobnait leans over Siúr Sodelb, pressing a cloth to her head and the side of her flushed cheeks. An arm flails and nearly hits Máthair Gobnait on the head, but she takes hold of the arm and replaces it at Siúr Sodelb's side. Siúr Sodelb mutters and then shouts a word.

Áine moans softly, puts her hand to her mouth, turns from the door and runs down the path to the entrance of the *faithche*. This time her feet slip all too easily and she is on her back, the force of the impact giving her body a severe jolt. A wail of despair escapes her and she lies there for a moment, the soft rain wetting her face and joining the tears that have begun to flow.

When she rises, she lets her feet take her south, through the *faithche* entrance, down the hill, away from the oratory and the sleeping hut. The journey doesn't take long. The clouties are there, pieces of cloth dangling from the tree. She stops at the edge of the well and leans over the water. In the dim light of the misty morning, there are a few murky shapes of metal fragments and coins. She has only the cloth from her gown and *léine* that had once belonged to Siúr Sodelb that she can give.

She lifts her gown and tears a strip from the *léine's* hem. She mutters some words, a little prayer from the back of her mind that comes forth unwittingly, dips the cloth in the water and ties the cloutie around a tree branch. Again she bargains, but this time it was with a different deity, one that is used to such bargaining, and she hopes that the reply will be different. A few moments of silence, her breathing coming in rapid bursts, and then she is up on her feet again, a tiny kernel of hope still present inside her.

This time she walks slowly, her feet taking her up the hill, her face bowed against the thickening rain that the heavily clustered trees do little to abate. It might have been the mist that dampened the sound, but the noise she first hears she ascribes to a moving branch, though there is no wind. She hears it again and stops to listen. This time when sound comes, she realizes it's a moan. She heads toward the direction of the sound, the dampened ground and pelting rain muffling her steps. In a small clearing she sees a naked figure bent over and an arm swinging a corded rope upon its back. Moving closer she recognizes Siúr Ethne, her ribs so prominent now they can be counted from a distance. Her grey hair, usually covered with her veil, hangs in limp hanks along her bony shoulders.

Áine watches her for a few moments, transfixed, as she swings the rope along her back, scoring the flesh, creating great weals that ooze blood. Before each stroke she closes her eyes and mutters, *'Mea culpa, mea culpa,'* and when the rope hits her back, she emits a low moan. Áine is horrified at first; she can't understand what purpose such action can achieve, until slowly it all becomes clear. The pain, the act of scourging the body to such physical suffering, was the most extreme offering to God imaginable. That she must suffer like Christ, suffer his wounds, his pain in order to know God's grace. In that light Siúr Ethne's actions have a certain beauty, a wonder that few can match. She slips away quietly, leaving Siúr Ethne to her purification.

She walks slowly the rest of the way up the hill, past the garden and through the *faithche,* deep in thought. Was that the path she must take? If so, she's committed a greater sin at the well than any Siúr Ethne might have done the whole of her life. She will find rope and expiate these sins with the greatest force she can muster. But she will also ask Máthair Gobnait for penance as well.

She finds Máthair Gobnait where she's left her, at Siúr Sodelb's side. This time Epscop Ábán stands above them, his arm raised in benediction, a small pot of holy oil in his hand. Siúr Feidelm, Siúr Mugain and Siúr Sadhbh stand to one side, their heads bowed in prayer. Áine seeks out Siúr Sodelb's face, sees the stillness and that the flush of fever has vanished. Her eyes, so round and beautiful, stare upward, their transparent blueness emphasized in death. Máthair Gobnait leans forward and closes them.

'No,' says Áine. The word chokes her, stops dead in her throat. She rushes to Siúr Sodelb's side, takes up a limp hand and begins to chafe the wrist. 'Sodelb, hear me, you cannot die, please. You mustn't leave me.'

Epscop Ábán places a hand on her shoulder. 'Come away, child. She's at peace now. You must thank God for that.'

She turned to Epscop Ábán and shrugs off his hand. 'Thank him? Thank him for taking the dearest woman of all?' A moment later she is through the door, back into the drenching rain.

~

She says nothing as they begin to wash Siúr Sodelb's body. She merely takes the cloth from Siúr Feidelm and runs it along each limb and steps back to allow Máthair Gobnait to dry her. She washes her hair, massaging the scalp and rinsing it thoroughly before combing it carefully to prevent snags and breakage. Once she is finished, she spreads the hair along the pillow to dry to its polished brightness. Máthair Gobnait gives Áine the fresh linen *léine* and head covering, woven with Siúr Sodelb's own hands, and the wool gown that her needle has plied so that Áine might find comfort in dressing her this one last time.

They lay her, sewn in her shroud, on a bench in the oratory, where the *cailecha* and Máthair Gobnait gather round her. Epscop Ábán stands at her head. Áine still hasn't spoken. It's only when they began the *Beati* that Áine opens her mouth and sings, filling the music with the pain and sorrow, belying the words. She lets the music take her over, offering it not to God, but to Sodelb, whose soul hovers and whispers in her ear, encouraging her on to fuller sounds, higher notes, ringing a descant that has not yet been tried.

She closes her ears to the rest, living only in the music that still carries on in her head. She blocks out the *Pater Noster*, the prayers of faith and the words of the Gospel. She remains when the others process out and kneels by the figure laid out with arms not extended like the one on the cross, but folded in prayer beneath the shroud. She pulls away when it's time for Cadoc to carry the body to be buried, interred in the holiest of places, for the holiest *cailech,* beneath the packed earthen floor of the oratory.

When it is time for the offices, she attends in silence and stares at the newly turned earth that is Siúr Sodelb's grave, only opening her mouth for the singing, because Sodelb comes and whispers in her ear. She longs for these moments and sits for hours in the oratory, after the offices and meals are finished. When her eyes aren't closed, seeking Sodelb's voice, they remain fixed on the fresh grave. She wonders if they will put a stone over it. Weigh her body down as her soul flies up to heaven. Heaven is where she'd be, if Epscop Ábán and Máthair Gobnait are right. But Áine knows her soul is here, right beside her and no amount of empty words can convince her otherwise.

She spends the night there, sitting on a bench. No one can persuade her to move. Her limbs stiffen and her back protests, but she ignores them. It's only after the first office of the morning, when Siúr Feidelm sits beside her, places a mug in her hand and orders her to drink that she blinks and recalls herself. She sips the liquid, realizes her thirst and drinks some more. Her stomach clenches against the invading liquid, too long empty, and she retches slightly.

'Come away, Áine,' Siúr Feidelm says.

She resists for only a moment, but then her limbs turn soft, her mind fades and she allows Siúr Feidelm to lead her to her bed.

~

She rises a few hours later, her tongue thick and her mind groggy. Outside, through the open door, she sees a watery sun breaking through the clouds. She goes to the door. It seems impossible that it would shine, the birds would chitter and sing, the cows provide milk, and the bees remain busy. Even from this distance she can hear the bees hum.

'Come, Áine, I need your help.' It was Máthair Gobnait, striding up to her, a cloth, gloves and heavy veils in her hand. 'There is another king and he will be looking to establish a new hive, I think. I want to coax him into the one I've prepared.'

Áine sighs. After slipping on her shoes, she follows her down to the hive nearest the *faithche* wall, her steps slow and heavy. She dons the gloves and veil along with Máthair Gobnait and gazes off into the field, while Máthair Gobnait explains what she intends to do. The words float around her but never settle and she can only blink when Máthair Gobnait asks her if she understands.

'Have you heard anything I said?'

'Heard? Yes, I've heard.'

Máthair Gobnait frowns. 'Have you understood it? It's important that you do, otherwise you or I might be stung.'

'But the bees rarely sting you.'

Máthair Gobnait tilts her head. 'You think they haven't stung me often? You can take nothing for granted, Áine. It's only by their grace and God's that I'm allowed to tend them, take their honey and wax. Part of that grace is respecting their will and His.'

Perhaps it is the drink the night before that permits such a release, for she knows some drug had been slipped in it, but the words collapse the defences she's built up in these past few days and ignite her, like a spark to dry kindling, that becomes immediately hot and crackling.

'His will? Is it his will to take such a pure soul as Siúr Sodelb?' Her voice rises to a higher pitch, ringing loudly. 'What kind of god is that who would strike Sodelb down? What did she do, what possible sin could she have committed that she would be taken like that?'

'We cannot fathom all of His actions. His ways are beyond our understanding as mere mortals.'

This answer is no answer and it only enrages her. 'How do you live with a god like that?' she says. 'That he would strike down such innocents as Domnall and Sodelb.'

'You're angry. And it's natural that you should direct it at God, since there is no one else that is clearly to blame.'

She can hear the bees buzzing beside her. They accuse her even if Máthair Gobnait does not. 'I'm to blame,' she shouts. 'Me! If I hadn't been so cowardly, Siúr Sodelb would never have insisted on accompanying me to the fair, and she wouldn't have contracted the fever. Siúr Feidelm agrees.'

'You're not to blame. We know nothing of how the fever came to her, only that it came.'

Áine shakes her head, the tears flowing. Máthair Gobnait tries to put her arm around her, but Áine flings it off with a wild thrust of her arm. The top of the hive slides off with the impact and she turns in horror as the bees buzz louder, clustering and hovering, until, by some secret agreement, they rise up into the sky in a deafening roar.

Máthair Gobnait makes a soft cry. 'Bring the *beachair*,' she says. 'We must follow them.' She clasps her skirt and the woven sack and goes in pursuit, Áine following, carrying the hive. They go down through the *faithche* and across the field, onto the next, to where the bees have settled in a tree. Máthair Gobnait stands below the branch that holds them, lays the large sack on the ground and the empty *beachair* on top, and speaks in a low, calm voice words of encouragement and praise.

'Sing your song, Áine. See if we can get them to settle on the cloth.'

Áine stares up at the bees, the words frozen on her lips. She knows she must sing to make amends for what she's done to the bees. She takes a deep breath and squeaks out a few notes, but they end in sobs.

'Ssssh,' says Máthair Gobnait. 'Take your time and try again.' She gives the branch a gentle shake.

Áine closes her eyes and stills her breathing and this time she manages the notes. It's a feeble effort compared to her previous performances. This time she has no firmly held hand, no whispering presence to give her support. When she finishes she looks at Máthair Gobnait and shakes her head. 'It wasn't my best effort.'

'No matter,' says Máthair Gobnait. 'The bees have heard you.' She points to the sack where they hover and fly around the *beachair*.

Áine views them and looks up at Máthair Gobnait in disbelief. Beyond Máthair Gobnait, at the far end of the field, movement among the cows and heifers catch her eye. The bull is there somewhere, doing his late summer duty. Despite the fading light, she can see something moving carefully among the cattle. 'What are those men doing in the field?'

Máthair Gobnait turns and looks in the direction Áine indicates. 'My cows!' she shouts in surprise that quickly turns to anger. 'They're taking them. How dare they! Quick, Áine, go and alert Siúr Mugain, Siúr Sadhbh and Cadoc.'

Áine nods and runs off back to the *faithche*. She pauses near the entrance to catch her breath and turns to see Máthair Gobnait in the distance waving her arms. The bees swarm up around her and become a large dark cloud, and even from the entrance Áine can hear their thunderous noise.

~

The sisters talk about it during the simple meal after the evening office, their words bursting forth like an overflowing dam. It is a *sceál* of the highest value, to be savoured and discussed in the most particular detail. Something most miraculous happened in that field. The bees responded like God's instrument to punish the wicked, stinging them mightily, so that they abandoned their theft. The men are clearly sent from the Fidgenti, for who else but heathens would dare steal the cattle belonging to a nunnery under the care of Epscop Ábán? Wasn't it their workmen who were clearing the field across the river? This is a strong challenge to the Érainn here and the Eóganacht who rule in Cashel. The sisters talk all evening and give thanks to God, to Máthair Gobnait and the bees, and ask that they may be safely returned from the tree in which they now lodge.

Áine shakes her head when anyone questions her. She is unworthy to tell the tale. God punishes the sinful; that is clear from the moment she sees the bees wreak havoc among the thieves, stinging mightily the arms and limbs that flailed at them. Is this God's justice, his retribution? Would that she'd been stung, perhaps the pain of it might take some of the sin she carries. Such a fit punishment for her cowardice and her denial of God's will that she go to the fair on her own.

She slips away quietly, while the rest are still at their meal, Máthair Gobnait's calm voice ringing over them, reining in the more outrageous claims. She heads toward the sleeping hut. Once inside, she makes her way over to Siúr Ethne's cot, where she slips her hand under the straw pallet and finds what she hoped would be stored there.

She walks quickly down the path, the feeble light from the moon just enough to guide her over to the wooded area. There, in the small clearing she visited once before, she removes her gown and *léine* and assumes the posture she remembers. It is time she stopped cowering behind others, she thinks. She must face her just punishment.

She swings the knotted rope along her back. The sting of it is fierce, just as she imagined it; bigger, larger than anything a bee could manage. She swings again, harder this time and she keeps swinging until she feels her flesh open. She pauses, puts a finger to her back to check the blood is running and resumes swinging.

The moon disappears and a soft rain begins to fall. The sting has long since been replaced by a burning and searing pain. It's at that point the roaring comes, the shouting, the screaming that eventually descends into blackness.

CHAPTER FOURTEEN

She opens her eyes and sees a dark figure bending over her, a small corona of light outlining the veil on her head.

'Máthair Ab,' she says.

'At last child, you're awake.'

She lies on her stomach and attempts to turn over, but the agony in her back stops her.

'Remain still. You're back is in a terrible state. You must let the salve do its work.' Máthair Gobnait lifts a bowl and a spoon. 'Do you feel well enough to take some broth?'

She swallows and licks her lips. Her tongue, furred and thick, seems only barely capable of it, but her stomach rumbles at the smell. She nods.

In the end she manages half of it, but the effort of lifting her head and the sharp little pains that stab her back each time she moves eventually prove too much. She thanks Máthair Gobnait, closes her eyes and tells her she's tired. It's true enough, but she is also reluctant to engage in any kind of conversation, to answer any of the questions that she can feel hovering around her. She needs more energy for that, and above all, she needs to think.

There is much to think about. The rage, fear and blame are almost too much to bear. To share it all would endanger more than her life this time, and the anger and frustration that is so strong it obscures the pain in her back makes her think only that she must act. The thought fills her mind before she collapses.

~

She wrinkles her nose and catches the scent of mint in the air. The salve is cool on her back and eases some of the burning pain as it finds its way into the welts and open wounds that are only just beginning to scab over on her back. The air is thick with unspoken words. Máthair Gobnait doesn't press her though, and speaks only about her physical pain.

Áine hardly notices the pain in her back. Her thoughts are directed towards the pain that makes her heart ache, and the tears that fill her eyes are not the result of over energetic fingers, but from the memories that are all too plain to her now. These memories make her a different person and Áine is no more, and she grieves that loss, just as she grieves for the memories themselves.

Máthair Gobnait finishes and stands before her. 'Your back is already much improved. The skin is healing well.'

'Thank you for your help. And Siúr Feidelm's.'

'You're welcome.' She pauses a moment. 'I've spoken to Siúr Ethne about the scourge. It was her scourge you used?'

'It was.' Her voice is faint.

'I know some religeuse follow a path of asceticism and penance and feel the scourge is an integral part of finding God, but it's not the way here. Such a path is dangerous because it can sometimes lead to extremes where we confuse ego with God.'

It's a view that Áine hasn't considered. Her own speculations of Siúr Ethne's choices have been drawn solely on her observations and experiences. Observations and experiences that belong to someone she really is no longer. But still, she listens to Máthair Gobnait, mulls over the words and sees that Siúr Ethne could easily fall into that situation.

'I've thrown the scourge into the fire. I know that others are just as easily made and applied in secret, though. Can I ask that you will not indulge in such an action again?'

Áine notices her choice of words, smiles at the subtle innuendo implied by the use of 'indulge' and the phrasing of the question. This woman is clever as well as kind. She can bend people to her will with her careful eloquence and compassionate smiles. It is something to be aware of.

'You can rest assured, Máthair Ab, I won't use the scourge again.'

There is a pat on her shoulder. 'I'll let you get some rest now.'

~

It is some days later, when she is able to walk a little, that Colmán arrives. He finds her sitting on a bench spinning wool. The day is dull and overcast, and there's a slight edge in the air, one of the many small signals that the seasons are shifting.

He stands in front of her, legs slightly apart, arms folded. His pose is as a legal representative of the rank of *aigne*. 'You are Cuimne,' he says, his voice firm.

She looks up at him. He examines her carefully, taking in her uncovered hair, her pale face, her mouth firmly set and lastly, her eyes. 'You know,' he says.

'I am Cuimne.' There is no emotion in her voice, she just states the fact. She notices then his travel-stained clothes, the dishevelled hair. She's put him off balance now and inside she smiles.

'Your father was one of the Eóganacht of Irluochair near Lough Leane, a king.'

'Yes, a minor king, like your father.'

'And your father's dead, now.'

She nods and resumes her spinning because she finds such a routine task can shift her mind from her fear. The anger she keeps, knowing it will nourish her and stiffen her resolve.

'They say you had a brother, too.'

She raises her eyes, caught by the remark. 'Who are *they*? Did *they* tell you that my mother died in childbirth when we were both small, so that it was just the two of us, so close in age we were nearly twins? It was only when we were fostered that they managed to part us, but still my brother came to visit, when he was able.' She stops and gasps that she would let that much slip. Her hands start to shake.

'I'm sorry for your loss. To have both your father and brother die within days must have been terrible.'

She bites her lip, stung by his pity. She does not need pity. With her decision to abandon her desire to remain unnoticed, unrecognized, she needs resolve and courage. She tries for calm. 'Did they tell you how my brother died?'

'I talked to your foster family and they explained about your father's accident. A blow to the head from a fall. Of your brother they said little, only that he was cut down in a fight.'

She considers his words and knows it is all a matter of perspective. 'Has anyone said who cut him down?'

He shakes his head. 'Only that they presume it was one of his father's men because a few of them disappeared at the time he was killed.' He narrows his eyes and gives her a careful look. 'Have you a different story? They did mention that they were surprised when you didn't appear for your brother's burial, though men were sent to recall you from your journey back to your foster family.'

She returns his gaze and strives for composure. The spindle is tight in her hand and her nails are digging into her other palm. It is those very men who went after her she is certain attacked her on the road to An Dhá Chích Danann. Instead of recalling her, they killed the loyal men who accompanied her. And these poor loyal men are now thought to have killed her brother. There is no one else but her to claim otherwise.

'What is it?' he asks her.

She looks away. His eyes see too much, and right now, she knows she is on the verge of speaking, despite its potential danger.

He sits beside her, unfolds her hand from around the spindle and takes it in his own. 'I know there is something you are keeping back. Some information that is related to your brother's death, I can see that.' He gently turns her face to his. 'You fear something. Tell me what it is.' His voice is soft, persuasive. All the probing tone of the legal representative is gone. Now there is something more dangerous there.

'I saw,' she whispers. She chokes on a sob and the terrible images that have been so blessedly well hidden fill her mind now. His arm is around her shoulder and she leans in, thinking that just for a moment she will draw on his strength. She can't help but linger though, and then finds she can't pull away. A deep breath gives her no more than an intake of air. It does nothing to help her speak the words that tell the tale of the images. Somehow, though, she manages eventually and tells him what she knows.

An arm with a sword. That's what she knows. A man's arm wielding the sword that kills her brother, cuts him down as he turns his back after a word or two spoken in anger. Those words are innocent by themselves and tell her nothing of the argument. What can 'enough' and 'I will say no more' become to provoke a slaying?

This is all she saw and heard when she went to bid her brother goodbye, after he promised to leave the hunt and meet her by the well near the wooded track she took east. The light was poor and the trees thick, but she could hear the stir of horses and men nearby.

'The blame is with me,' she says softly. 'I should have called my few men anyway.' And that is the bitter core of it. That she did nothing but run away. Run to An Dhá Chích Danann for protection before making her way to her foster family to persuade them to help.

'It would have been of little use,' says Colmán. 'They would have slaughtered all of you.'

'As they did eventually,' is her retort. She recalls the slashing swords cutting her men to bits and shivers. Where were their bodies?

'But not you.'

'They thought they had.' She remembers managing to crawl from under one of her men and make her way away from the track. 'But I think now, they know I am alive.'

'You are alive and you have the protection of the law on your side. Who is the person who killed your brother?'

'I don't know. I didn't see his face.'

'Was there nothing about him that you recognized?'

She pulls away and shakes her head. 'There is no law that can protect my situation, I think. My father is dead, there is a new king, and my family can find no favour with this king, a distant cousin.'

'But we can seek justice for you. Your brother is killed and you must have compensation for such a terrible loss.

It demands a high price. We'll find out who has done this and bring the law to bear.'

'The law? You think I want to enact the law? I want to cut him down as my brother was cut down. He deserves nothing better.'

'It's natural you would want to do that, but let me find out more of the particulars, first, though. You are safe here, for now.' He pauses a moment. 'What exactly do you remember of your own attack? What number of men?'

'I rode behind my servant, Ciarán,' she says. 'And two of my father's men were with us when five men came up out of the furze and attacked us.'

'Did you recognize the men?'

She shakes her head. 'The light was poor and the men wore *bratacha* that covered their heads. They pulled me from the horse, and that's the last thing I remember.' She looks away.

He opens his mouth as if to say more, but closes it after a moment. Silence settles over them. 'Have you mentioned any of this to Máthair Ab, or any of the sisters?' he asks, eventually.

'No.'

'Not even Siúr Sodelb?'

She lowers her head and picks up the spindle again. 'She's dead.' She states it as a fact now, though a wail of grief echoes in her head.

'Dead? When did this happen?' His voice is full of concern.

She tells him with only a few words, still staring at her spindle. There is no reason for him to see the pain it causes, though she might try and convince herself that these emotions she feels belong to someone else. He says the words that all say when hearing of someone passing.

He even pats her hand and tells her that she's suffered too much loss of late and needs time of quiet industry to allow her soul to absorb it all. 'I know what I speak of,' he tells her.

He takes his leave soon after, giving her the promise that he will try to find out more about the circumstances of her father and brother's deaths and her assault. He cannot promise when he will return, but he's certain that it will be within the month. She shrugs at those words. She has her own ideas, her own plans to make.

~

She sits staring out across the fields and woods, picks out the sheep in the far field above, little dots with even smaller dots tagging along. Some of the lambs are still young enough to want their mother. Down along, she sees the cows with Siúr Sadhbh and her two young helpers trudging up the hill to them to do the evening milking before *Nocturns*.

She looks down at the spindle in her hands. Even now, she knows Siúr Ethne will be sitting at the loom in Siúr Sodelb's place, weaving the wool into cloth for Epscop Ábán's *manaigh* and the two fosterlings due soon. She wonders if one of the fosterlings will train in the kitchen with Siúr Feidelm, or learn the vagaries of producing a crop from Siúr Mugain. Perhaps Siúr Ethne will teach one of them the skills of fine sewing and embroidery while she fills their ears with specially selected passages from the Bible. If she had the choice now, she'd choose the kitchens, immerse herself in the safety of the mysteries of garden botany and plant lore, as well as the mundane tasks of counting loaves and sacks of grain. But that is finished. There is no choice before her now. She has hidden behind these women for too long. Once she tells Máthair Gobnait all that's in her heart, her time here will be done.

Up to now, she's avoided attending the meals and the offices and avoided all personal conversation by pleading the state of her back. Today, though, she goes to *Nones* at midday, stands at the back and eases herself down carefully on her knees when the time comes to pray. But she can utter no prayers. She is unworthy of any of the Lord's grace or forgiveness, for she will never be able to forgive herself for Sodelb's death, her brother's death or forgive the man who killed him. She cannot see how it will ever be possible. Wicked and sinful, that's the person she is now. That's the person Cuimne is. The woman that was Áine, who loved a *cailech* above all others is no more. She realizes this fully as they say the final *Pater Noster* and when the office is finished, she removes her veil.

CHAPTER FIFTEEN

She finds Máthair Gobnait at her forge, the special hearth set up behind the *Tech Mor* that few go near, except the young boy who pumps the bellows set in the ground that blows air through to the fire. This place that serves as a site where wondrous transformations of metal occur creates unease among many, and though they understand that Máthair Gobnait wields those transformations through her skill and use of fire, it does nothing to shift the awe and wariness they feel. Máthair Gobnait uses the forge only on rare occasions, to create a sacred vessel, shape a cross, or fashion an item Epscop Ábán might request.

This time she works a simple cross, the hot metal already made liquid in the crucible and poured into the mould to form its new shape. She takes hold of the shape and turns the ends with tongs so easily, it is as if the tongs are extensions of her fingers. She looks up when she hears someone approaching, and her head is limned in light. She raises the back of her gloved hand to her forehead and draws it across to wipe the sweat that gathers there from the heat of the fire. There is no doubt in Cuimne's mind that Máthair Gobnait, as her name suggests, is indeed a woman of power, an ancient power that all *goba* who work the forge and metal possess, stretching back as far as the god, Gobniu, himself.

'Áine,' she says. 'Sit over there. I'm nearly finished.' She indicates a hefty rock that juts from the ground. The rock is part of the hillside that intrudes in various places of the community's land and now provides a resting place.

She watches as Máthair Gobnait plunges the shaped metal into the small vat of water beside her with the metal tongs she holds, and then, once cooled, places it on the cloth on the ground. The tongs are laid down, the gloves removed, and she walks over and sits down.

'I'm glad to see that you were well enough to attend *Nones.*' She touches her uncovered hair. 'But I feel it is something more than that which brings you here now, Áine.'

'Cuimne,' she says. 'I'm called Cuimne.'

'So Colmán told me when he mentioned he spoke to your foster father. He said your father was a king.'

'Yes.'

'And your brother was the *Tánaiste*, until his death.'

'Yes.'

The two sit in silence for a while, Máthair Gobnait content to wait her out. The words don't come easily. Though she knows Áine is no longer, it's still difficult to utter the words that make it unalterable. For a few moments she wants to hold on to that feeling that she too is one of Máthair Gobnait's daughters.

Eventually though, she starts her tale, explains her deep love for her brother and how he was slain, and her part in the events. Her voice drops to a whisper when she tells Máthair Gobnait of her terrible but unalterable fear, and determination to face the fears and unearth her brother's murderer.

But Máthair Gobnait will not accept these words. 'If only for your own safety, you must lay aside such thoughts,' she says. 'And let time heal your grief and calm your anger and help you to understand that you are blameless in this matter.'

Cuimne knows Máthair Gobnait's words are full of reason, but such reason is beyond her. She is a king's daughter who should fear nothing in the face of what she feels for her brother. 'I cannot.'

'You would unearth this person, and do what? Bring him to justice, extract vengeance, or perhaps kill him, though it might even be your kin and knowing that type of murder is of the worst kind?' asks Máthair Gobnait.

'I-I would have vengeance.' Was that what she wanted? She stiffened her resolve. She must do something.

'They can answer to God. It's not for you to judge.'

'They're not Christians, they answer to me.'

'They answer to the law, should a case be brought.'

'No. There is no amount of cattle, no gold or silver or the equivalent of seven cumals in honour price to satisfy my lack of father or brother to provide for me.' Is that what she believed? The words had come out of her mouth before she knew what she said. She would not back away. She would stand firm.

'Give yourself time to try and find it in your heart to let this go, to forgive. The Lord does ask us to turn the other cheek.'

'Siúr Ethne says that God tells us to seek an eye for an eye.'

Máthair Gobnait purses her mouth. 'Forgiveness is not just for the transgressor, but it also is to heal the one who has been transgressed against.' She places a hand on Cuimne's shoulder. 'Think, child, think.' Her voice rises and there is a hint of anger in it.

'Is that what the Church would say? What Epscop Ábán would say? I don't think so. I can think of no other way but this, Máthair Ab. And for that reason I know I can't be a part of your community any longer. I must go.'

'God can be merciful and he would teach us of that mercy. Stay here for a while until the situation becomes clearer. Someone wished you dead, and here you are safe from that danger.'

Cuimne considers her words. She needs some time, in any case, to make her plans, to contact her kin and see how she might best proceed. 'I will stay a while,' she says in the end.

Máthair Gobnait rises and moves over to the cloth where the newly created cross lays. She stoops over, picks it up and returns to Cuimne. 'This is for you. Keep it with you, whatever you decide to do, if only for my sake.'

Cuimne takes the cross from her hand and sees there is a small loop where she can string a cord and hang it around her neck. She knows this is a special gift, a sign that Máthair Gobnait has accepted her as one of the community. 'I will try,' she says and gives Máthair Gobnait a wan smile.

~

This time, when she visits the well, it's not in desperation and hope. Now, she searches for peace. There is nothing surreptitious about her journey; she walks through the *faithche* entrance and down the well trodden path with a purposeful stride. The limp no longer troubles her. Once she arrives at the well, she pauses to allow a young woman who kneels beside it to complete her own prayers and invocations before she makes any of her own. The woman is fair, her hair nearly the colour of the strip of wet linen she clasps in her hand. For one moment Cuimne thinks the woman is Sodelb, until the woman lifts her head and she sees the rounder chin and shortened nose. She pushes aside the pain and observes the woman's earnest face, the moving lips and wonders if anyone will hear her prayers.

She's not seen this woman before, either coming for healing or helping on the farm, but then she doesn't know everyone, especially women who remain in the safety of their own *les*. Her needs, her story, are something she can only guess at. That this fairly well born woman risks coming to this sacred site on her own, speaks much for its serious nature, though so near to Máthair Gobnait's community, under the protection of the Church, many might feel it safe enough, even if they didn't subscribe to the Church's beliefs.

The woman rises, and in the one hand clasps her linen strip, fresh from its dip in the well. In the other hand she holds a small earthen jar of water. She nods to Cuimne as she passes by and follows the path away from the well. Cuimne moves forward and kneels down. She casts her mind back for the prayers she used to offer so diligently with her foster mother, a prayer to the Daghda, a prayer to Lugh and most important, a prayer to Anu. The words pour from her now fast and repetitive, invoking protection, a *lorica* against what she must do. The words uttered, she sits back in stillness, testing her mind and body for the peace she seeks. With peace might come the forgiveness Máthair Gobnait desires of her. She certainly has found no peace in the oratory, where the new grave accuses her every time she is there.

After a moment she grows restless, her mind shifts from the well to the home she left those many years before to be fostered among the Eóganacht of Glennamain. Until her father's death, she'd been back to her own home only once since that time, when her father's cousin died of fever. She must have been all of twelve and had noticed her father's greying beard and her brother's height and handsome face. Though her father had seemed distracted, he had allowed her to play the harp for him and the rest of the people gathered there for the funeral. It was an old harp, belonging to the family, and its sound so much better than the one she played at her foster home. He'd praised her skill then, learned from the bard at her fosterage, told her she had a fine touch and he was proud that a daughter of his could play such a noble instrument and bring honour to the family. It was then he promised her that one day she might have the harp, take it with her on her marriage.

She'd been happy that day, basking in the certainty of her skill and what was to come in her life. Diarmait, with a laughing tug at her hair, had told her she should stop growing so beautiful, for he would soon have to beat a multitude of men coming to her father to bargain for a marriage contract. This he'd do with great earnestness, he'd told her, for hadn't Óengus, his foster brother, noticed her. She'd laughed at him and asked him why she would ever marry that *bastún*, though she blushed with pleasure, flattered. 'Then you think me nothing but a *bastún*?' he'd answered. 'For I'm the spit of him; we're a pair with no difference between us but the colour of our hair.' Perhaps that's why she found such pleasure in the thought. That she might marry someone like her brother, someone who would tease and joke with her and wish for her company.

And what of such plans now? She looks down at her hands, notes the knotted knuckle on her small finger, one reminder of the change since those days when she was twelve. She flexes her hands and wonders about the family harp with its finely carved pillar and polished

soundbox; the harp that should be hers. She thinks of
Óengus, a vague figure whose hair she knew wasn't dark
like her brother's, someone who laughed and teased but
was well skilled with a sword. What did he know of her
brother's death? If he was anything like her brother, she is
certain that he will help her look for the killer and keep
her safe in the process. But these questions and thoughts
cannot be posed in a message. Somehow she must find a
way to go to him.

~

She turns from her place at the loom when she hears
Colmán hail her from the doorway. She's been weaving
for a few hours now and her back is aching, so though
the opportunity to stop is welcome, the cause makes her
reluctant. She rises to find someone to fetch refreshment
for Colmán and it occurs to her that his arrival might be
opportune.

It is only the serious cast of his face that gives any hint
of purpose of his journey here, and so she is slow to ask
him the news. She chides herself that there could be no
news that would make her fearful now. With all that she
has suffered, what other events could possibly be worse?

'You are well?' he asks.

She nods, though it is a lie. Her heart gives regular
beats in her chest and she is able to eat, drink and walk
about doing simple tasks like weaving, carding and
spinning wool, sewing the cloth, fashioning the clothes.
She can even measure out herbs for the infusions without
serious consequences to give to the people who come to
the community for the coughs and wheezes caused by the
autumn rains already upon them. But she still cannot
attend the offices, bow her head in prayer, or even sing
the psalms. There is no forgiveness present in her heart
and no desire to confess its lack again and again.

Her mind, instead of finding peace, has grown ever more restless with the passing days, darting everywhere to seek answers and form plans. Sleep has become an infrequent visitor, especially with the empty place in the cot beside her. She finds it much easier to work at the loom, or sit on the bench and sew while the hours stretch before her and her mind goes racing. Máthair Gobnait says little, and even allows her the extra pine resin candles such work requires. There is no place for her at the hives, not since the swarm, though Máthair Gobnait has only said that her own restlessness would infect the bees and she would rather not have anyone stung.

But Cuimne can see that he understands some of this because his eyes suddenly become sympathetic, though he says nothing of it. Instead, he professes that he is well enough too, and on further questioning from her, says that he believes his parents and wife fared well given everything, though he's not seen them since he left them.

'I've been to see your cousin.'

'My cousin who is now king?' The bitter note creeps in, though she tries to prevent it.

'Yes, as you guessed, he's king now, but duly elected by the *tuath*.'

She frowns. 'Of course Ailill would have his supporters, who would ensure his election as king.'

He nods. 'As your father probably had for his election. Wasn't his predecessor this man's father?'

'Yes, but he was less able than my father. He was a simple man, liked to spend time with the herdsmen and the matters concerned with the farm. He wasn't interested in furthering our connections or expanding our lands. My father said he knew all ends of the cow but couldn't fathom one contract from another.'

'That might be true, but Ailill seems capable enough. And he was glad enough to hear news of you.'

'You told Ailill what happened to me? He knows I'm here?' She feels a small grip of panic and forces it away.

'I said only that you'd suffered injuries on your journey back to your foster family and had lost your memory for a time. Ailill seemed genuinely surprised and relieved that you are recovered. He assumed you were staying with my family and that I'd come only in that capacity. He assured me he would be glad if you returned.'

'You told him nothing more?'

'I told him I had come to inform him about your injuries and recovery. I only listened, observed and then later indirectly questioned a few of the old servants. They explained that your father died during an argument with Ailill and some others who had been asked to come to help in a cattle raid.'

Cuimne steels her expression. This is no surprise to her, she knows all about it. She knows that the argument got out of hand and her father fell, struck his head upon a rock and died. It does nothing to erase the cloud under which Ailill had become king, election or no. And it is no help in calming the tension that is building inside her, or the tightness around her eyes.

Colmán continues to speak, explaining the events in detail, but she shuts it out. It's not the power of the words to invoke terrible grief that make her do this, it's the knowledge that each word is another stone on the pile of reasons that tell her to act.

'Did you hear anything of my brother's death?'

He gives her a look that is filled with such compassion and sympathy she can only turn her head away from it. 'Áine, please hear what I'm saying. Your brother was in a scuffle, another argument, only this time swords were used, your brother's included. Hot-headed youths with too much drink in them. His death was an unfortunate outcome.'

She thinks about this and compares it against her memory, wondering for a few moments if perhaps she misunderstood what she'd seen. She shakes her head a fraction, willing a clearer picture. All she can recall is an arm, well muscled, gripping a sword. Still, there is something about the tale that seems wrong. Why would she be struck down in such a manner if it was an innocent fight?

'What was the cause of this fight?'

'That I don't know.'

'And is it known who struck my brother?'

'No. At first it appeared that he was slain by an enemy, and his foster brother demanded that someone be brought to account for it, but Ailill was persuaded otherwise when it was clear some of your father's young men went missing at the time.'

'And they pursued it no further?'

'On the contrary, they searched for the men, but they were never found.'

Cuimne gives a grim smile. She has no doubt they were never found, because they were the men who had travelled with her and were slain themselves when she was attacked.

'Have you thought of what will you do now, Áine? Will you return to your home or stay here among the sisters?'

She straightens. 'I am not Áine, I am Cuimne.'

'Of course, I'm sorry.'

She nods and lets the silence fall between them while she contemplates all that he's told her. The pile of stones is higher than ever, now, and it is impossible to pretend otherwise. She must make the journey home, no matter that it might be more dangerous than ever to venture out of this community. She is no closer to knowing who had slain her brother, and while it might appear safer for her now that others seem to believe it was an accident, committed in the heat of the moment, she needs to know who it was. Not just for the overwhelming desire to take some sort of action, but because she knows in her heart there is something more to these events than Colmán was told.

She looks up at him eventually, sees his concern and something else. 'No. I cannot stay here. I must return home. I will hear from Ailill himself what happened to my brother.'

'You still believe it was a wrongful death?'

'I must find the truth for myself. Only then will I know what my future holds.'

'Please, Cuimne. You don't have to do any of this. You could remain here with the sisters.' He reddens slightly. 'Or you could come and live with me, be my wife, as I mentioned before. I haven't changed my mind.'

'It's impossible for me to remain here. I no longer have the mind or heart for this community. I'm unworthy of their company, especially Máthair Ab's.'

'What do you mean unworthy? How could you be unworthy?'

She nearly smiles at his words. That he should be encouraging her now to join this community when in the past he'd been clear how little he thought of the idea. 'There's nothing more to be said. I will return to my home.'

'And you will not consider my offer?' The words are spoken softly.

She sighs and gives him a direct look. 'No. For many reasons. Though it's for my cousin, Ailill, to decide, I doubt he would agree to such an arrangement. Nor would I want him to. If only for the reputation of the *tuath,* he would want me to have the full honour of *cétmuinter*, no second wife or mistress. As for me, I wouldn't want to do such a thing to Bruinech. She has suffered enough.'

'We've all suffered enough. My parents, Bruinech, me, we've all suffered the pressure to produce children, a pressure now doubled since my brother's death.' There is pain in his voice and bitterness too. 'I thought by bringing in another wife or mistress, I might lessen the pressure on Bruinech, so that she might be happy. You were known to her, and you are compassionate and wouldn't introduce more strife into our household.'

She considers his words and she notes the distress in his face. The points he makes now are so different from the impression of his initial offer. She finds herself moved by his situation and for half a moment she's tempted to accept. She shakes her head. 'No, I'm sorry. I cannot help you.'

'I see.' His tone is more formal now and his face schooled to a neutral expression.

'I would ask you one more thing, though. That is, if you wouldn't mind.'

'Yes?'

She took a deep breath. 'Would you take me to my home?' She reads the mixture of emotions on his face. She knows there is too much honour in him to refuse and his worry over her welfare will compel him to ensure she is well settled in her home. It's that element of his character and his feelings for her that she puts her faith in. It helps her to insist on her return home and look for her brother's killer, because only she can recognize the arm that wielded the sword.

CHAPTER SIXTEEN

'Are you certain you won't stay here?' Máthair Gobnait sits in her stone chair, the throne from which she surveys the land she loves.

Cuimne shakes her head, avoiding any glance towards the mountains and kneels before Máthair Gobnait. Underneath her knees the grass is damp, its wetness already penetrating her wool gown and *léine*. 'I'm sorry, Máthair Ab, but I must go home.'

Máthair Gobnait rests her hand on Cuimne's head. 'I understand your need to visit your family. I think it's important for you to go there to make some kind of peace with who you were, and who you are now.'

'I am still who I was: Cuimne, daughter of King Fergus of the Eóganacht of Irluochair and sister to Diarmait.'

'You are that and more. Much more.'

'As much as I might wish it—might have wished it, I am only what I was. I can pretend nothing more. I am no Christian. I'm a woman who will not forgive what happened to those I love.'

'Forgiveness that is easy to offer doesn't come from the deepest heart. Cuimne, give yourself time to absorb your grief and all that you have suffered, so that it can find its place beside all the other things that are you.'

'I cannot. I must go, Máthair Ab.'

Máthair Gobnait clasps Cuimne's face in her hands. Her eyes are glittering, full of emotion. 'You, my child, must decide which path you are to follow, but it must be done only after full consideration. Harm lies ahead, for your soul and possibly your life. Think, Cuimne, think!'

Cuimne blinks under the force of Máthair Gobnait's tone. And for a moment she pauses to consider the words, but in the end she knows there is no other choice for her. She pulls Máthair Gobnait's hands away and shakes her head, tears in her eyes.

'I'm sorry, Máthair Ab, I must go.' Cuimne bows her head, unable to face the disappointment in Máthair Gobnait's face. She hears her sigh.

'And Colmán is willing to taking you?' Máthair Gobnait's tone is weary, accepting.

Cuimne bites her lip. 'Willing? Well, he isn't happy about it because like you, he'd rather I didn't go.'

'He's wise in that.' Máthair Gobnait rises from her seat and lifts Cuimne up. 'Then, my child, I can do nothing more but give you my blessing and ask God's protection for you.'

Cuimne feels the cross traced across her head and hears the familiar words uttered. She sighs, knowing it will be the last time she'll feel this kind of comfort from this dearest and holiest of women.

~

She rides behind him on his horse, her arms around his waist, clad in an old *brat* and the grey wool gown and linen *léine* that had once been Sodelb's. Behind them ride only three other of his men. He has chosen to take only a small number so that the journey is quick. Already, he has been away from home too long. And there is no need to impress the king with his standing or his wealth.

Cuimne feels this keenly as she clasps his waist. She is no longer a king's daughter and her position is not as certain as it was the last time she made the journey home. Then, though her father had died, there was no doubt she was the sister of the future king, and she rode proudly with her small entourage. Now, she shares a horse with a legal representative and feels guilt for taking him and his small group away from home too long.

Colmán has spoken little since their departure from the community and Cuimne is glad. It will take a few days to cover the distance to her home and she thinks she would rather not have the journey filled with mindless chatter, even though she knows that isn't Colmán's manner.

It is in this relative silence that they stop to eat at a small clearing. She draws the *brat* around her, its once bright blue now faded almost to grey. Grey as her mood and the sky above them. Grey as the beard of Colmán's servant, who looks tired and drawn. It has only been a short time since his brother's death, she realizes, and her guilt increases. He should be marking his grief at home.

'Do you journey much in your capacity as legal representative?' she asks him.

'I am on occasion called away to disputes. But most are in our *tuath* and don't require much travel. I go to Cashel sometimes and to the annual law meetings, but that would be all.'

'But now I've taken you from your home for a long period of time. And your brother only just dead. I'm sorry for that.'

He pauses, considering her remark. 'The length of time I spend from home is much of my own making, if you remember. I chose to look into your background. I chose to make the journey to your foster family and to your home.'

'I understand that, but you did it for me. And now, you're on another journey at my request.'

She hears the sigh, sees the small frown. 'Did it occur to you that, for now, I might prefer to be away from home? That for me, it might be so unbearable to see my parents' grief, my wife's suffering, and better to do something I have some considerable skill in?'

He says it kindly, but it still strikes her dumb and she realizes how much conceit she possesses to have assumed he preferred to tangle himself in her affairs because of his regard for her. She says nothing for the rest of the meal, savouring neither the food, nor the humility that has been thrust upon her.

A soft rain starts to fall and mist descends from the mountains, so that there is no sight of An Dhá Chích Danann to give her pause of either comfort or challenge as they near the place she was found beaten. She grips Colmán tighter, for even in the thickening mist, she knows it's nearby. After a moment's thought, she decides to offer a prayer to An Máthair Anu, the goddess whose breasts rise so full and high, but she cannot still the trembling that shakes her legs and arms.

Colmán halts. 'There is no cause for fear. My men are well armed and capable. And I have my own knife and sword.' He withdraws a sword from the pack one of the men carry and places it in front of him, across the horse's back. With a quick motion he leans over and takes a knife from the leather casing strapped to his calf and hands it to her. 'There, hold that, if it makes you feel safer.'

She takes the knife, clutches it in her right hand and replaces her arms at his waist. 'Thank you,' she says. After a moment she leans her head on his back.

They travel in that manner, the men following, until the light begins to fade. 'You know a place to stop somewhere for the night?' she asks. In the past, she had always stayed with distant kin or kin of her foster family, or her own family, to ensure a suitable welcome. It is only now that it occurs to her Colmán might not have such connections in this area. As far as she knows, his people were mostly linked to *tuaths* and lords east of his home.

'I do. There is another legal representative whose home is very near. I stopped with him before, and I'm sure he would provide a welcome for us now.'

'He wouldn't deem it unseemly that I am in your company, without servants of my own?'

'I'll say nothing of your true identity. I'll say only that you're my cousin and I'm accompanying you to the home of your prospective husband.'

She grimaces at that statement. It is a wise choice, but she rankles at the idea she might be on the way to marry someone. It seems too close to the matters that hover between them.

'If he is a legal representative like you, are you certain he won't see through the lie?'

'It's what I told him before when I journeyed. That I was seeking a marriage bargain for my cousin, so he won't be surprised to see me come through again, this time with said cousin.'

It seems plausible when he phrases it in that manner, and she allows herself to be content with that, so when they ride through the *les* entrance she feels no sense of anxiety. Her early fears have disappeared as the distance from the mountains has lengthened, and she is able to appreciate the sight and smell of the friendly smoke curling from the roof hole, and the sounds of animals settling from the night.

The welcome from Colmán's friend Murchad, his parents and his wife, Almaith, are fulsome. They lead Cuimne to a seat by the fire to work off the chill from the wet ride and give her a warming drink. She is grateful for the fuss and allows it to distract her from the larger issues. A servant offers her a bowl of boiled cabbage and meat and she takes it eagerly, glad that she can at last feel her hunger.

Opposite her, two sleepy children lean across the grandfather's lap, the older of the two playing with his grandfather's gnarled fingers. The talk flies over her head while she eats, Colmán falling into easy conversation with Murchad and Murchad's father. Words of the weather, crops and families fill the air, the natural way of conversation to friends such as these. Actions of the king of Mumu at Cashel and the growing power of the bishops are left to the later hours of the night, when all are settled into their seats, and beer drained countless times from all the mugs.

Almaith regards Cuimne only with mild interest and offers her a dry *léine* for sleeping. They have made the small cubicle ready for her, she tells Cuimne after a while, but adds that Cuimne will have to excuse the young toddler already asleep in the bed, promising he will do nothing to disturb her sleep, as he is harder than the dead to wake.

Cuimne nods and murmurs all that is expected of her, though everything seems no more than a blur in her travel-fatigued state. The last remnants of tension that had gripped her the whole day have slipped away under the influence of the meal, the beer and the warm fire. She rises and follows Almaith into the cubicle after a faint goodnight to the others. Almaith hands her the dry *léine* and waits while Cuimne removes her damp clothes.

'I'll hang your garments up by the fire overnight. With some luck and the gods on our side you should have dry clothes for tomorrow, when you resume your journey.'

Cuimne finds the words to thank her, but her tiredness makes it difficult to utter anything more than that.

Almaith suddenly becomes talkative. 'It's the least I can do for a kin of Colmán's. Are you *derbfine,* cousin to his father's family?'

Cuimne makes an effort to rouse herself and answer sensibly. 'I am from his mother's family, but distant only. Colmán was kind enough to offer his legal expertise in this matter.'

'Colmán is a good, kind man, alright. Such a shame so many troubles have beset him of late. I would hate to see any more come to pass.'

'As would I, Almaith.'

'His wife has suffered terribly, *a stor.* But she's the anxious sort, as was her mother, so.' Her tone contains no special emphasis or hint at a double meaning. Still, Cuimne feels a twinge of unease.

'You knew her mother?'

'No, not directly. But anxiety does nothing to help conceive children. Bruinech was the only child her mother delivered safely.'

From the cover of her lowered lashes Cuimne gives Almaith a speculative look. She cannot help but feel there is some hint of a message behind Almaith's words. How best to tell her that her future has nothing to do with Colmán or his family? 'I hope Bruinech will find some way to alleviate her anxieties, though I doubt I will hear little of how she or Colmán fares after this journey is completed.'

'You'll be married soon.'

Cuimne nods. 'All being well, my affairs will settle into place by the season's end.'

'And you are happy with the choice?'

'Happy enough. It's my family duty that's uppermost in my mind.'

'Yes, we all must be aware of the importance of our obligation to our family. But in the case of marriage, sometimes what sets out to be a duty can be a pleasure. There are children, the satisfaction of a well run household, and the comfort of a good husband. These are all things that can give much joy.'

'Yes. I'm sure you're right.'

Almaith presses her hand. 'I hope it becomes the case for you, Cuimne, kin of Colmán.' She gives a warm smile and it lights up her round face. 'For now, though, I bid you goodnight.'

~

They are ready to depart early the next morning and Cuimne is relieved to see that the day is fine enough, though a bracing breeze cuts through her *brat*. Colmán's men hug their own *bratacha* close and draw them up around their heads.

After they take their leave of Murchad's household, Cuimne mounts the horse behind Colmán as before, and they resume their journey. This time her arms feel more at ease around his waist and she settles into the slow trot that marked their pace the previous day. And this time there are no fears, no tense moments of recall and the track they follow, though stony and rough, is well worn and provides few surprises. They break for a meal somewhere around midday at a spot sheltered from the wind. They settle as best as they can on rocks. One of Colmán's men lights a small fire, so that they might all share in a drink warmed by a small heated metal rod.

'You've known Murchad a while?' Cuimne asks Colmán eventually. The question has hung in her mind all morning and the other questions that follow it. How much had he said to Murchad and Almaith on his first journey? What did they know of her really?

'Yes, I've known him a long while now.'

'And his wife, too? She seemed to count you a familiar face.'

'His wife, nearly as long.' He eyes her carefully. 'Murchad and I attended the *nemed* together.'

She considers his words and understands then how they would know him and his family so well. It was not a case of two legal representatives meeting on the occasional law case, but fast friends from youth, schooled together, perhaps even as close as foster brothers. 'They know your family, your wife.'

He only nods; the statement is obvious.

She reasons with herself that Almaith's words were nothing more than an expression of her concerns for the wellbeing of Colmán and Bruinech. Cuimne reminds herself to stop seeing conspiracies where none exist and focus her wits on the place where conspiracies are more likely. Her home.

CHAPTER SEVENTEEN

Even before they entered the *dún* she can see changes, despite the soft rain that falls. The mountains still rise tall around them, but where sheep had grazed before, there is a field of oats, and where oats have been, cows wander around, their dark hides standing out like shadows on the landscape. Two women working in the vegetable garden, preparing it for winter onions, raise their heads at their approach and give a nod, but Cuimne has no idea of their names, or who their parents might be. Once inside the *les,* she notices the sheds are different, some new and larger, while others that she remembers are gone. The stocky woman feeding the hens in the yard might be the daughter of the woman who once managed the hens, but Cuimne can't be sure, and doesn't want to reveal her ignorance. In the end, she merely nods to the woman and asks if someone might tell the household she is back home.

The woman gives a small wink to one of Colmán's men and wipes her hands on the back of her worn gown. 'You were here before,' she tells him.

The man reddens slightly. Though he is not a lord, he is a man of some standing and certainly would prefer not to be so obviously known by this woman. Cuimne can only imagine the circumstances for this acquaintance and suppresses a smile. 'I was, so,' he says after a moment.

The woman gives a quick obeisance and hurries into the house while they all dismount.

A small group emerges from the house and makes its way to them. At its head is a tall thin man with dark hair, and Cuimne knows that this is Ailill, and the men clustered around him are his men, and relatively unknown to her.

'You've returned, Colmán. And with my cousin.'

Ailill examines her carefully, his face wary. 'You are welcome to our home, Cuimne.' After a moment he moves forward to embrace her lightly.

She bristles slightly at his phrasing. That he should welcome her to her own home, calling it *his* in the process, is difficult to bear. She steps back and he releases his arms, while she tries to steer her face into a more neutral expression. Her eyes go unwillingly to his arm and she examines it carefully, but the light is poor and she is unable to study it for long. Her stomach is a knot.

Ailill indicates the woman behind him. 'Cousin, this is my wife, Sárnat.'

A young dark-haired woman moves forward, her manner shy and unassuming. There is no harm in this woman. 'Welcome, dear Cuimne,' she says in a soft voice. 'We were so relieved to hear you were safe.'

There is distance between the two women, one that is mostly of Cuimne's making, and she dares the other woman to try to close it. There will be no embrace for the two of them. A nod and a guarded greeting suffices for Cuimne, and with it is carried an unspoken message that makes it clear she will not be won over.

Ailill sweeps his arm out towards the doorway. 'Please, come inside.' Cuimne cannot help but notice there is tension in his voice and she glances down once again to his arm. It strikes her that she would be better to play the warm cousin rather than let him see her animosity. Cuimne looks at the doorway to her home. She hesitates a moment, her heart flutters and threatens the hold she has on her emotions. Even Colmán's reassuring hand at her back does little to help.

Perhaps because she expected more dramatic alterations after what she has observed in the fields and inside the *les*, it seems little changed inside. The rush lights are lit and fixed in their usual position, clamped in the iron pincers. She can see her father's chair is there, the same trestle table leans up against the wall and the loom is still in its place at the side, a linen cloth stretched on it. The heavy wooden chests, beautifully carved and painted with intricate patterns, seem no more faded than when she'd last been here. The *léine* and gown that hangs on a rack near the fire could have been her own. It is the same, and yet it isn't. Ailill takes her father's wooden couch at the fire next to his mother, who she suddenly remembers is called Lassar. Lassar is an old woman, there is no mistaking that. Even in the poor light, Cuimne can see traces of skin showing through the sparse grey hair that covers her scalp.

Lassar leans on her stick and makes to smile. 'You'll forgive me for not greeting you at the door. These old legs aren't as nimble as they once were.'

Though her limbs might be feeble, her voice is firm and the keen eyes say it all, that the mind is as quick as ever. Cuimne remembers that her father had never cared for this woman, describing her as someone who failed to remember her place. Her place is clearly marked now, elevated once again to the king's side.

Cuimne regards Lassar with narrowed eyes. Her own vague memories of this woman are limited to painful pulls on her hair when Lassar attacked her head with a comb, and a few heavy slaps to her face when she was caught in some scrape with her brother and dared to answer back. She does have a clear memory of Diarmait calling Lassar a cow behind her back and imitating her large-breasted appearance with a *léine* of Cuimne's stuck inside his tunic.

Sárnat gestures to her. 'Please, have a seat.' She flutters nervously over to the bench on the other side of the fire and pulls at the sheepskins covering it. 'We'll eat soon, once the meat is finished.' She glances over at Lassar and bites her lip. 'I'll just go over and see how the cooking fares.'

'Some warm mead for them first, Sárnat,' says Lassar.

'Yes, yes of course.' Sárnat moves to a bench where a jug of mead rests.

Lassar motions to a young man, little more than a boy. 'No, it is the *rectaire's* place to get Barrdub or one of the serving girls to do that. Ask him to check also that the meal is ready.'

Sárnat replaces the jug on the bench and looks uncertainly at the *rectaire,* who has jumped up from his seat at the side and has headed for the door. Cuimne is surprised that they would have such a young man in such an important position. It is no one she recognizes, so she has no idea if there is some blood connection that has him placed here.

Lassar is not finished with her instructions to the *rectaire.* 'Tell whichever one you see, though Barrdub would be best, to get one of the lads to come in and put up the table. It's time enough now.'

The *rectaire* nods and disappears out the door. The men and few women who cluster in around the fire and off to the side murmur throughout this exchange that is clearly common enough. Cuimne thinks she recognizes a face or two. There must be some client farmers and lords whose lands are tied up in their land that are among them and would remember her. Beside her, Colmán takes her hand and squeezes it under the cover of the *bratacha* that drape their shoulders. The *bratacha* are only slightly damp. It seems that Colmán is as reluctant to remove his *brat* as she is hers. It's only later, when awkward glances come their way, that they both slide them off their shoulders and Colmán places them next to him on the bench. By this time the slave girl, Barrdub, comes tripping in, heads directly for the *bratacha* and hangs them on the rack next to the *léine*. That chore completed, she serves up the mead.

Lassar nods across to Colmán and Cuimne and sighs. 'You must excuse my daughter-in-law. Sárnat is newly wed and is still finding her way here. I know her foster mother well enough to have expected more from the girl, but given her family, I guess it's no surprise.' She glances over at her son and shrugs as if to wash her hands of any part in such a poor decision. Sárnat lowers her head, but not before a tear escapes down her cheek.

Cuimne only half hears this plaintive speech. She cannot stop noting Ailill's tense posture, the leg crossed and his hand tightly clasping the wooden mug he lifts periodically to his lips to drink deeply. It's not just the actions that hold her attention, it's the place he sits while doing them. It is still her father's wooden couch, the couch from which he heard disputes, gave his decisions and planned the *tuath's* future. This man sits in it now, drawn up to the fire, as though her father had never sat in it. Catching her eye, he gives her a tight smile and it stirs her anger. His eyes narrow and they hold her, and she is certain she sees a question there. It's their own private exchange, while Colmán recounts their journey, making unremarkable things remarkable, until the men come in to erect the table with the *rectaire* in their wake.

During the meal, Colmán answers Ailill's questions about various law cases he's dealt with in the past, the different tanglings of *tuath* and kin groups, and the variations of the law in Mumu, in comparison to other parts of the country.

Cuimne listens to this exchange, her thoughts taking increasingly darker turns. What was Ailill's purpose in quizzing Colmán about the law? Was he testing his knowledge to confirm that he was in truth a legal representative? Did he suspect that Cuimne had brought him for some other purpose? Or was it that Ailill sought some legal information for himself? Cuimne thinks carefully about the questions she's heard. They had focussed on fine points of the law regarding orchards, cattle, as well as a few general questions about land ownership. There could be many shades of meaning to any one of these remarks.

Colmán answers all the questions courteously and without hesitation. Yes, a client farmer who is negligent with sheep or cattle could be made to replace any ailing animal. No, a farmer whose fruit tree overhangs a neighbouring farm wasn't entitled to all the fruit the tree produced; the fallen fruit belonged to the neighbour. Cuimne is certain there is nothing innocent here. She only wishes her brother was here so she could discuss it with him.

The women and the other men contribute nothing to this discussion and remain silent for most of the meal. Sárnat glances periodically to check that mugs are filled and plates are never empty while the *rectaire* hovers nervously near Lassar. Lassar concentrates on her meat, sucking and working her remaining teeth along the bones she holds to her mouth. The bread she dunks into the beer, softening it enough to manage easily. Colmán's amusement at Lassar's unabashed actions is obvious, and for some reason that irritates Cuimne.

Lassar catches her look and raises a brow. 'The belongings you had here,' she says. 'I've had them moved to another sleeping cubicle. The one at the back.' She indicates the north end of the house. 'My bones can't tolerate much cold and damp, so I've taken your old cubicle.'

Cuimne gives her a frosty look and glances at Ailill. 'All of my things?'

Ailill nods. 'Your foster family sent them on after you left and nothing could be discovered about what had happened to you.'

'What steps did you take to find me?'

Ailill frowns and looks at Colmán. 'Your foster family waited a while, thinking you had been delayed. Eventually, they sent word to us that you hadn't arrived and wondered if you had decided to remain with us. Did Colmán not tell you? We sent out men to inquire, but by that time no one could find any trace of you.'

Was that information among the maze of all the words Colmán had laid upon her, trying to convince her that she was mistaken in her assumption? She cannot remember. So many times the buzz of her fears and anger had drowned out the words he'd spoken.

Colmán mentions that he did explain all of it, but adds there was too much for her to take in at the time to pay much notice to these details. Ailill gives Colmán an assessing look and nods before regarding Cuimne. 'Your foster family sent your belongings after it was clear you wouldn't be returning there.'

'It appeared you were dead, then,' says Lassar. 'But we were wrong, it seems. She looks Cuimne up and down and snorts. 'There's no mistaking that sulky mouth of yours.'

Cuimne gives Lassar a dark look and recalls more encounters with this woman during Lassar's occasional visits to her father's home. The mean little pinches, the biting criticisms whenever she was near. Colmán, on the bench beside her, touches her leg briefly, counselling caution. She takes a deep breath and tries to smile.

But there is no one counselling Lassar to still her tongue. 'You were such a wayward child. Badly in need of some sort of discipline. Your father left you run wild, and much good it did you. Your foster family despaired when you first went to them.'

'That's not true,' says Cuimne, with a little more heat than she would like, but she cannot help herself. 'I was young, not used to being separated from Diarmait and they understood I didn't mean half of what I said then. Do you have any idea what it's like to feel alone and no one to listen to you? That you're not allowed to see the most precious person in the world to you, but you must spend your days instead learning such dull tasks as sewing, spinning and weaving?' She halts her diatribe, shutting her mouth with force, so that she will say no more of the bitter memories and have them understand the depth of her grief.

Lassar looks at her with contempt, but Ailill's face shows only pity and that she will not stand. 'You must excuse me. The journey was long and my tiredness has overcome me.'

'Of course,' says Ailill. 'The *rectaire* will show you to your bed.'

Cuimne forces a smile. 'I don't need to be shown, I know where it is.' She bids the others goodnight. To Colmán she asks, 'You will stay a few days, at least?'

Colmán glances at Ailill, who nods. 'A few days only. I must return home, it's been some time.'

She sees the fatigue in his face, but the eyes still show the kindness, and something more. She cannot place what it is, but it's been there for some time and it makes her uncomfortable. 'Thank you,' she says eventually and hopes he understands that the thanks she offers is for more than his consent to remain here for a few days.

~

She wakes early, the habit of the past few months too ingrained now to break, and makes her way outside, soft leather boots stuffed on her feet, her wool gown hastily thrown on, and a *brat* wrapped around her. It seems strange that she isn't standing or kneeling, reciting, praying, singing, but instead now in her home, surrounded by the familiar distant mountains covered in mist, and the fields and woodlands that dot the landscape. The light is soft, the air is moist against her skin and small droplets cling to her hair. The smell is fresh and new, but underlying there is the distinct tang of decay that marks the tail end of autumn.

From her place leaning against the wall of the house Cuimne notices the signs of the day beginning. She watches the women at the milking, the men having herded the cows in with the help of the farm dog. The cows, crowded into the confines of their pen, are milked in the same order every morning. That much is clear from the manner in which they gather, ready for the firm hands to press the teats into service. It's another difference from her father's time, but, she concedes, perhaps a good one. The cows are quiet, the women know their jobs, whether it is emptying the buckets, sitting on the stools, or leading the cows to their appointed place.

There are more cows than she remembers, a reflection of the farm's expansion. Is this increase born of theft, or underhanded bargains and trades made with their overlord? Or the king at Cashel? She moves over to the shed where the horses and ponies are housed, inhaling the smell of the manure, oats and horse sweat that pours through the open door. One of the men is just leading the ponies out to the field nearby for the day's grazing. She nods to him, asks his name and discovers it is Aed, the small boy she would often find crouching by the horse shed years ago, watching the men whenever they were working there.

'Shall I help you?' she asks. 'I remember you used to follow me when I insisted on leading my own horse to the field.'

'Of course, Mistress,' he says. He offers her a rope placed loosely around the pony's head.

With a lightened heart she takes the rope and follows Aed towards the *les* entrance. She feels at home among the horses and ponies, recalling the times she spent on their backs, or playing with them in the field. Here are happy memories and nothing more. For the moment it's all she wishes for, a few quiet moments where she is in company of her own choosing. A quiet moment like those she found singing the psalms, reciting the prayers, or just sitting silent in front of the altar.

'Cuimne!'

Cuimne looks over and sees Lassar leaning on her stick, a dark *brat* thrown around her shoulders. Her whole face is creased into a frown. 'Would you please come here a moment?'

'I'll just help Aed take the ponies to the field.'

'Let Aed take the ponies by himself, I need you to come now.'

Cuimne sighs, gives Aed a rueful look and hands over the rope. With a deliberate pace, she makes her way over to Lassar. 'What is it you want?'

'It's not for you to run raggle taggle with Aed, or anyone else who works on this farm,' Lassar says in a low voice. 'You're no longer a wild seven-year-old, or even a twelve-year-old child with a father who knows nothing about what is appropriate behaviour for the daughter of a king.'

'But I'm no longer the daughter of a king,' she mutters.

'Perhaps not, but soon you will be someone's wife who wouldn't appreciate that sort of conduct.' Lassar throws in the last comment as she stalks off back to the house and her seat by the fire.

Cuimne watches her retreating back, struck by the parting words. She has been a fool not to realize her potential marriage was the main reason for the welcome here, such as it is. She would be a tool to bargain for the *tuath*, to secure a marriage for her that would benefit Ailill and his family. She knows it's only to be expected, she'd been raised in the hopes of an advantageous marriage. It is her duty, a duty that includes providing heirs for her husband. Almaith had spoken truth about what Cuimne must face on her return home when she spoke to her a few days ago.

She puts her hands to her face, and lets the darkness it provides fold over her, like a cloak. If she must make a marriage she will do it, but it will be on her terms and serve her purpose as well, if she can manage it, though she concedes that her aunt and even Ailill are forces that will take careful planning to overcome.

'Is there something amiss?'

She lowers her hands and sees Colmán standing before her. She attempts a smile and greets him. 'I'm still a little tired, I think. I didn't sleep that well.'

He nods. 'I suppose there are some changes to get used to.'

'Yes, even last night I could see that.' She gives a rueful smile. 'Thank you for remaining here for a few days. It does help me to deal with all of this, if you're present.'

'I must leave tomorrow, though. I'm sorry.'

'I understand.' She sighs. 'You've done much for me.'

'I hope you've dropped the idea you must find out more about your brother's death? I'd hate for you to do something foolish.'

She gives him a steady look. 'I promise you I will do nothing that's foolish.'

'What you and I think is foolish, might be two different things altogether.' He frowns and his face fills with concern. 'I mean what I say. I would not have you plotting to kill anyone, or even injuring them.'

'Colmán, your rank, law experience and the help you've given me earn you the right to voice your opinion to me, but that doesn't mean I must be guided by it.' She pats his arm. 'But I do appreciate your concern. I must find my own path here, and I will. I would ask only that you leave me a knife. For my protection.'

He narrows his eyes and frowns. She assembles her face into a passive look but refuses to be drawn by his expression. He sighs and passes over his knife silently. It is the one he'd given her on their journey and she notes the fine workmanship. She quickly blinks back the tears that come to her eyes.

'If you should ever need me,' he says, 'you've only to ask.'

She smiles and stretches up to kiss him lightly on the cheek. 'I will.'

CHAPTER EIGHTEEN

She feels bereft after Colmán's departure. All her energy and desire to come home and pursue her plans evaporate in the wake of his leaving. Now, she feels her last connection to the woman who was Áine, the person who loved Sodelb so well and flourished under Gobnait's nurturing, vanishing with the last sight of Colmán.

Leaning against the doorway, she watches the rain running off the thatched roof overhang to the stone gutters below. Colmán will have a wet ride. He said little to her when the time came to leave, something she marked down to the presence of Ailill, Sárnat and especially Lassar. He only clasped her to him briefly and gave her a meaningful glance, before turning to the others for a more formal farewell. And now she is alone and must make her own way.

'Come away from the door, Cuimne, you're blocking the light.'

She turns and looks over at Lassar, who sits in her chair, spinning the wool. 'Instead of standing there like a door, put yourself to use and comb some of this wool in the basket. Better yet, sit at the loom and weave for a while. I presume you learned that much from your *muimme.*'

Cuimne glances at Sárnat who sits on a bench on the other side of the fire, sewing a fine *léine* for Ailill. She can see some of the embroidered tracery at the neck and cuffs. Though this fine work is more fitting for a daughter of the king, she has no stomach for it, not for lack of ability, but because it reminds her of Sodelb's skills. She sits down on the small stool by the basket after a dark look from Lassar, and begins to card the wool. She tries to lose herself in the repetitive motion. Forward, backward, forward, backward, the words fix in her mind and remind her of her own situation. Sárnat says little besides expressing the hope of improved weather. She casts nervous glances towards her mother-in-law, her words eliciting no response from Lassar, who appears lost in thought.

'Colmán seems a clever enough man. Do you know anything of the law cases he's worked on?' Lassar says eventually.

She thinks of Fionn's theft. Such an odd case, with subtle political overtones, yet Colmán had made no enemies there. That in itself counts for something. But is it his law experience or his cleverness that Lassar is curious about? Is there some angle of the law that might suit her situation, and Colmán either hadn't mentioned it or didn't know it himself? 'No one in particular,' she says, finally. 'But I understand he is well respected by the law courts and other legal representatives.'

Lassar seems satisfied with her answer, for she falls silent again, her gnarled hands working the wool with practiced ease. 'And what is his father like, his family? Is their farm as prosperous as this one? What cows have they?'

Cuimne blinks under the force of the questions and strives to answer them as evenly as she can, while her mind searches for the cause that prompts the questions. Status and comparisons seem foremost in Lassar's mind and she assumes that Cuimne had spent these past months with Colmán's family. It is natural enough for her to be curious about it. She digs through her memory and tries to answer Lassar's questions calmly, while feeling gratitude that Colmán hadn't mentioned Máthair Gobnait's community. Besides the desire to avoid the snide remarks, comments and biting questions that Lassar would have tossed around, she also wants to keep the memories and experiences of Máthair Gobnait's community for herself, to take out and examine privately in her own time. Even now, one of the psalms threads itself through her mind, keeping her company.

It is there that Ailill finds her, sitting on the stool, her hands going backwards and forwards carding wool, while a psalm sings its way through her mind. He comes through the door, shaking his hair free of the rain and stomping his feet. Sárnat looks up, the pleasure written on her face, and goes at once to lead him to the warm circle of the fire before whisking off to get him a hot drink from the kitchen shed.

'Let the *rectaire* do his job,' says Lassar when she reaches the door. She motions to the young man, who scuttles forward from the water vats where he was overseeing their placement. 'Give Barrdub a shout,' she says to him. 'She's probably over with the girls who tend the cows. Aren't they churning today?'

'Oh yes, I forgot to tell you that they said some of the cheese from this last batch has failed,' says the young man.

'They did, did they?' Lassar rises and takes up her stick. 'I'll just have a look at this failed cheese. More than likely one of them has spirited it off. Even so, we can't afford to have carelessness of that sort.' She pulls her *brat* over her head and makes her way out of the door. The *rectaire* looks after her helplessly.

Sárnat bites her lip. 'Do you think she'll tell Barrdub to come?' She looks over at Ailill. 'Perhaps I'd better go anyway. It's partly my responsibility.'

'It is your responsibility,' says Ailill in a gentle tone. 'It is your responsibility to instruct young Liam to do his job properly.'

She nods and hastily takes up her *brat*, wraps it around her and motions to Liam to follow her. Ailill sighs and shakes his head. Clearly he meant for Liam to go on his own.

The exchange comes as no surprise to Cuimne. Lassar's authority over the household is clear. Now, with her father and brother dead, she has free rein to apply her harsh judgements and reprimands without restraint.

Ailill rises and moves over to the bench, where he pours himself a mug of beer. He picks a poker out of the fire and places it for a moment in his mug, heating it up. He drinks in silence for a while, while Cuimne observes him from the other side of the fire. She can see he is tired and remembers the *bothach, fuidir* and *ócaire* who work the land and give portions, and the *aire déso*, the *bóaire* who lease farms under her father's care when she was young that seemed to bring no end of work for everyone. It is a hard task to eke a living from land that might be less boggy than Boirneach, but still has its share of rain and damp. At least her father had always claimed. He had argued it was best to accumulate more land inland where the trees and fields weren't bent over by the winds in the winter. He'd looked ever eastwards. Even her own fosterage had been contracted to further those plans.

'You are settling well?'

Startled, she looks across at Ailill and tries to collect herself. 'Well enough,' she says at last. Her brother had once described Ailill as sly. She has no idea why he thought that, but she remembers his words. They were close enough in age, he and Diarmait, though what little she recalls of Ailill makes her think of him as much older. Still, with little enough to go by, she will watch her words carefully.

'I know it must be difficult for you to return home with many things changed.'

'I'm managing, thank you.' She continues carding the wool and starts to count her strokes.

'Still, I would like to give you some time before we think of your future.'

She keeps her head lowered so he will not see the defiant flash in her eyes. 'We?'

'All of us, since all of us will be affected by the decision.'

'I will have some say in this decision,' she says, her voice firm.

'You will, of course.'

She looks up now and studies his face. She can detect no mockery, no lie there, but still she can't be sure.

He returns her stare with a mild look, but she finds she can't trust it, though she reminds herself not to make an enemy of him yet. 'I'm sorry,' she says. 'As you say, there's still a lot to get used to.'

He raises a brow that says he hopes her words are truth, but she can see now there is caution in his face. The man is no fool. 'You have no need to worry,' he tells her. 'Soon you will have your own household to run as you please.'

'This is my home.'

'You would have had a new home someday, whether your father lived or not. You know this.' His voice is mild still, but she knows there is steel behind it.

'I do know it. I'm just not ready to leave this home yet.' She thinks to play for time, show a little resistance so that he might agree to her choice of husband.

'I'm prepared to give you time, but we need to set things in motion soon. Negotiations can last months, even years.'

'You have someone in mind?' Though she knows he'd said he would defer the discussion, she is curious about his choice. Would his strategy be her father's? A link with an Eóganacht in the east had been his plan, a family related to her foster father. Though she'd been happy enough with that plan in the past, now she looks to an entirely different direction.

'I know your father had begun negotiations with a family, but they had progressed little. And in the time since his death and your disappearance I believe the man in question has found another wife.'

It's a tidy solution, already accomplished, and she is glad of it. Though her father would have been disappointed, the situation is much different now than when he was alive. 'So you would look elsewhere?'

'I would look where it would most benefit us now. In my view that might be someone from the Corco Duibne, or the Eóganacht of Raithlinn.'

She nods. Diarmait's foster brother, Óengus, was of the Eóganacht just north of here and she wonders what Ailill thinks of him. 'I see. There is no one specific, though.'

'No, not as yet. Is there someone you have in mind?' He gives a slight smile. 'A certain legal representative, perhaps?'

'What? No, not at all. He has a wife. I wouldn't want to look there.'

'You're certain? It appeared a little differently when he was here.'

She bristles at his words. It's certainly not the case. What she would wish, deep in her heart, is impossible now. She could never be Áine again.

'There is no need to look in that quarter,' she says. 'I'm surprised you would consider it, for I would be at best a second wife. That's hardly worthy of the status of the family, or me.'

'I'm not so sure. They are an influential family and would be a good alliance.'

'What would be a good alliance?' Lassar comes through the doorway. She removes her *brat* and shakes out the raindrops, leaning heavily on her stick.

'I was suggesting a few possibilities for Cuimne's future.'

Lassar draws herself up, the stick in front of her. 'We are Uí Chearbaill. She will marry someone to our advantage.' Her tone is firm.

'That's what I was just explaining. I wondered if perhaps she was considering a match with Colmán.'

'Colmán?' Lassar moves over to the bench and sits, landing with a thump, as if to emphasize her view. She asserts that they can do better. A strong ally is needed in such times.

'The Eóganacht of Raithlinn are not strong enough?' asks Cuimne. She wonders if there is dissension between mother and son and if she might use it to her advantage. She tells Lassar that accepting Colmán as a second wife would not place her in any position of influence.

Lassar concedes the point and says they should look away from the Eóganacht of Raithlinn, but find someone who would meet with the approval of the king of Mumu.

'You feel he carries that much weight with Fiachra, though we are so far from Cashel?' asks Ailill. 'I'm not so sure. I feel Fiachra would just as soon we look closer to home.'

'No, don't be foolish, Son.'

'Would you consider Óengus?' asks Cuimne. In some ways she finds their wrestle for power amusing, but mostly she would rather just get on with the matter and settle it to her liking.

'Óengus? But he's an outsider, one of the Múscraige.'

'Does that really matter? I'm sure his father will pay a handsome brideprice that even Fiachra or the king of Mumu wouldn't object to.'

'But Óengus was Diarmait's foster brother,' says Ailill, a slight edge to his tone.

'Yes, so you know him, Cousin, and see that he is a fine and honourable man. And he will assume his father's role and will have some of the choicest lands.'

'Óengus is unsuitable,' Lassar says curtly. 'He's far too hot-headed. He'd quarrel with a snail for crossing his path if he could.'

'We're in agreement on that,' Ailill says. 'I don't think he would be suitable, on many counts.'

Cuimne flushes. 'You're being unfair. Óengus is an honourable man and I'm sure he'd be glad to have me as his wife.'

'Oh I've no doubt of that,' says Lassar. 'He'd do anything to secure a future with a family such as ours. But I won't be dragged into his fights, or his father's. No matter that he was a good friend of your father.'

Cuimne wonders if it is jealousy that makes them object so strongly. Óengus was tall, broadly built and handsome, and could charm people effortlessly. In short, he was nothing like Ailill.

'Have you seen Óengus of late?' asks Cuimne. 'What I remember is that he was given to high spirits, like my brother.'

'He was here just after your brother died,' Lassar says darkly. 'I saw no remarkable change then.'

She doesn't leap at the mention of her brother's death, though it galls her that they should even remark on it so casually in her presence. She uses the opportunity instead to study their faces in an effort to detect anything that might be deemed suspicious.

'He is—was—my brother's closest companion, so I would at least like to meet with him. It would bring me some comfort to spend time with someone who knew my brother so well.'

Ailill glances at his mother, a frown on his face. Lassar narrows her eyes and casts a sceptical look in Cuimne's direction, but Cuimne keeps her face impassive.

Lassar starts to open her mouth but Ailill nods. 'I suppose it could do no harm.'

'Thank you,' says Cuimne.

'We'll ask him here,' he adds. 'I'll send word when one of the men is free.'

'On one condition,' says Lassar. 'When he comes, you will meet him only in our presence. Is that agreed?'

Cuimne forces a smile. 'Of course.' She will agree now, and in the meantime, she'd think of some way to meet with Óengus on his own, without Lassar and Ailill's knowledge.

CHAPTER NINETEEN

'The harp, where is it? It wasn't among my things.' Sárnat stares up at her from her seat at the loom, her face every bit as startled as a deer about to leap away. Lassar continues with her spinning as though no one had spoken.

Cuimne had looked for the harp the first night she'd arrived, searching among the large chest that contained her possessions, pulling out the fine embroidered *léines*, the brightly coloured gowns in red, blue and green and her old plaid *brat* so they lay scattered on the floor. At the bottom, among a small pair of leather shoes and the odd sandal she had only found her pouch of copper brooches and her old comb, given to her when she was young. Angered, her first impulse had been to run out to Lassar and Ailill and demand the harp's return. Her father had promised it to her, after all. In the end, she'd decided to bide her time and look for it about the house, and when she found it, decide what to do then.

She'd searched the house, even managing to slip into Ailill and Sárnat's sleeping cubicle on the pretence of wanting to collect a *léine* of Sárnat's to embroider a pattern she'd learned from Colmán's mother, but found nothing. In desperation, she'd even searched the kitchen and the other sheds, though she knew they wouldn't have put something so valuable in there. The only place she hadn't searched was Lassar's cubicle. Lassar rarely went outside the house without leaving at least one of the women behind to notice every move she made.

Now she is certain the harp is gone and makes her query as calmly as she can. Ailill enters the house, shutting the door behind him. The wind has worked itself up into a hard gale with the approach of evening and now the fire blows up a protest and sparks fly. At the hearth Barrdub jumps away and the turf she is placing on the flame tumbles from her arms. Another servant scuttles over to help her pick up the turf.

'My harp, what's become of it?'

This time she directs her question to Ailill. He raises his brow and then shakes his head. 'The harp isn't here.'

'Not here? Where is it?'

'The family harp,' says Lassar, with great emphasis on the word 'family,' 'is with Fiacra. He requested it for his son who studies to become a *file*.'

'But I'm a *file* and my father promised it to me.' She is aware she is whining and though she hates herself for it, she cannot help it. As usual, there are other women in the room, though most are servants at this time of the day. She glances around at the young woman who is sitting with Sárnat at the loom. Cuimne recognizes her as the daughter of one of the minor vassal lords and flushes. Her father would never have approved of such public behaviour.

'It was not for your father to promise that harp to anyone, especially someone who would leave this family and marry,' snaps Lassar. 'Fiacra's grandfather gave it to your grandfather. It was a great honour then and it's a great honour now for Fiacra to remember it.'

'You gave up that precious harp?' she says. 'I don't believe you.'

'It's true.' Ailill's voice is kind.

Lassar frowns and pauses, as if she were considering how much to tell such a foolish troublesome girl. 'We did not go unrewarded. Our cattle are more numerous and we have additional land for them to graze on.' She glances over at Sárnat. 'And someday, should my son be blessed with children, we might have an opportunity for an even greater connection to Fiacra.'

Ailill's kind voice had almost unravelled her, but as soon as Lassar launches into her explanation in her stern tone that carries with it underlying criticism, Cuimne's tears vanish and she maintains a stony calm.

'We assumed you were dead,' Sárnat says. She rises from the loom and moves over to Cuimne and takes her hand. 'There seemed no need to keep the harp, for none of us played it.' Her tone is meant to soothe, but it has no effect on Cuimne.

'I see. Well, I'm not dead and I'm here now and still a member of this *clann*.'

'Yes,' says Sárnat. 'But perhaps when you go to your husband's home there will be a harp there for you. Or one could be obtained.' She looks across at Ailill. He shrugs and mutters an agreement.

Lassar frowns. 'First you have to get a husband, which might not be such an easy task.'

Ailill interrupts and tells her he's heard word from Óengus that he's coming here as soon as he is able. She knows Ailill means it as a kindly change of subject and the knowledge irritates her, so she asks why he hadn't mentioned it earlier.

He glances at his mother. 'I'm saying now.'

She lets it pass and concentrates on the news. 'There is much to make ready. Sárnat, you must let me help you in any way I can. He will no doubt come with several men

211

and baggage, though he does love to ride at a fast pace.' There are so many things to think about to ensure the visit will run smoothly. She thinks to smile, assuring herself that at last her plans are finally moving forward.

~

She hears the herd dogs barking first, until someone shushes them. The dogs have only just arrived in with the calves and the dogs nip and nudge them into their pen for the night. A short while before, they had done the same for the sheep that are vulnerable to the many wolves and foxes that prowl the land. Now the sky is darkening quickly; the autumn days are closing in as they head towards *Samhain* and winter.

Barrdub looks up from her work placing the wooden plates on the table when she hears the dogs bark and glances at Lassar, who nods. Liam is out in the yard. Barrdub moves to the door and nearly collides with Sárnat, who is making her own way there. Sárnat sees her and halts, flustered, and resumes her seat on the bench while Barrdub goes out into the dusk. Cuimne rises from the stool, brushes her gown and straightens her hair. Though it has only been a few days since Ailill's announcement about Óengus, she has no doubt who has just ridden in.

Lassar frowns at Sárnat. 'You'd better check with Liam that there is enough food for a few extra guests.'

'Yes, yes of course.' Sárnat bobs up again from her seat and heads to the door. It opens before she can reach it and a large, grizzled-haired man in dark robes, belt and sandals strides in.

'Epscop Ábán.' Cuimne moves forward and starts to kneel before him, until she collects herself and steps back. No one here thinks she's had any contact with a bishop or any Christian community, so how to explain Epscop Ábán's appearance?

'You're most welcome to our home, *A Thiarna Epscop*,' she says, her voice formal. She launches into lengthy introductions of Sárnat and Lassar and their connection to her, and is even grateful when Ailill appears only moments later. She fusses around the bishop, taking his cloak and offering him a seat, while trying to ignore the puzzled glances cast her way. Through her babbling narrative, Epscop Ábán only accepts her offer of a seat and smiles. She avoids his penetrating eyes and hopes that she can think of some explanation that will suffice for all of them.

Lassar gestures for Sárnat to arrange for some refreshment and issues an open invitation for the bishop to remain with them. This is only what any guest would expect and Cuimne derives no comfort from the words. Their dislike of Christians has always been clear, and is no different than what she had felt before her attack. Their ways are different; their outlook is something that doesn't always coincide with the traditions of the past. Now, she isn't certain what she thinks, and for that alone she wishes Epscop Ábán would go quickly. But there's also the matter of his knowledge of her as Áine, and all that means to her presence here and what she is determined to do.

The conversation follows its usual course among strangers. The weather is dissected and the health of all those present. Cuimne knows she must use this borrowed time as wisely as she can, but knowledge and action don't always coincide, especially when paralysis of thought comes into play. It's with a sinking feeling that she notes the talk winding down and everyone but her begins to look at the bishop in expectation, and still no suitable explanation has come to her mind.

'Colmán knows Epscop Ábán well. They had a law case together recently.' It is the only thing she can think of and she snatches it in desperation.

The bishop gives her a cryptic look. 'That is so. A most complex case.'

'Such a case would while away the evening. We look forward to hearing about it,' Ailill says politely. 'I had no idea a Christian priest would hear a case concerning a non-Christian. Are you part of the law courts?'

'I'm not, no, but everyone involved in the case was a Christian. It was heard at Máthair Gobnait's nunnery.'

'A nunnery?' asks Lassar. She glances at Cuimne.

'Máthair Gobnait and one of her women tended Colmán's brother when he was ill and dying. They eased his way, poor man. He died a short while later.'

'I see,' says Lassar. She looks at Epscop Ábán. 'This woman, Gobnait, she is under your authority?'

'Yes, she's under the Church's authority.'

'Ah, so that explains your presence at the case. But surely, in the end, it is Colmán who decides?'

'As I said, it was a peculiar case and called for a different approach.' He describes the events in a succinct manner, his voice calm. It seems simple as he lays it out, omitting as he does all the tension and underlying currents Cuimne remembers.

The topic is well explored, the fine points carefully examined, first by Lassar and then Ailill, while Sárnat casts anxious looks at Liam, at the table and the door. The responsibility of a meal gone cold or burnt looms ever larger for her as Liam stands nervously, casting glances her way. Cuimne gives Sárnat sympathetic looks, but is content with the discussion's direction. Moments later several of the men enter, giving a subtle hint that it is way past time for the meal to be served.

Sárnat jumps up. 'Should Barrdub bring in the meat? It must be ready now.' She gestures to Liam and her relief is apparent. The conversation ceases and everyone's attention shifts to the meal.

It is after the meal, when all are replete and Epscop Ábán sips his mead with slow appreciation, that the words Cuimne dreads most come out and the bishop mentions that there is a purpose for his visit.

He smiles at Cuimne. 'There is more besides a wish to greet and visit with your cousin, whom we all knew as Áine.'

It is almost like some bit of planned entertainment the way all eyes turn their gaze from the bishop to Cuimne. She flushes, despite her efforts to keep her face expressionless, and knows that her work is undone. The questions will not come at once, but they will be waiting for her.

For now, Epscop Ábán takes back their attention. 'I'm on my way to meet with Fiacra. I hope to discuss with him the possibility of acquiring some land here to establish a monastery.'

The statement creates a stir. Shocked looks and sceptical expressions are exchanged. Any speculation of Cuimne's relationship with this man disappears in the face of this unwelcome information. There are enough places, in their view, for any Christian to worship, or a *manach* to seclude himself. That there should be more suggests a future they are unwilling to accept.

It is for Ailill to make the point. 'There is no need for a monastery, here. You would only be spending time and effort to erect buildings that would remain empty.'

Epscop Ábán gives a benign smile. 'It will not be large, and there are some *manaigh* from my own monastery who have expressed a desire to come here. We grow apace in Boirneach.'

The bishop's words do little to allay their concerns and the underlying meaning brings a small flash of anger to Lassar's eyes.

'You would have men who are not from this *tuath* come to live here?'

'They are all Christians, regardless of their *tuath*,' says Epscop Ábán.

'We are not,' says Lassar.

'I understand that. And in time, that may change.'

'Not in my lifetime,' Lassar says in a curt tone.

Epscop Ábán nods as if to concede her point. Cuimne knows he is used to these pronouncements and has heard many variations of them in his years with the church. She also knows that he realizes making pronouncements or presenting philosophical arguments will do little to persuade those like Lassar to his belief.

Ailill, conscious of his hospitality responsibilities, gives his mother a warning look and makes some conciliatory remarks. The bishop brushes his hand in the air, accepting the words as if Lassar's comments were of no matter.

'Well, I can't imagine what Fiacra would want with a monastery in these lands,' mutters Lassar.

Ailill redirects their attention to a request for tales of his journeys and suggests they move to the fire. With only a glance at Cuimne, Epscop Ábán nods and moves away from the table. The glance tells Cuimne everything. He will hold her confidence and remain silent about her deeper connection to him but he will seek her out later.

~

It's not until the next morning that he finds her alone. It is impossible for her to remain in bed until everyone was about their tasks, because Lassar would only drag her out with accusations of laziness. And sojourns in the sheds with any of the animals or their keepers would be another transgression for Lassar to root out, like a pig hunting nuts in the woods. Her tasks are clearly marked and are inside the house, or in close proximity to it, as befits any other woman of her status and Lassar is there to ensure she keeps to them.

Still, she makes her way to the back side of the house, hoping that it is out of the range of any of the keen eyes on the look-out for her. She stands there, shivering in the chill breeze, her red *brat* wrapped close about her and watches the cattle grazing on the rise above, the range of mountains looming over them.

'Contemplating the psalms? Or perhaps offering some prayers?' Epscop Ábán makes his way to her side. 'It is a view to be admired, I must admit.'

'It is.' She hears her nervous tone. He gives her Máthair Gobnait's greetings and tells her that Máthair Gobnait misses her terribly. Cuimne stares at her hands while he passes on Máthair Gobnait's words and feels a tightening in her chest. Silence falls for a moment and she wonders if it is best just to get the conversation he wishes over with. 'I'm sorry I wasn't forthcoming about our connection, Epscop Ábán. You can see how it is here. No one is a Christian, and there is little sympathy for it.'

'Yes, my child. That was evident. But you mustn't forget that you are a Christian. You could show them by your excellent example that there is nothing to fear from God and that only good things can come. He did grant you the return of your memory, and with it, your identity.'

His words are a sour taste in her mouth. She wonders if it had been God's will that she be granted her memory. If so, it is a punishment, and an apt one. Who better than Him to know it for what it is? But really, she knows it is her own doing, her chosen fate to take her current path, and she must follow it to its end.

'I am no longer the woman you knew. I'm Cuimne now, not Áine. And Cuimne is not a Christian.'

'On the contrary, you may have been given the name Cuimne at birth, but now you are born again as Áine, baptized into the Christian faith as that name. It's not something you can shrug off like a *brat*, or a gown.'

'Please, *A Thiarna Epscop*, it's not possible for me to continue in your faith. My circumstances are changed.'

'How so?'

She looks up at him, gauges the shrewd blue eyes, now lined with the experience of many journeys and encounters, and notes the firm mouth. He is a priest and *anam cara* to many, including Máthair Gobnait. If he still regards her as a Christian he would keep his counsel. Should she tell him what is in her heart?

She lowers her eyes and looks at her folded hands. 'I have obligations, plans I must carry out for the sake of my brother's honour.'

'Plans?' The words he chooses are always few, but cut to the matter at hand.

'I believe my brother was killed by my cousin in order for my cousin to become king.'

'But that is *fingal*. No *tuath* would permit a kin slayer to become king unless he was immensely powerful. How did this come about?'

'I don't know the exact particulars. I only know that there was an argument, my father was struck down, and soon after, my brother was killed outright in a fight. I think the fight had something to do with my father's death.' She pictures the arm wielding the sword, compares it to Ailill's and she knows she cannot be sure.

'I see.' Epscop Ábán sits in silence, contemplating her words. 'And you know no more than that?'

She shakes her head. 'I can hardly get the truth from my cousin or his mother and wife, or any of their servants. And I've not been able to question anyone else who might have been there. I hope to do that soon, when my brother's foster brother, Óengus, comes to visit.'

'Is there no servant or client labourer whom you trust that you could ask? While you might get more particulars from your brother's foster brother, it is possible you would hear a more even account from someone else you knew in the past.' He takes her hand. 'I find it difficult to believe that your cousin would commit kin slaying in such a manner and there would be no fuss.'

'Even if he had no hand personally, I'm certain he was behind it. He had so much to gain.' The words are heated and spill from her mouth before she can stop them.

'You're risking much if you're determined to prove your cousin is this killer.'

'Óengus will help me if it's necessary. He and my brother were very close.'

'So you would put him in danger as well. This can only go badly. Do you plan to bring the law into this? Or would you kill your cousin? Is that your plan? What would the *tuath* feel about that?'

The question startles her because she realizes that her plan has little shape. All her purpose and commitment seemed to have dwindled lately, and what even a few days ago was a strong desire to meet with Óengus to drive this purpose forward, is now reduced to a genuine wish to see and talk with someone who knew and liked her brother well. As for her safety, she will look after that. She thinks of the knife that she keeps strapped to her leg and close by her in her bed at night.

'I'm not certain, but Óengus might have some idea how we may proceed.' The words are feeble and she knows it, even before she hears Epscop Ábán's reply.

'If you have killing in mind, you must remember it is still against the law of God and the law of this land,' he says firmly. He speaks reason, reminding her that such action would affect her future, whether she is linked to the killing or no. 'Think what Máthair Gobnait has taught you,' he adds.

She promises she has nothing of the sort in mind, though privately she remains uncertain. She only knows that she must face this killer, when she can find the proof to be sure who it is. He takes her hands and coaxes her to kneel before him while he blesses her, his hands moving in solemn motion to form the cross. She isn't certain why she has allowed him to persuade her to kneel and she blinks back the few tears that come. The tears are for her confusion and for the other times she has knelt in this manner. She rises and thanks him, and turns. A short distance away Lassar stands, her stick in her hand, and a frown on her face.

CHAPTER TWENTY

Lassar waits until Epscop Ábán has departed before she seeks out Cuimne. Even though Cuimne expects Lassar's questioning, when the moment arrives it is still unnerving. Cuimne has no idea how much she has heard of her conversation. She tries to stir up the old anger, feeding it with thoughts of Lassar's certain involvement in her brother's death, but has no success. Her defences are dissolving. She feels vulnerable now, prey surrounded by predators. Epscop Ábán's visit has done nothing to help the feeling.

'Sit here where I can see you, Cuimne.' Lassar points to the bench on the other side of the fire. It's early afternoon, with no one but the three women inside. Ailill and Liam have gone off with a couple of *bothach* and a slave to oversee the hauling of stones from some fields. Barrdub is churning butter with some of the other women in the kitchen shed. Cuimne looks over Sárnat's shoulder discussing cloth to use for the coming baby as Sárnat sits at the loom, newly strung linen thread ready for the working. Sárnat has only just told her of her pregnancy and Cuimne has seized upon the news to distract Lassar from the unspoken questions that hang in the air. It is a ruse that Cuimne knows Lassar sees through, but she had to try. Now, at Lassar's instructions, she takes the designated seat and sighs.

Lassar tilts her face and narrows her eyes and asks her what her connection is to Epscop Ábán and why she was kneeling in front of him. She doesn't mention his name, she merely labels him as a 'holy man,' but her tone and emphasis make it clear she thinks there is little that is holy about him. Cuimne reminds her of Colman's court case, but Lassar will not accept this explanation.

'I am not a half-wit,' she says. 'Colmán is not a Christian, no matter that the man has his monastery nearby. It is Cashel singing the tune there, giving land away, not his father. He has little love for Christians.'

'His father asked Máthair Ab to attend his ailing son. His feelings have changed.'

'Máthair Ab, is it? And how well do you know her that you would call her "mother?"'

Cuimne could bite her tongue off for the slip. It was a foolish thing to say. 'Everyone calls her that now. It's a title of respect.'

Lassar gives her a doubtful look. 'Perhaps, but that doesn't explain why you knelt before that Christian priest just now while he uttered words and made motions over your head that belong to his faith.'

She tries to remain calm and offers up the best possible explanation she can think of. 'I did it because he asked me to. It means nothing. He thinks because I met him before and think kindly of him I might soften you towards him.'

Lassar grunts. 'There is no hope of that, no matter what kind of useless Christian prayers he may utter over you.' She falls silent and Cuimne prays now that the conversation has ended. Her prayers, so quick to come to her mind, are directed to the Christian God that she's just denied and Lassar has whipped her acid tongue against. Despite her poor behaviour towards Him, her prayers are answered. Lassar says no more on the matter and Cuimne moves back over to the loom.

~

The day is as listless as she feels. The air, still and heavy with unshed rain, engulfs the mountains in dark grey clouds. Cows disappear and re-appear on the higher fields like some *sídhe* from the next world, their lowing ringing eerily across the valley.

Cuimne pauses for a moment to watch them before she searches out Aed, her brat slung quickly across her shoulders. In the days that have passed since Epscop Ábán's visit, the bishop's words have continued to haunt her. And this morning she has finally decided to question Aed about what he knows of the events surrounding her brother's death.

She hears the clop of hooves before she sees the horses. The mist parts and Óengus appears, his thick, light coloured curls glistening with moisture. He stands in a chariot pulled by a fine horse. It is no cart with a *capall*, but a warrior's vehicle, even though the roughness of the tracks and paths would make it a bone shattering journey and the chance a wheel would break. Behind him, his mounted men emerge, one by one, as if they were sheep to be counted for shearing. Óengus jumps from the chariot in a swift graceful motion. Cuimne is overcome with a joy she does not question and launches herself into his arms like she is a young girl again.

For a moment he stands stunned and her arms hang around him. He pulls her back and searches her face, his eyes intent. 'Ah, *mo storín*! How good to see you,' he says finally. He gives her a tight embrace, then drops his arms and puts a hand to her face. 'And you've become such a beauty.'

She regards him under lowered eyes. His own appearance would make any woman's heartbeat. Under his loose *brat* the muscled girth of his chest and arms are evident. There is no trace of softness in him, even his face, once a little rounded, is all angles that no amount of beard can hide. The boy is gone. A warrior at the height of his power and ripe for admiration stands before her now. He kisses her lightly on the forehead, his lips lingering perhaps a moment longer than is proper. His beard tickles her. A glow spreads through her body.

Cuimne sees Aed approach and calls out. 'See who's finally come? And welcome he is, too.'

Aed gives her a weak smile and nods formally to Óengus. He moves to the servants and the other men and they begin to lead the horses away.

'No need for formality here, Aed,' she says. 'This is Óengus, though you may not recognize him under all that hair.' She reaches up and tweaks his beard.

Óengus gives a hearty laugh and puts his arm around her. 'Ah, there is a punishment for girls who do naughty things, if I remember. Since you no longer have braids to pull, it seems my only recourse is tortuous tickling.' He lifts his hands and twirls his fingers in mocking threat at her neck. She smiles, recalling her brother's love for this game.

'Cuimne!' Lassar stands at the door. Óengus drops his hands and straightens, but Cuimne refuses to let Lassar ruin her good spirits. 'It's Óengus, he's only now arrived. We were just having a little tease as we used to.'

'You're a grown woman now, not a girl.' She turns to Óengus. 'Come inside then, instead of cavorting like a ten-year-old for all to see.'

Óengus bristles. 'It is not for you to tell me how to behave, old woman. Nor should you reprimand Cuimne so.' He glances at Aed, who stands uncertainly by his horse, his hands on the reins. 'Go on, man, take the horse and chariot and lead the men to the sheds.'

Cuimne asks Lassar in a soft tone to let the issue pass. 'Óengus is a dear friend, a brother almost, and Diarmait's closest companion. I would hope to give him a loving welcome.'

Lassar nods stiffly and the welcome proceeds as it should, a door opened, the guest ushered with due ceremony across the threshold and made to settle in the best chair by the fire. His men filter in and find benches to sit upon. The orders are given for refreshment and all polite conversation is exchanged about the weather, his journey and the health of his family and theirs. In short, all the requirements are met.

But it isn't how Cuimne wishes it. The lack of warmth, the stiffness of the exchange, only serve to underscore how it might have been had her father and brother still been alive. She thinks of all the joking, laughter and easy banter that would be shared among loving companions, all enjoyed with the best mead and the choicest of meats. And afterwards perhaps she might have played the harp, heard tales of his exploits and how he became such a fine warrior. Now, there are only wary glances and a few questioning looks that mix with the smouldering anger that filter around the room to manifest in the occasional sly reference, dark look or shifting foot.

Cuimne tries her best to lighten the mood. She sits on the stool by Óengus and smiles fondly at him. 'Are you still easy just as easy to beat at *fidchell*?' she teases.

He looks up from his mug and pauses before answering her to assemble his face into a winning smile. 'I'm certain I could find skill enough to win against you.'

'There is much to be learned from playing *fidchell* well,' Ailill says.

'I am skilled at it,' Cuimne says.

'I understand that your brother was not so skilled.'

'*Fidchell* is not a game for women,' Lassar says. It's clear her comments are meant as a criticism of Cuimne rather than a determination against women's general involvement.

Cuimne frowns a moment and her anger flares, but just as quickly the flame dies and she find she has no interest in sparring with Lassar. She does feel gratitude, however, when Óengus gives her hand a sympathetic squeeze.

'Playing *fidchell* well is for those who are unable to fight battles in real life,' he says.

'Just because someone is skilled with a sword and can fight battles doesn't mean they will win the war,' Ailill says. 'There is more to war than swinging a sword around.'

'What are you trying to say?' There is an edge to Óengus' voice.

'I'm saying nothing but that there is subtlety to *fidchell* you may not have appreciated.'

Óengus rises from his seat, his face flushed with anger. 'You think me stupid? That I have no subtlety?'

Cuimne puts a hand on Óengus' arm. 'I'm sure Ailill wouldn't be suggesting anything like that. You are known for your cunning and skill with a sword. You, and my brother. Even at games you were unbeatable when we were young.'

Óengus gives Ailill a dark look, resumes his seat and collects himself with visible effort. 'And I remember you could never run fast enough to catch us.' His light tone is forced but it is enough to ease the tension in the room.

Ailill curls his lip but says nothing. The conversation is directed toward safer subjects, in as much as Cuimne can manage it. Safety is relative, for topics of all nature hold hidden traps and it requires all her energy to think ahead and keep the conversation harmless.

They can eat, drink and they can talk about crops, animals and the forthcoming winter. Cuimne touches only lightly on her recent experiences. That subject is filled with too many quagmires and potential flashpoints to discuss with Óengus in any depth in front of Ailill and Lassar. She knows that Óengus is not making a favourable impression and she can only pray in time that he will be able to shift their poor opinion. Tomorrow, she might have an opportunity to take him aside and approach him about everything that is on her mind and get a better idea how he might feel about the idea of a marriage between them. The notion raises no objections for her. She can still feel the connection of her brother through him, and at this moment that outweighs her desire to unearth her brother's killer. But the two goals may fit neatly together, because she has noted that Óengus's feeling for her brother is still strong and his fighting spirit keen.

~

She is still contemplating these ideas as she lies in her bed, the rest of the household retired long since. The certainty with which she initially formed her plans is losing its shape, more melting ice than hardened rock. Ailill's death no longer fills her with satisfaction and the thought of Sárnat a widow with a baby on the way gives her no comfort at all. She can still take some pleasure from the image of Lassar supplanted by another mother of a different king, though if she marries Óengus she would

227

have no involvement in the future here. In that light, what befalls Lassar should be of little consequence.

A cold hand steals across her neck and a kiss is planted on her cheek and her lips. Her eyes fly open and she reaches instinctively for the knife. But it is only Óengus bending over her, clad only in his *léine*, his blond curls tangled around his head. He presses his lips harder against hers, prying them open with his tongue. Stunned, she lies speechless while he slips under her sheepskin coverlet with practiced ease. She pulls away with a gasp.

'What—'

He puts a finger to her lips to quieten her and whispers in her ear. 'You don't want them to hear us, do you? They might think we're plotting.' He gives a soft laugh. 'You are so beautiful, *a stor*.'

He pulls off his *léine* and nuzzles her neck and nips her ears before resuming his kiss. She is stunned by its heat and for a moment she allows the slow response of her own body to take over so that she might enjoy the moment. His hand moves quickly across her shoulder and down inside her *léine* to cup her breast, squeezing it hard, while the other hand scoops up the hem so that it bunches around her waist. He swings his bare leg over her and she tries to move out from under him, but his weight is too heavy. She can feel his erection hard and full of purpose. He kisses her again, his tongue searching while his hand arranges her legs, separating them.

She manages to pull her lips away. 'No,' she whispers. 'Not yet. Not here.'

'You have no need to worry,' he said. 'Ailill can hardly refuse us marriage then.'

'He spoke to you of that?'

'No, but it's what we always planned, Diarmait and I. I thought you knew. I thought you wanted it.'

'I do, I mean I didn't know about your plan, but that is why I asked you to come. That and to know more of my brother's death.'

His face darkens. He rolls off her then and props his head on his hand. 'Yes, we must talk about that. But not here. Tomorrow we'll find somewhere private.' His face softens. 'For now we can turn our mind to more pleasant things.' He runs his hands along her legs lazily, his green eyes still hazy with lust. For a moment she considers giving into him, but is caught by the thought that it might anger Ailill even more and cause a violent confrontation. It would be one way to achieve his death, for she has no doubt that Óengus would beat him in any swordplay. But it's the price of it that makes her hesitate. She would not have a war with Óengus' *clann*.

Óengus draws her against him and buries his mouth once more in her neck, this time biting hard. His hand pushes down between her legs seeking an opening. She wriggles in pain at his bite and pulls away once again. 'No,' she said. 'Ailill will be furious and that would do us no good.'

He draws up and looks at her, confusion in his eyes. 'What do you mean?'

'We need Ailill to think we aren't forcing his hand. It's better to persuade him, make him think we respect his will in this, so that he doesn't suspect any darker intentions.'

He considers this idea for a moment, weighing the greater good against a moment's intense gratification. The battle is difficult. Eventually he sighs but cannot resist a few lingering kisses to her belly and breasts before he takes up his *léine* and pads out of the room. In the dim light she can see his retreating figure, the broad muscled back, the thick well-shaped legs and buttocks, and for a moment feels regret. Perhaps she is being a fool. She fingers the side of her neck where the sting of his bite still smarts. Then again, perhaps not. There might be something to be said for subtlety in bed, too.

~

Despite the dull day, Óengus takes Cuimne for a walk. He grabs up her hand the moment they are outside and runs across the field to the woods nearby. She is breathless by the time they reach the dense forest, a place that has lost some of its familiar paths she remembers from childhood and is now given over to large bushes and taller, fuller trees. It seems darker too in the heavy grey day, darker than it would normally. She leans against an oak, her hand loosed from his, her chest heaving.

'Ah, Cuimne, you're no longer used to running.' He stands in front of her, his face alight with laughter, his breath even and untroubled.

'I've had little cause to run these past months, and for some of the months, no sound legs to run with.'

'Your legs were injured in the attack?' His face clouds. 'I knew only that you had lost your memory from a blow to the head.'

She grimaces. 'They beat me everywhere, my arms, my legs, fingers and broke them all. They stabbed my side as well.'

'In truth?' He searches her face, a curious look in his eyes. 'Who did this?'

She pauses a moment. 'I don't know. I remember little. My men, my horse, all gone. I thought at first it was connected to my father and brother's death, but I know now it was more likely a group of outlaws.' She holds her breath, hoping he will believe her. She's not certain why she hasn't disclosed her suspicions or what she saw of her brother's death. It might have been the dark look in his eyes and what that might wreak from a few unguarded words. She knows only that for the moment, she has decided to keep it to herself. Until she has a better idea of Óengus and his plans and what more she can discover on her own.

He pulls her into an embrace. 'From now on I'll be here to protect you, I give you my pledge on that.' As if to prove the point he lowers his mouth on hers and kisses her fiercely. She allows it, appreciating the sense of security his words provide. She tightens her arms and feels his strong body against hers. Noting her response, he presses her in tighter, runs his hand along her back under her *brat* and then moves to her breast and kneads it fiercely. He pushes her back against the tree, his breath ragged, and begins to raise her skirt.

She pulls away. 'We must talk, Óengus. Tell me what happened, please, with my brother.'

After a moment his eyes clear and darken, his attention diverted. He nods. 'You're right. There's time enough later.'

'Were you there when my brother died? Did you see what happened?'

He shakes his head. 'No, but I have no doubt that your cousin is a murdering bastard.'

'What have you heard about it?'

'There was an argument—'

'About what?'

'Your father wanted to raid some cattle, take back some of his own after Úa Cahill insulted him at a gathering.'

She holds up her hand to stop him. 'Yes, I know that. They told me when I returned for the burial.'

'Then you know Ailill was among those who were against the raid. They had no heart for such things, the cowards. They've become old women and so they wanted your father out of the way and killed him.'

She regards him now and notices the vein that pulses at his forehead. His anger is still strong. She thinks of what they told her when she arrived home and recalls the grief and remorse, but also the strong underlying current of tension. 'He fell and hit his head on the hearthstone. Do you know otherwise? You and Diarmait were out hunting at the time.'

'We were. But when we returned with the two boars we'd discovered what happened. Your father was there in the house, dead, and a great lump on the back of his head. Of course they would say it was an accident. Diarmait was furious. There was much shouting and accusations flew back and forth. We stormed out, both of us, and went off. Diarmait couldn't forget it, though. And I'm certain that Ailill and his men attacked Diarmait when he went off to meet you.' His face simmers with anger and he clenches his hands. The effort to control his temper is evident.

She considers his statement and can feel some confusion and uncertainty now under the force of the conviction he uses to underscore each word he utters. She puts her head in her hands a moment to create a small private space so that she might organize her thoughts into some sort of order.

'What would you do about it?' she asks finally.

'Diarmait was my brother. I shared everything with him and he did the same. Always.' The words clip the air, precise and forceful. 'He promised to share you.' Grief supplants the anger now, narrowing his face and darkening his eyes.' He takes up her hand and strokes it repeatedly and examines her face. 'He promised me we would marry and that's what we must do first. Then together we can plan how best to kill Ailill and despatch him to the sorry death he deserves.'

She knows she should feel no surprise at his words. Hadn't her first urge been to kill the man who had cut her brother down? But the idea repels her now and she desires only to persuade Óengus to a different course of action. She looks at her hand, still clasped and tries to decide what steps she will advise. He has stopped stroking, but both hands still clasp hers firmly.

'Perhaps we should go to the law courts and ask for recompense.' She knows before she finishes the sentence that he will reject this step out of hand, but the idea has niggled away at her for some time now.

The rejection is swift and severe. 'No, we should never consider that path.'

'Well, if he killed my brother, or had a hand in his killing, then some recompense would be due for both. It would be a hefty price for Ailill. He'd be ruined.'

'Surely, no price can be put on Diarmait's or your father's death that would satisfy us.'

'It would be one way to get land, or cattle at least.' She says the words quietly, wondering at herself. Colmán would laugh to hear her now.

Óengus strokes her hair and she can feel the strength of his fingers against her head. 'No, I would not follow that course, though I can understand that you, a woman, would be averse to violence. But don't worry, I will have a care and ensure that any killing will be done secretly, and if you prefer, without your prior knowledge.'

She considers all the duties, obligations and influence she had as the king's daughter. But her father is dead and her brother, too, and though she has fewer obligations, she also has little influence to bring to bear on any case that might come before the court. She would never be able to give evidence of anything, even if she had it to give.

'You have nothing to fear,' Óengus says. 'I'm here now. We'll see this through, Cuimne. You have my word on that.' He gives her a reassuring smile, cups her chin and leans down for a kiss. She accepts it, but wonders at her choice.

CHAPTER TWENTY-ONE

She thinks no one sees her return. She'd insisted that Óengus wait a while before following in her wake, so that she can slip into the house before anyone notices she's been gone a while. On her way, though, she decides to stop at the horse shed in the hopes she will find Aed there, but the shed is empty, the horses out grazing and Aed most likely turning his hands to whatever task is necessary.

With a sigh, she leaves the shed and makes her way back to the house. In the distance she can hear the herd dogs barking their commands to the sheep. She pauses a moment and sees men on the side of the hill herding in the strays from the furze and rocks to follow the other sheep that are heading toward the lower lying land. The ewes are in heat now, ready for the rams. Ailill has mentioned that this year, with addition of another shepherd and more herd dogs, the numbers of sheep falling prey to wolves and foxes have fallen dramatically. Now she counts the evidence.

It is evidence that could tally with a man seeking to usurp a cousin from his position, but is it evidence of a man who would commit *fingal*? Or is it just good husbandry? She shakes her head, still uncertain where such thoughts will take her, and decides to leave it go for the present. She glances in the direction of the forest and sees Óengus. Quickly, she turns and walks the rest of the way to the house.

Inside, Cuimne pulls her brat from her shoulders as Lassar emerges from her sleeping cubicle and makes her way over to the fire, her progress slow. Sárnat jumps up and goes over to give her hand to Lassar's arm, but she throws it off.

'I'm not a cripple yet. I can manage.'

The harsh bite of Lassar's tone causes Sárnat to flush and pull back. 'I'm sorry, I could see you were in pain and thought only to help. Shall I get you a warm drink?'

'It's only my knees acting up. This damp grips them tight. I'll be fine in a moment.' She reaches the chair and drops herself into it with a thump and shuts her eyes. After a moment she opens them and looks at Cuimne. 'What are you gawking at? Haven't you any work to do instead of wandering outside looking for trouble?'

Cuimne can see the pain etched in Lassar's face and gives her a muted comment about watching the herd dogs. She sits down and takes up the hanks of wool in the basket, noting now the fine soft quality of it. With an unconscious motion she sweeps her hair to her back, away from her eyes, so that she can examine the wool better.

'What's that on your neck?' asks Lassar. She leans over for a closer look. Cuimne's hand flies to cover the offending mark created there the night before under Óengus' rough mouth. She'd no idea the evidence of his work was still there.

'It's only a bruise. I must have given it to myself in my sleep.' The excuse is so feeble she lowers her eyes in embarrassment.

'You're some clever *cailín* if you can bite yourself in your sleep,' says Lassar. 'I told Ailill he'd sniff around you and more, if he didn't watch it. You be careful girl, or you'll wind up with more than a bruised neck as a memento.'

'But if we're to marry, there is no cause for concern.'

'Who's decided you two will marry? Not Ailill. Not yet in any case. We've yet to hear anything that convinces us that it would be a good match.'

For some reason Cuimne rises to Óengus's defence. 'Óengus is an honourable man, from a good family. His father is old, but he is a king. It would be a good match.' Her words lack force at the end and she winces at the slight edge of doubt that creeps in.

'Bah, the man is a hot-headed idiot and his father beats his slaves for sheer pleasure. Even your father saw that.'

'I wouldn't call him an idiot.' She throws out words to replace Lassar's description, though in her heart she knows they aren't true. 'He is kind and compassionate.'

Lassar eyes her. 'Passionate you mean. Is that the attraction, he can rut like buck in heat? Or is it that you see him as a substitute for your brother?'

'No, it's nothing to do with any of that.'

'What is it then? Is it that he seems like a hero from some tale? If that's the case, then it is time you recognized those heroes as only tales to while away a long night. There are no perfect gods out there who will honour and protect you from all the harsh realities of the world. Everywhere there is someone who will undermine you, plot against you, even those in your own *fine* or *clann*. The tracks and forests have many a kinless man who would kill you for the price of your leather sandals or the food you carry in your sack. And if it isn't men, there are fevers, plague, injuries and childbirth that can bring a woman down.' She glanced at Sárnat, who sits staring at

Lassar, stunned by her outburst. 'And the children, they too can be lost, even before they are named. Think on that, before you try to think to marry the warrior hero you believe Óengus to be.'

Sárnat gives a soft whimper and puts her hand to her belly.

'I'm sure Lassar didn't mean you would lose the baby, Sárnat,' Cuimne says softly. She frowns at Lassar, angry at her outburst on Sárnat's behalf. This surprises her for only a moment, for she knows that some of Lassar's words are true enough and the others matter little to her.

'I meant nothing in regard to your babe,' Lassar snaps. 'You have good health and all the signs so far point to a safe delivery.'

Sárnat nods and bites her lip. She turns her attention back to her sewing, taking up Ailill's woollen tunic to mend the tear near the hem. The women fall silent and it is only the sounds of servants working in the background shaking out coverlets, sweeping, and stirring the fire, that fills the room. Cuimne is grateful for this small respite, if only to sift through the growing mire of feelings and thoughts. She picks up the wool hanks again with a plan to card them, but Sárnat asks her shyly if she will help her with the embroidery design on the dress they'd discussed before. Cuimne agrees willingly and moves over beside Sárnat.

The two are deep in conversation when Óengus enters, his large frame blocking the light that shines through the open door. Cuimne puts on a smile and greets him evenly. Lassar glances at him and snorts and resumes staring into the fire. She issues no more taunting remarks that might stir Óengus to anger and action that he might later regret and Cuimne is grateful.

'Did you want to join the men over in the hillside?' she asks. 'They're working with the sheep.'

'Sheep? No I don't think so. I'd be of little help with sheep.' He walks over to the bench she'd vacated earlier and sits down, his feet spread before him. 'Hunting, now that would suit me. Shall I take Aed and my men and see what I can find? There should still be a few bucks around.'

Lassar snorts softly again. 'No, Aed is up on the hillside, I think, herding the sheep with the others. They are where they're needed for now. If you feel the need to stick your spear in something, you'll have to wait.'

Cuimne reddens and lowers her eyes. The reference is obvious and she can only hope that Óengus won't pick it up.

Óengus shrugs. 'Perhaps I'll go tomorrow. For now, I'll remain here.' He stretches out his feet once again and gazes at Cuimne.

Cuimne catches Lassar's look and sees the raised brow. Her meaning is clear. You cannot still believe this man is not a fool. Cuimne lowers her head. She isn't certain that he is a fool, or just stubborn in his choices. Stubbornness she needs to take into account. She pulls the metal teeth through the wool, watching it separate the fine hairs. Some of them tear or break with ease, but there are a few tiny knotted areas she has to tease repeatedly before they smooth out like the rest.

~

She feels the weight of him in her bed before she hears him. A kiss on the neck, a hand along her thigh and up along her waist to her breast and a soft moan in her ear. She jumps.

'Óengus, what are you doing here?' This time she must do all she can to suppress the frustration in her voice and her only answer is a kiss pressed hard against her lips and his tongue forcing her mouth open.

She pulls away. 'I thought we agreed this was not a good idea.' She keeps her voice a calm whisper. 'Lassar has already noticed the mark you put on my neck.'

He kisses the bite lightly. 'Ah that is nothing, *a storín*. I would give you a thousand marks of my love if it would speed our plans to marry.'

'It won't speed our plans, though. It will only anger Lassar and Ailill.' She sits up. 'We must behave well and I will do my best to persuade Ailill that the match would be good.'

He pulls down the neck of her *léine* and kisses her collarbone, considering her words. 'You're certain that would be a better approach?'

'I'm certain.'

'I will have my father send a formal letter outlining an offer and explaining that it was your father's wish. He won't refuse us then.'

'My father wished it? He said nothing to me.'

Óengus waves his hand in the air. 'It was always understood, my father knows that.'

'A letter to Fiacra might add weight to the plan. If your father can explain how the *clann* would benefit from the marriage, Fiacra would give it serious consideration, I'm sure.' The idea has come to her, not because she feels it will succeed, but because she is almost certain it will not. There was little Óengus's father could offer Fiacra that he would not get elsewhere, especially if Ailill has already approached him with a specific person in mind.

He strokes her cheek softly. After a moment he nods. 'Perhaps you're right. We must think this through carefully.' He raises himself up and gives her a rueful look. 'Still, it would be nice to give ourselves a little taste of what is to come.'

She gives him a sweet smile. 'I know. But this is for the best, believe me.'

He leaves her with a kiss and squeeze of her breast and a promise that when the time does come, she'll remember it always. She touches her neck as she watches him leave and feels a small pang of regret that she cannot find it in her heart to marry this man who had been so close to her brother.

~

Óengus, Aed, and the other men go hunting, even Ailill. He trails behind reluctantly, and they head for the forest with spears, long knives and short swords in hand. Óengus leads the way, his brightly coloured *brat* slung across his chest, his face flushed with the promise of the day. Cuimne watches them go, lifts her hand for a wave in response to Óengus's and wishes them all good hunting. Beside her, Sárnat knits her brow and places her hand on her stomach. It isn't unknown for serious and even mortal wounds to occur in any hunt. And for that Cuimne finds herself praying, and her prayers are offered along with Sárnat's. She adds one that includes the hope that Óengus will heed her and refrain from taking matters into his own hands and spear Ailill.

The farewells complete, Lassar herds them both inside while she mutters to herself inaudibly, though her tone clearly indicates her own assessment of the situation. If she has anyone in mind to blame for this day's hunting, she keeps it to herself and gives over the rest of the day to ensuring everyone is kept busy. Hunting men work up great appetites, even if there is nothing killed. There is food to prepare.

When darkness begins to fall, Cuimne's eyes start seeking out Sárnat's, the two women united in their desire for the men's safe return. Barrdub appears to be the only one who doesn't feel the heightened tension and hums lazily at her tasks, until Sárnat snaps at her to hush. Stunned, Barrdub looks at her in surprise, but keeps her mouth firmly shut and her thoughts to herself.

The darkness is well settled when they hear shouts. The words are unclear, as are their owners. Cuimne and Sárnat meet at the door as if cued and Sárnat flings it open. It takes a while to count the number of figures making their way through the *les* entrance and up to the door and discover they are less than they should be. Cuimne searches for Ailill first and when she sees his face, her relief is palpable. She can detect fatigue under the grime of dried blood and dirt, but no sign of injury or pain. It's then she sees that Óengus has his arm slung across Aed's shoulder and is limping badly. He is whole as far as she can tell, otherwise.

The two women step aside to allow the men to come in. Liam rushes forward to help. When they enter, Cuimne can see that Aed's face is red with the effort of supporting Óengus. They settle Óengus on the wooden couch. He is nearly white with the pain and his mouth is drawn tight. The servants take the men's *bratacha* and bring hot water for them to wash off the blood and grime of the day.

'The others are coming. We left them to finish stringing up the large buck that was killed,' says Ailill. 'We came ahead to get Óengus back, but it took longer than we thought because we had to stop often to rest.'

'What happened?' Cuimne asks in a quiet voice. She kneels down by Óengus's leg and begins to remove his leather boot. It's undamaged but also too tight for her to shift.

Óengus groans in pain at her efforts. 'My ankle, I think I've broken it. The feckin buck led me a merry chase, and just as I threw my spear, I tripped over a root and fell.'

She pictures the scene but keeps the smile to herself. It was not the stuff of heroic tales. 'A good kill, nonetheless. The buck is dead.'

'Only after Aed threw his spear to finish it off,' Ailill says. 'It was a kill that all shared, to be fair. The men played their part.'

'If that bastard buck hadn't decided to double back, I'd have had him long ago,' Óengus says.

With some firmness Cuimne changes the subject to the possibility of cutting his boot to remove it. Óengus raises noisy objections until she gives a small tug on it to prove her point. He relents after a howl of pain. It takes a sharp knife and Aed's strong fingers in the end to cut through the leather without damage to the skin, but finally the boot is removed and the true state of his ankle revealed. Bruising already darkens the stretched skin that envelops the ankle bone. For a moment it's as though she is back beside Máthair Gobnait, treating yet another injury during the harvest season. Giving it little thought, she issues instructions to Barrdub without fuss, her voice calm, while Liam and the other servants tend the rest of the men.

Later, when the patient is duly settled, Aed excuses himself to go check that the men have arrived and hung up the buck safely in one of the sheds. Moments later, Cuimne picks up Aed's knife from behind the bowl of water where she'd hidden it earlier and tells the others she will go after him to return it. Before anyone can say a word, she is out the door in pursuit. She catches up with him just by a storage shed, where she can hear the voices of the other men joking and talking inside. Breathless, she grabs his arm and pulls him away from its entrance to the side.

'Lady, you startled me,' he says.

'I would have a quick word with you now, Aed. In private.' She keeps her voice low.

'What is it?' His tone is cautious. Private meetings alone with women of noble birth could easily cause trouble later.

'It is nothing to alarm you. I would just like you to tell me what happened when my father died.'

'What do you mean?'

'Just tell me what you know. I understand you were out hunting with Diarmait and Óengus, but I would like to know what you've heard.'

He gives her a curious look. 'Only that there was an argument and your father fell and struck his head on the hearthstone.'

'And you have no reason to doubt that?'

'No. When I arrived, it seemed to be the truth. There was blood on the hearth. Barrdub had to later scrub for ages to remove it. You wouldn't want something like that to remain in plain sight for all to see when they came through the door.' His tone is cautious and there is a touch of uneasiness, but she realizes that it could be the manner of her questions that put him on guard.

'Did my brother see the blood on the hearthstone?' When she'd met him at the burial, her brother had conveyed little to her other than anger that her father had died. She had heard nothing from others. It was not the type of information people shared when they offered condolences and she'd been too overcome with grief to notice anything in particular of Diarmait's distress.

'Your brother was so upset he saw nothing but your father, dead on the bed. He roared in anger, throwing around all sorts of accusations. We had to pry his fingers away from Ailill's throat.'

'And what did Ailill do?'

'Nothing. He kept shaking his head and telling Diarmait to listen. But Diarmait wouldn't. He continued arguing and insisting someone would pay for his father's death.' He pauses a moment, a silent check to see if she would have him continue. She gives a nod. 'There were four of us holding him, trying to get him to calm down, and him like a *ban sídh*, screaming and wailing. And then Óengus tried to come at Ailill with his fists. The other lords held him off and they tumbled around until both Diarmait and Óengus took off. We didn't see either of them for the rest of the day.'

'And after my father was buried, after I left?'

This time he looks down at his feet as if to find the answers and the courage to speak them lying in the grass. 'I-I don't really know, Lady. He was off with Óengus and some of the men. On some wild ride or other.'

'He was going to Óengus's father. He told me before he left he wanted to meet me at the sacred well near the bridge at Úa Cahill so we might say farewell in private.'

He looks at her in surprise. 'And did you meet him?'

It is her turn to look uncomfortable. 'I-I. No,' she says finally. 'Well, I waited, but there was no one there, so I left.'

He nods slowly and appears to accept her story. 'It seems your brother did show up. But I suppose you know that, now. There was some sort of fight, perhaps the men with him said things about his father's death. In any case, it was clear there was a scuffle and he was found later, struck down by a sword. Some of your father's men had disappeared and it was thought that they might have had a hand in it.'

'There were no other witnesses to speak of it?'

'No. Óengus said he rode off with a few men and they continued on their journey.'

She takes in the whole tale and finds that it is still difficult to bear. Not enough time has passed and she wonders if there will ever be enough. She collects herself, thanks Aed and returns his knife.

He takes it and nods. 'Is there anything else you would know?'

She shakes her head and turns away, lest he see the tears that are filling her eyes. It is more than grief that causes the tears now, she knows that, but the reasons are more complex than she is able to understand at the moment. She wipes her face carefully and moves back towards the house.

CHAPTER TWENTY-TWO

Each day she calculates afresh how much time it takes to heal a broken ankle. She searches her mind for all the remedies, salves and brews she can remember that Siúr Feidelm explained to her that promotes the knitting of bones. It isn't that Óengus is a bad patient. On the contrary, he sits in the chair by the fire, his foot and leg wrapped in splints, propped on the stool and praises and thanks her at every opportunity. He also grabs her and plants a kiss on her lips if no one is present. There are the occasional jibes to Lassar or Ailill, though. It is perhaps the jibes that make his ever lengthening visit seem tiresome. That and the constant mediation between him and Lassar she feels compelled to do, which at times leave her frustrated or irritable. Eventually, to her shame, she follows Ailill's strategy and finds pressing tasks outside of the house.

'They work you too hard at things beneath your status.' Óengus offers this remark when she returns from allegedly helping with the bread baking. In truth she'd just stood and watched the bread bake.

Lassar grunts from her seat by the fire. 'No one asked her to do such a thing. She did that of her own choosing.'

Óengus gives her a questioning look. 'Leave such tasks to the others. I would have you here, near me.'

Cuimne reddens. 'I-I can't stay in here all day, there are numerous things I must supervise, especially with Sárnat expecting a baby.'

'But surely there are tasks you can do in here, out of the damp cold.'

Cuimne searches for a suitable reply, but Lassar is ahead of her. 'What she really means is that she would rather be working at some lowly task than have to be in here listening to your mindless prattle all day.'

Óengus face darkens. He opens his mouth for a retort but Cuimne cuts in. 'That's not true, Lassar. I am glad for Óengus' company.'

'Then sit down and stop flitting in and out,' Lassar snaps. Her knees are too stiff and swollen to be able to leave the warmth of the fire and her temper is clearly frayed from Óengus's daily presence.

Cuimne is determined to prove her point and forces herself to remain inside for the rest of the day without any break and tries to be bright and attentive to Óengus' conversation. By evening, she feels she's earned a break and volunteers to go call the men in for the meal. Ailill is close by, just outside the hen coop, examining an egg and he calls her over.

'How long is it before Óengus is able to mount a horse?'

She suppresses a smile. His tone is neutral, but there is no mistaking his motivation.

'Ten days, perhaps, I'm not sure.'

The sigh is audible. 'I see. And in this time have you thought about our discussion regarding his suitability as a husband?'

She frowns. She is not prepared to talk about this now. There are no clear answers in her head and she cannot bring herself to press Óengus's suit or reject him out of hand. She makes an excuse and asks for more time to consider his words, adding there hadn't been enough time.

'Truly?' he says.

He searches her eyes and she lowers them, fearful of what they might betray. He sighs again. 'I see. Well, we'll let it go for now. In the meantime, if you can do everything in your power to speed his recovery, I would be eternally grateful.'

'Of course,' she says. 'I think we all want to see Óengus returned to health.'

She leaves him with that cryptic remark before she is tempted to say more.

~

In the days that follow, it becomes more apparent to her that she is trying not to think about Óengus's suitability as a husband. The reasons behind that prevarication are even more troubling and she avoids thinking about them as well. At night she is too tired to do anything but sleep. His determined and loving manner makes her feel worse and she fears she will lose her temper altogether if she doesn't find a way to have a day without his continual presence. Lassar, whose sharp eyes miss nothing, seems to know how she is feeling and takes delight in finding ways to keep her near Óengus. She reminds her to tend his bandages, asks her to make healing brews and to tell him tales to pass the time.

It is Sárnat who provides her with an excuse in the end, though Cuimne has no idea whether it is deliberate or not. Cuimne's knowledge of herbs and the remedies they provide prompts Sárnat to ask her to review the household's herbs and check that all the remedies that aid childbirth are among them. Cuimne accepts quickly, before Lassar can create a reason for her to refuse. It is a thorough process; she examines each patch in the garden and each pot inside the storage shed, questioning Sárnat or the women who cook. She uses the pretext of foraging for some needed herbs as a way to have time on her own, even though there is little hope of finding them at this time of the year. She even forgets her knife, so eager is she to escape the house. Nevertheless, she squats by a random patch just near the forest and relishes the quiet for a moment. It is in that quiet that *Um la Mholadh Beacha* comes to her, a soft melody in her head. She smiles at the memory and begins to hum it, letting the sounds wash over her. Before she realizes it, the words form and she is singing them. There are no bees to hear her now, but still, she can feel a response inside her. By the time she finishes, calm has descended. The bees have told her. They work as a group, live in hives. She sees that clearly now and knows she is not alone. She closes her eyes a moment and says a prayer of thanks. This time it is not to any god of Sárnat's.

~

Arriving at the decision is easier than imparting it, though it seems the household conspires to have her convey this decision with fair speed. It is only a day or so after her forest foraging, when she is mixing a healing brew for Óengus, that everyone vanishes from the house. Even Lassar manages to be elsewhere. Cuimne sits on the seat beside him and waits until Óengus has drunk the brew she'd handed him before she broaches the subject.

'There is something I must tell you,' she says.

He hands her back the mug and smiles. 'Nothing could be that serious for such a face.' He takes her hand and tries to pull her to his lap, but she resists. Instead, she holds on to his hand and clasps her other hand over it.

'Óengus, I'm not the Cuimne you knew before. I've changed.'

'Of course you're the same person. Why would you be any different?' His tone is confident, reassuring.

'I'm not, truthfully. Not since the beating, at least. Something happened then, that I haven't told anyone in this household. But I feel I should tell you.' She looks down at his hand, searching for the right words.

'I'm sure it won't be as awful as you think.'

'It's not that it's awful, it's just important.' She takes a deep breath. 'Immediately after the beating, a farmer and his son took me to a woman who was known widely for her healing ability. She was the head of a Christian community for women. She cared for me and brought me back to health. Without that care and help, I would certainly be crippled, if not dead.'

'And I'm sure they had your thanks. Would you like us to give them something in return for all of their help as well? That could be easily arranged.'

It is difficult enough to form the words in the manner she thinks best, but his interruptions make it worse. She holds back the impulse to tell him to allow her to finish before he speaks. 'No, not that. I was there for many months and got to know them so very well. I was drawn to their singing each time I heard it. I even composed a piece with one of the other women. I began to share in their worship, learned the prayers and the psalms they sang. It-it gave me a sense of calm and wellbeing I'd never before experienced.'

'What are you saying?' His tone is guarded now, his brows draw in a question.

She clears her throat and blurts out the words. 'I'm saying that I asked them to baptize me. That I became a

Christian and lived among them as one of the *cailecha* until I came here.'

'*Cailecha*?'

She explains what a *cailech* is, and what she'd pledged, pleading for understanding with her eyes.

'Why didn't you say something before this? Why are you telling me now?' His voice is cold. There is nothing of the idiot about him now.

'I-I didn't tell Lassar or Ailill because I knew they had no great liking for Christians. But I think Lassar eventually guessed.'

'But why have you come home, then?'

She searches her mind for an answer and is surprised to some degree by what she says. 'I wanted to come, to see my home one last time and to learn as much truth as I could about my brother's death.'

'But me, why did you lie to me?'

She lowers her head, unable to meet his eyes. 'I didn't lie, exactly. I just never mentioned it. But now it seems I must tell you because it's become impossible to stay here any longer.'

'But I still don't understand. You know the truth now. You know your family wished us to marry. You can give back the veil and marry me.'

'That's just it, Óengus. I feel the truth is never going to be clear. And as a Christian and a *cailech* I can't bring myself to take any kind of action. I thought to deny all that, to marry you and honour my brother's wish, but I find I can't. My vows are too important.' She searches for a meaning he can understand. 'I swore an oath, Óengus.'

'You're saying you want to forget our marriage? Set aside the promises your family made to me and to my family?'

She looks at him this time, so that he can see she is in earnest. 'There can be no marriage between us. I will never marry.'

'Not marry?'

She shakes her head. 'It may seem strange to you, but it's true. When you mentioned it, I thought I could come to it because it would be the best choice for the family, but I find I can't break my oath. Please, believe me, it's not you, Óengus, but my commitment to my faith that compels me to say this now. I can't deny it any longer. I've been unable to sleep and every time I see your face so welcoming and full of love I can only feel guilt.'

He studies her, his face grim. Moments pass and she can see he is considering all her words and is relieved when eventually his face clears and he smiles.

'You would never be held to a Christian oath, so don't worry.' He pulls her into his lap, his arms pinning her against him. 'I won't let you get away that easily. My father will arrange it.' He holds her eyes and she can see his are steely and unwavering. 'No one will steer us from this course, Cuimne. I promise you that.'

He releases her after a few moments and rises from the chair. 'I'll head away tomorrow and set things in motion.'

'But your ankle—'

He waves his hand. 'My ankle is well enough, I'm sure. I can hobble now with a stick, so I should be able to manage a journey on the back of a horse. My men should be able to ensure I arrive home in one piece.'

She is too surprised to do anything but nod and make a mental note to explain to the servants how to keep the splints firmly in place and to prevent his ankle from swelling on the journey. These thoughts keep her face from revealing the utter dismay she feels.

~

Her revelations have been almost as much a surprise to herself as they are to Óengus. When she was foraging, singing the piece she'd composed, something had firmed up inside of her and only became clear the moment she started speaking to Óengus. She knows her change of heart has not occurred in one flash of insight, but that it has been creeping up on her since she'd arrived and Óengus only hastened it. That much she can admit to herself. For the rest, she feels herself a coward that she couldn't press the matter enough with Óengus to convince him she would never marry him. Perhaps, with the strength of her sisters behind her, she will be able to, eventually. She tries to brush away the moment's anxiety she felt when he pulled her into his lap, his arms firmly imprisoning her body, but she knows that forms part of her decision.

Though it is clear everyone knows something has changed between the two of them, no one says a word that evening, not even Lassar. Óengus remains determined in his path and keeps a cheerful voice while speaking of his need to return home, citing family matters and other obligations. Everyone says the appropriate words, but bemused looks are cast in Cuimne's direction. Ailill asks Óengus twice if he is certain of his fitness and the first time Lassar adds that they wouldn't wish him to tumble from his chariot. But Óengus is firm and each time they ask, he gives her a secret smile that she knows bodes ill for her. She forces herself to smile back, nonetheless. For now it's the best she can do. She has bought some time to make her own choices and persuade Ailill of them.

In the morning, while a heavy drizzle of rain falls, Óengus is loaded onto his chariot with much effort and groaning. He is no longer the warrior hero. He sits in the chariot now, his leg propped awkwardly and his back against the chariot side. One of his men stands beside him, holding the reins. She knows his journey will be rough and uncomfortable. Taking pity on his situation, she leans down and gives him a quick kiss on his cheek. He catches her head and whispers in her ear, 'We will be married by spring.' Startled, she pulls up quickly and blinks, but makes no reply. He gives her a reassuring smile. The chariot moves forward with a jolt and his smile becomes a rictus of pain.

Cuimne watches him leave. There is relief, but also some sadness at the sight of his retreating figure, because so much of her old life is departing with him.

'Whatever you said to him, Cuimne, I give you a thousand thanks. We're finally rid of him,' Lassar says. She pulls her *brat* tighter and makes her way inside, Sárnat following in her wake.

Cuimne starts to follow, but Ailill places a hand on her arm and speaks in a low voice. 'A quick word with you, Cuimne, before you go in.'

She glances at the darkening sky. The drizzle is quickly turning to heavier rain. He pulls her to the sparse shelter under the eaves of the thatched roof.

He makes straight for the point. 'You've decided against Óengus.'

'Well, I tried to explain that to him, but he finds it difficult to accept.'

'Oh. I'm glad to hear you at least have decided it's not a good match. There's someone else I'd have you consider.'

'Who?'

'Colmán.'

'Colmán? I told you that he has a wife. That's no great match, an *adaltracht*, second always to his *cétmuinter*. I told him that.'

'You told him? You mean he asked you to marry him?'

'He did, but I refused.'

'You could change your mind.' She starts to speak, but he holds up his hand. 'Hear me out, Cuimne. He is a good man, but he's also an influential man, someone whose ear could be of great value in troubled times. It would be no dishonour to be his second wife.'

'Perhaps not when he asked me, but now, I cannot.' She forces her voice to sound firm, to convey a certainty that her mind wouldn't be changed. She clutches her arms to keep her hands from shaking.

'What's different now?'

'I am a Christian, a woman pledged to God.'

He stares at her for a moment, all words fled. 'I don't understand.'

'Before I came here I wasn't living with Colmán's family, I was in a Christian woman's community, Máthair Gobnait's.' She explains the rest patiently, as she did with Óengus. This time there is no hurt or confused reaction, there is only cynicism.

'This Christian conscience seems to have arisen suddenly,' he says. There is no tone of compassion or even a hint of the friendliness she detected earlier. 'I'm afraid I can't help but think this is a ruse of some sort. My only problem is that I can't figure out why.'

'I'm speaking the truth. The men who found me beaten took me to this Christian community where Máthair Gobnait tended me. She is known for her healing. Epscop Ábán will confirm that, and everything else I've told you.'

Realization spreads across his face. The curious pieces, so awkward before and made more so with her clumsy explanations, fall into a seamless narrative. 'I see. And now, after all this time, you find that you want to become a Christian *cailech*.'

'I am a Christian *cailech*.'

'Then why did you leave?'

She flushes. Her explanation to Óengus won't serve her well now. 'I needed time to think. Time to be sure that the path I'd chosen was the right one. I came here, to my home, to the place I grew up and formed my ideas and my relationships. I thought I would know if I belonged here instead, but now I am certain I belong with Máthair Gobnait and her women.'

He considers her words, the cynicism easing from his face. His attempts to understand her point of view are noticeable and she is grateful. It also allows her anxiety to ease and give space to the surprise she feels at the words she'd spoken. She knows part of her desire to go to Máthair Gobnait was born of her cowardice in the face of Óengus's plans. How better to press her point and avoid him than in the protection of Máthair Gobnait's community? But she now knows that the words she spoke to Ailill are true. She does belong with Máthair Gobnait. She is part of their group, their hive. She can accept their support, stand with them and share their strength, instead of cowering behind them. The bees have reminded her of this. She accepts this now, and the relief is almost overwhelming.

'Please,' she says. 'I would like to return to them, take up my obligations as a *cailech*.'

'This is a huge step. I'll have to think about it, consult others. You're not the only person who would be affected by this decision. The family, the other lords, all of them would lose out from any alliance your marriage would bring.'

'Joining the community would bring you the good will of Epscop Ábán and others connected to the church. Surely that would count for something, though you're not a Christian.'

'Are you certain they would look on us favourably despite the fact we don't share their faith? I'm not.'

She cannot answer that. She has no clear idea how the Christian Church or even Epscop Ábán would regard such an idea. She bows her head and shakes it.

Ailill sighs. 'I'll look into the possibility over the winter. I'll write to your bishop and Fiacra and ask about it. In the meantime I'll talk it over with the others here. That's the best I can promise you.'

'I'm grateful, Ailill, truly I am. You've been more than kind to me and I know I don't deserve half of it.'

He leaves her with a nod. She stands under the eaves for a moment, then lifts her head toward the sky and prays in earnest that all would come to pass as she hopes, preferably before spring. As an afterthought she also asks for the patience she knows will be required before her hopes can be fulfilled.

CHAPTER TWENTY-THREE

A desire for patience becomes a regular feature of Cuimne's prayers as they enter winter and the weather confines most of their daily activities indoors. Sárnat's belly grows ever larger, the one element that seems to mark the passing days that are filled with chores and tasks that never vary for Cuimne. Occasionally, the fabric on the loom changes and a woollen length with vibrant colours replaces the solid colour of linen, or from a plain hem or neckline of a gown in her lap there emerges a beautifully embroidered pattern.

They mark mid-winter and the solstice and Lassar seems more languorous, spending much of the time huddled in front of the fire, warming her joints and drinking hot brews and whatever else Cuimne can think to give her to relieve her aches. Such is the pain and the measure of the relief that Lassar is even on occasion disposed to thank Cuimne for her efforts. Cuimne also uses her skills when needed to ease Sárnat's indigestion and leg cramps. Sárnat accepts her ministrations with warm gratitude and makes a point to share the happier side of her pregnancy with Cuimne. When the baby first kicks, it is Cuimne she tells, placing her hands on her belly so she can feel the movement there. It is a surprising sensation for Cuimne of a force created by a life within Sárnat and independent of her. A wonder. It makes her think of music. But the music becomes the laughter of children, rather than some abstract lullaby.

The music stays with her, and though there is no harp to inspire her further, she composes a small piece, a little ditty with lilting words for Sárnat to sing to her child who kicks with such might. She sings it to her that night.

'Again!' cries Sárnat when she's finished the piece. And so she sings it again. Even Lassar smiles when she sings it this time. The confidence she feels then fills the tune with a lovely lilt. They laugh and clap when it's finished.

Ailill enters the house, asks about the commotion and Sárnat tells him about the song. 'One more time?' he asks her with a smile. And one more time she sings. Sárnat joins in at the end when Cuimne gestures. There is more laughter then and it lingers around the room.

'We should be sorry to lose such an adept musician and *file*,' Ailill says when the laughter has eased.

'Lose her?' Sárnat asks. 'Has a marriage been arranged?'

'Not exactly. I've had a summons from Fiacra. He wants to discuss Epscop Ábán's recent visit to him. It seems he made a favourable impression.'

'What has that to do with Cuimne?' Lassar asks.

Ailill glances at Cuimne. 'She wants to go and live in that Christian woman's community.'

Lassar gives her a speculative look, but Sárnat frowns, her face filled with sadness and regret.

'You mean the woman named Gobnait that she and Ábán mentioned?' asks Lassar. 'And what's brought on this desire to live there?' Her tone is clipped. There is no trace of anger, but something else. When Sárnat speaks, Cuimne realizes what it is.

'Oh, but I thought you were growing accustomed to us. And now you've found a place in my heart, you cannot want to go.'

'It's not a decision Cuimne made lightly,' Ailill says, his tone soothing. 'And I don't think it comes from her dislike of us, or the time she's spent with us. But we must see what Fiacra says. He is the one to make this kind of decision.'

Cuimne shakes her head. 'Truly, Sárnat, if not for my growing commitment to the community and the faith, I would happily stay here with you and the baby.'

'Oh but you must at least stay for the birth,' Sárnat says, her voice all nerves. 'Your knowledge and kind comfort would make all the difference.'

Cuimne gives a weak smile, conflicted by the wish to be gone well before Óengus or a letter might make an appearance and the desire to help Sárnat. 'We don't know if I'm to leave, or when. God willing, I shall be here to help.' She braces herself for their reaction towards her overt indication of her intent and faith. It is the first of many she hopes to make, so that they might grow used to the idea. And she also admits that it will help her prepare for what lies ahead. Glances are exchanged, Lassar purses her lips, but nothing is said. For that she is grateful. For somewhere along the way she has lost her sense that her safety is threatened and has grown to care for the people she once thought of as enemies.

~

It seems God is willing for her to remain through the rest of the winter and past the feast of *Imbolc* that heralds the spring. Ailill is away during that time and Sárnat frets while Lassar withdraws into dark moods. The task of overseeing the farm and dealing with the various husbandry issues of the *aire déso, bóaire*, the *ócaire*, the *fuidir*, and *bothach* is left to Cuimne.

Though she is kept busy, Cuimne finds time daily to offer her prayers, sing the psalms and perform what she remembers of each office. Portions of the Gospel that she can recall she speaks aloud, reminding herself of them, and like any good *seanachaí*, she becomes word perfect. These moments of quiet shape her days and wrap her in a cloak of wellbeing that allows her to tend Lassar's moody spirits with patience and Sárnat's anxieties with warm assurances. It also helps to keep her from searching the hills and tracks for any sign of Óengus or his men.

The days that God wills she should stay there mount up and still there is no sign of Ailill. Even she is worried now, especially with Sárnat's belly swollen to an alarming size and her ankles and face puffed. Sárnat cannot perform any tasks, whether they are done sitting, standing or walking. The movements create a pain or ache in some part of her. Even lying down seems to cut the breath from her at times and she can manage only a little sleep.

The situation is serious enough that Lassar pulls Cuimne aside to voice her concerns one morning when Sárnat lies abed, propped up enough to ease her breathing.

'This pregnancy doesn't progress well. Something is not right.'

Cuimne nods. 'I only have a little experience with childbirth from my time with Máthair Gobnait but I've seen nothing like this. The swelling in her ankles and legs don't bode well.'

'Her belly is too large for a spring birth. It will be sooner than she thought and I don't think it will be easy.'

'Do the servants know anything? Would Barrdub?' She realizes it's a feeble hope but she's desperate enough to clutch at anything. 'Maybe one of the women in the other households might help.'

Lassar gives a doubtful shrug. 'Ask them and send Barrdub to the nearest farm. It can't hurt. And while you're about it, you may as well pray to your god. We'll need all the help we can get.'

She doesn't wait long to seek out all the women. She makes inquiries among the servants and wives of *bothach* who are giving their time to their lord's farm in the spring rush of lambing, as well as other tasks in preparation for the planting season. They all have opinions and none of them hopeful, including the woman, Ornait, who acts as midwife. Several recommend herbal draughts or rituals. Only one ancient crookback whom Cuimne approaches one morning as she sits on a bench, wrapped in her *brat*, while her daughters milk the cows, gives Cuimne anything that could be construed as sound experience.

'I remember one like this before, when I was young,' she says. 'They all died, in the end.'

'All?'

'They were twins. Two girls, neither strong. Nor was the mother. The birth took too long, you see, and the cord was wrapped round tight on the neck of the first.' She shakes her head and when Cuimne presses her for more, she says there is no more to say. They all died.

'Is there something we could do to ensure a good outcome this time? Could you help, perhaps?'

'Me? Ah, no. I wasn't there the last time, so I've no idea what to do. I suggest you pray to the gods, child.'

It is that information that leads her to ask Sárnat if she can feel her stomach. She does it casually, a request couched in an expression of curiosity over the shape of the child in the womb. She has no desire to alarm Sárnat any further. Sárnat agrees, lying listlessly in her bed, and pulls back the sheepskin coverlet. Cuimne places her hands carefully, sliding them around the belly, pressing lightly and counts limbs. With no real experience she can't be certain, but it seems that she feels three feet. On the count of the third she halts, feels again just to be sure she hasn't mistaken it. There is no mistake.

Later, she shares her discovery with Lassar, who frowns at the news. 'We should get a physician or apothecary to tend her, though that may alarm her more,' Lassar says. 'I wish Ailill was here.' The comments communicate Lassar's state more than anything Cuimne has heard up to now.

'Shall I go? Take Aed with me? Or perhaps send one of the other men?'

Lassar considers a moment and nods. 'Ask one of the men. We need you here.'

Cuimne feels easier after she sends the man off. As she watches him make his way down the track, she sees Ailill ride in through the *les*, followed by his servant and some of the lords. She cries his name and he urges his horse toward her, his face full of concern. Once he dismounts she gives him a hasty embrace and explains the situation. He takes her hands and kisses them.

'Thank you for tending my wife so well,' he says. 'I only hope my news will repay in some degree.'

'We'll talk about your news later. For now I think it's important you see your wife.'

She draws him into the house and to Sárnat's bedside. The joyous hugs and kisses do much for Sárnat's spirits and her own. It is only later, by the fireside, when Ailill starts to pace, that her nerves are set on edge once more.

'What is your news?' she asks. Anything to distract him, set his mind far away from his wife's situation.

He pauses a moment, stares at her and his face clears briefly. 'It's good news for you. Fiacra has granted land to Epscop Ábán so that he might start a monastery nearby. After I spoke with him, he agreed to make your acceptance into Gobnait's community a part of the bargain. It will be, in effect, your *premortem* inheritance that would normally go with you to your husband.'

For a moment she is stunned, all of her fears and concerns about Sárnat flee under the weight of this news. 'Thank you Ailill, for all you've done on my behalf.'

He waves his hand, shoving aside her thanks. 'You will stay until after the birth?'

'Of course. I'll remain as long as Sárnat needs me.' She can do nothing else in the face of Ailill's efforts, but she knows she would stay in any case. Sárnat needs her.

He gives a wry smile. 'I'm afraid that might be a long time. I know she feels she could never be without you.'

~

It's as though Sárnat was only waiting for Ailill's return to begin labour. Her waters break soon after dark and the wails and pain follow a short while later. The physician is still on his way and all his experience and knowledge with it. The midwife, Ornait, is duly summoned and Lassar, Cuimne and Ornait concentrate all their efforts on the unfolding events. Ailill is banished elsewhere to fill his time and calm his nerves.

Sárnat has a small frame, and now, as they help her out of the bed to walk around in preparation for the birth, she seems nothing more than a huge belly. The walking proves difficult, though she tries her best to comply with the instructions, but her face, grey and beaded with sweat, betrays the effort it costs her. Cuimne encourages and soothes at the same time, periodically offering her sips of an herbal brew to relax her and ease some of the pain of the contractions. At times, when Sárnat can go no further, Cuimne rubs her back or her legs. Eventually, the women allow Sárnat to rest on a stool near the bed. She leans across to the bed then, propping her arms on the pallet.

The walking, the rubbing and the sitting become a ritual that goes on through the night while Sárnat's body slowly makes itself ready. The lengthy preparation fights against Sárnat's energy, which slowly drains and leaves her weak and increasingly distant from the women and all that is going on inside her. By the time the baby's head crowns, pushing its way to the opening, there is little left in Sárnat to follow the women's orders to push.

'Come, now, Daughter, press hard,' Lassar says in a firm voice. 'You are a strong woman, my son's dearest wife. If you cannot do it for you or the babe, do it for Ailill, for I know you love him.'

Cuimne wipes Sárnat's brow and whispers in her ear. 'You're too good to give up now. This household needs you and all that you give it. Your wonderful capacity for love, your quiet willingness. And most important, these babies will need you, too.'

'Babies?' Sárnat asks in a weak voice.

Cuimne curses herself for the slip. 'There might be more than one baby here.' Her tone is rueful, almost apologetic. The last thing she wants to do is frighten Sárnat.

Sárnat's face lights up for a moment and her cracked lips form a smile. 'Two. Now that is special. I thought I'd even failed at childbearing. That I carried a monster.' She takes Cuimne's hand, and at Ornait's signal, begins to push in earnest.

Ornait, positioned on a stool at Sárnat's parted legs, looks at Cuimne and gives a nod. The head is through.

Lassar smiles from her place on the bed, leans forward and strokes Sárnat's matted head. 'You're a great woman, you. The babe is all but here.'

'The first babe,' Sárnat says with a hint of humour.

A few moments pass, giving Sárnat time to gather her strength, before she is called on again to push. That final effort that thrusts the baby into Ornait's hands costs her and she leans against Cuimne for support.

Ornait holds up the baby. 'A boy, good and healthy.'

Sárnat nods weakly. 'That comes as no surprise.'

Cuimne goes to Ornait's side, Lassar taking her place supporting Sárnat. Cuimne takes the baby and holds it while Ornait cuts the cord. She marvels at his tiny fingers and toes. When the task is finished Cuimne washes the baby's mottled skin tenderly and carefully after she cleans the blood and mucus from the nose, eyes and mouth. When she reaches his hands, his fingers clutch her thumb and she notices how very tiny they are.

'Give Sárnat the babe for a moment, before the labour begins again,' Ornait says when she is done.

She hands the baby to Sárnat, reluctant to release him from her arms and face all the feelings he stirs within her. She watches Sárnat pull back the linen cloth to view his face and sees the glow, the shimmering that encompasses Sárnat. It is a perfect moment, a moment between a mother and her baby.

The moment stays with Cuimne, haunts her when Sárnat is gripped in the agony of the next child fighting its way out into the world. They've placed the other baby in a small wooden bed made ready and Cuimne finds herself glancing towards it at every possible moment, until Sárnat's cries ring out loudly and without cease.

Cuimne bends down beside Ornait. The midwife is pushing and massaging Sárnat's belly. 'Is there a problem?' she asks softly.

'The baby is turned the wrong way. I'm trying to bring it into the proper position.' She works quickly, her hands pressing and manipulating, while Sárnat's contractions push against her efforts and Sárnat's cries become screams. They change her position, putting her on her side, anything that might ease her pain and encourage the baby to shift.

'Her strength is going,' Ornait says.

Cuimne makes no comment, but she can see the pale face and the unfocussed eyes. 'Please, Sárnat,' she whispers. She utters the prayer that comes to her mind so often these days. The prayer to her Lord, the Saviour whom she now asks to save this good woman.

Lassar eases herself down on her knees, groaning. She takes up Sárnat's hands and chafes them hard. She whispers words Cuimne can't understand, but there is no doubt she is praying to her gods.

Ornait gives Cuimne a bleak look, though she speaks loud, encouraging words to Sárnat while she continues to work. Eventually, she looks up and nods grimly. 'The babe is turned and making its way out, now, but I don't think she has enough left in her.'

'Do your best,' Lassar says.

Cuimne can detect only the slightest rise in Sárnat's chest. Her eyes are dark bruises.

'The head is there,' Ornait says. 'I'll see if I can help it out.'

Cuimne puts her lips to Sárnat's ear. 'The babe is here, we just need one last push from you. That's all we ask. That's all your babe asks.'

Whether it is her prayers or Lassar's, or the words she spoke to Sárnat, or nothing but Sárnat's motherly instincts, her body tenses and the strength none thinks she possesses is gathered and given over to enabling the child to join his brother. Cuimne takes this boy, who seems even smaller than his brother, if that were possible, and washes and wraps him with just as much care. He too is sound and whole of body, all the fingers and toes the correct number. She strokes each of them with her finger and they curl in response.

'Cuimne.' Ornait's tone is sharp. She shakes herself out of the reverie and turns. Sárnat lies unmoving, her face waxen. 'She's only barely with us and I need your help to get the afterbirth.' She issues instructions rapidly.

With some effort they manage to persuade Sárnat to drink a little of the brew that is ready and then massage her stomach vigorously to get the desired results.

Ornait looks at the bowl filled with the afterbirth. She shakes her head. 'I hope all of it has been expelled.'

Cuimne stares down at the mixture of blood and mucus and tries to read its meaning. It tells her nothing and she turns away. Her knowledge is poor and her efforts are best directed toward more practical matters. She helps Lassar and Ornait wash and settle Sárnat into a freshly made bed. Sárnat remains unconscious, a pale ghost against the linen sheet. Her breath is faint and her hands are clammy.

Ornait frowns. 'We can only wait now. Hope there is no fever or any other after effects from such a birth as this.' She indicates the two infants lying in the wooden box. 'You'll probably need someone else to suckle them.'

Lassar nods and the two women thank Ornait. Lassar leaves to fetch Ailill and ask Barrdub to organize some food. Cuimne takes up the stool beside Sárnat and begins the vigil. As Ornait has said, there is nothing to be done now but wait.

CHAPTER TWENTY-FOUR

Cuimne looks down into the face of the sleeping child in her arms; the lips that alternately purse and open, the slightly crusted nose and the lids, so delicate and nearly transparent. She notes every detail and has done since his birth ten days before. She has seen his skin take on a lighter, less mottled hue and smooth itself to mould more firmly around the body.

Maél is the smaller of the two babies, and perhaps it is his small size that explains Cuimne's strong attachment. His efforts at suckling proved too weak at first, and she spent hours trying to give him some sort of nourishment, his feeble mewling making her increasingly desperate. She finally succeeded when she dipped a square of linen in a bowl of watered milk and squeezed it so the milk dripped slowly into his mouth. It was a tedious method but she'd been determined that this little one should live, after all he'd been through. Eventually, he'd found the strength to suckle and for that she is glad, though she misses the feeding that had become like a ritual for her.

His brother, Faélán, has managed better and has been feeding at the breast of Barrdub's aunt almost from the first. He found his voice all too soon and uses it with force when he is hungry. The two of them keep Cuimne busy, though any spare time she has is given over to helping Lassar nurse Sárnat.

271

Sárnat's recovery hadn't been certain. She'd been so weak and feverish in the days following the birth it often seemed she wouldn't last beyond the next sunrise. Ailill spent all the time he could silently holding her hand. They'd brought the babies to her and laid them beside her at different times, in the hope that such a sight would surely lift her spirits and encourage her recovery, but she did little more than briefly open her eyes.

It is only on this day, the tenth day, when Sárnat eats all the broth, drinks the healing brew given her and asks to see the babies that Lassar and Cuimne feel she is finally mending. Cuimne gives Maél one last fond look before she wraps him up again in readiness for his mother. She'd thought to bring Maél first, knowing this delicate quiet little babe would win over any heart. When she reaches Sárnat's side Ailill is there, smiling and talking. He falls silent when she hands Maél to Sárnat, watchful. The hope is palpable. Sárnat smiles down at Maél and lifts her face to her husband. The pleasure is evident.

Cuimne watches the three of them and feels a small little stab. 'He's a lovely sweet boy,' she says. 'So quiet. He's just beginning to suckle and you can see the difference it's made.' It is only then, when the words are out of her mouth, she realizes her choice of words is poor.

But Ailill deflects the sting. 'Ah, but he's a great little babby now, alright. And that's down to you, Cuimne.'

There are tears in Sárnat's eyes. 'All of us have so much to thank you for.'

Cuimne tells them thanks are not needed, insisting more than is necessary or even usual, hoping such emphasis would banish from her mind the feelings that suddenly arise without cause. It makes no sense to feel envy if that's what it is she feels. The source of the envy she refuses to examine because it is only borne of the tiredness she most certainly feels.

'I've sent word to the community about the arrangement.'

Cuimne gives Ailill a blank look, his words unclear.

'I wanted to let Máthair Gobnait know that you would be coming to her. Now that Sárnat is on the mend and the boys are doing well, there is little need to keep you much longer. We've stolen so much of your time already.'

'I was happy to stay. And I would willingly stay longer. As long as you need me. Until Sárnat has much of her strength back.'

'Ah now, Barrdub is here to help if you would rather go soon.'

She blinks back the tears and forces herself to reply. 'Yes, yes of course. I'll leave whenever it's convenient for you, then.'

Ailill nods and smiles. 'I'll arrange for Aed to take you, in say, three days' time.'

'Thank you. That should give me sufficient time to prepare.' Cuimne speaks the words with as much conviction as she can and hopes mightily that they will prove true.

~

Her parting is stiff; the words that she speaks are so formal they pain her ears. The others seem not to notice, the warmth of their manner so fully expressed it takes all of her concentration to avoid a breakdown altogether. She tells herself it should be joyful, this parting. Her kin have a growing, healthy family and she has escaped without any further sign of Óengus and his plans and is heading toward a community of dearly beloved women. In the end she can only manage to turn quickly to the small cart that contains her belongings and climb up inside of it, and give a strangled final farewell.

Aed is silent on the journey, leaving her to dwell on matters she knows she shouldn't as they meander along under a dull grey sky. She worries about the rash that has appeared on Maél's face and if Barrdub will remember how to mix the ointment she told her about. Lassar is there to watch Barrdub, she assures herself. Cuimne forces her mind on the road ahead, toward Máthair Gobnait. She will understand what troubles her and help her to smooth her path once again. And she will have the offices to occupy her, too. Prayer, singing, contemplation of the Gospel words. All of that would soothe her soul, give her peace and contentment.

Ailill had suggested distant kinsmen for her to spend the first and second night and she agreed initially, but then asked that they might visit Colmán's friend Murchad and his wife for the second night. For some reason she has a need to see them again, especially Almaith.

When they finally arrive at Murchad and Almaith's, Cuimne is suddenly nervous. It isn't the welcome that causes her anxiety. The welcome is open and full of warmth as they draw her inside, out of the coolness of the spring night. It's the sudden memory of the conversation she'd had with Almaith on her last visit and the desire to see a friendly face is quickly overshadowed by fear of Almaith's probing words. If she didn't know differently, Cuimne would have thought Almaith had obtained the rank of *aigne*, not her husband.

As before, the household is overflowing with family members, the children just as active and the talk just as far flung and relaxed. She explains away the imaginary marriage that Colmán had used to account for their journey the last time by saying unforeseen problems in the contract had occurred and it had been dissolved. Except for a raised brow from Almaith they accept her words without any question and Cuimne eventually relaxes and shares the story of the twins and Sárnat's fortunate recovery. It's the kind of happy news that needs to be shared and brightens spirits. Almaith, in particular, questions her carefully about the birth and all that had been done to ensure its success.

'Have you heard anything from Colmán?' Almaith asks when all the questions have been answered.

'No, no. Is something amiss with his family? Rónnat, is she well? I know she must have taken Domnall's death very hard.'

'No, no. Last we heard, all is well, but that was some time ago. I just wondered if you had heard from him.'

Cuimne can feel Almaith's gaze on her and she lowers her eyes, afraid they might betray things that even she doesn't realize. 'I've not heard from Colmán since he left my home place last autumn.'

'Oh, I didn't know. Not to worry. Last we heard, all is well there.'

No more is said about Colmán after that and the conversation shifts to another direction. Eventually yawns drive Murchad's parents to their beds and Cuimne rises to follow a little while later. Almaith shadows her to the cubicle to check on her son and ensure that Cuimne will settle without interference.

As before, the toddler is fast asleep, thumb in his mouth. Cuimne smiles at the innocent scene.

'It's so good to see you once again, Cuimne. I know we only met the one night, but I feel we're friends.'

Cuimne takes her hand. 'I'm glad. I look on you in the same manner. It's part of the reason I hoped to stop here on my way to Máthair Gobnait's.'

'Yes, Máthair Gobnait. Both you and Colmán spoke well of her.'

'She's a good and devout woman. She's been so very kind to me. I'm looking forward to seeing her once again.'

'I've no doubt about that.' Almaith pats her hand. 'You've changed, you know. The last time I saw you there was a darkness about you. It seems to have vanished, now.'

Cuimne smiles. 'Yes. I think it has. Much has happened in the months that have passed and it has fallen away.'

'I'm glad to hear it. I have to confess it had me worried and I could see that it gave Colmán cause for concern. He'll be glad to hear that you appear more settled.'

Cuimne blinks, her surprise strong. 'Colmán mentioned this to you?'

'No, he didn't. He had no need. It was plainly there on his face.'

Cuimne looks down and mumbles her reply. 'Colmán is a kind man.'

'He is,' said Almaith. She smoothes Cuimne's hair, like she would a child's. The two stand there in silence for a moment as she continues her stroking. 'Well, I'll let you get to your bed,' she says eventually. 'You must be exhausted.'

~

Under a watery sun that promises a bright day, Aed and Cuimne make their farewells while children weave quickly among laughing adults and barking dogs. Furze and tree blossoms scent the air and put a smile on Cuimne's face, despite a wretched night's sleep.

Once they are underway, the pair amble along and Cuimne makes a great effort to study the land around her, noting the signs of a deepening spring. This time when she sees An Dhá Chích Danann come into view, she can look at the mountains with appreciation; note the greening slopes that transform them from the rusty hue of winter sleep to the awakening signs of life. The two breasts, lush with their new growth reassure, and like all mothers, they are woven into the fabric of life. That her own mother has been missing throughout most of her life has always grieved her, but it's only now she can fully appreciate what she's missed. An Dhá Chích Danann has been the substitute mother of sorts, always prayed to on her trips between home and her foster family.

But she is turning from all that now. Her home is now with Máthair Gobnait, a different kind of mother, but surely one just as holy and more loving. She asks Aed to stop a moment. She climbs down and stands before the mountains, silent. The words, so familiar, come to her and she utters them one last time and adds her thanks. It must be done. It is her farewell.

~

Little has changed and yet everything has changed. The fields are greener, the cattle grazing in them more numerous and the buildings larger than before. She gets down from the cart to a series of warm embraces. Máthair Gobnait, Siúr Feidelm, Siúr Sadhbh and even Siúr Mugain, striding down the hill to her, take a turn at kissing her cheeks and holding her hands in greeting. Cadoc ambles up, a broad grin on his face, and begins to stroke the pony. Siúr Ethne is there too, hanging back from the others, but the smile and sincere greeting speak much for her feelings. Nearby, three young girls stand, their faces filled with curiosity. Their grey gowns and linen head wraps mark their status.

'Three girls, not two, Máthair Ab?' asks Cuimne.

'Ah, the Lord saw fit to bless us with three girls this autumn. And we're so pleased.'

It is a welcome she would have never imagined all those months before, and one so different from her first arrival here in the community. News is demanded amid laughter and Máthair Gobnait's reprimands them all about proper hospitality. She enters fully into the spirit and joy of the reunion and allows them to seat her on a bench outside, a mug of beer in her hand and begins to share all the drama and entertainment of her news.

Later, when she sits on her old cot, having changed from her bright gown into the grey one befitting her new home, she has a moment to herself. Sodelb's place in the bed is still there, though it is now clearly occupied by someone else. Siúr Sadhbh perhaps. Or even one of the young girls. For her, though, it will always be Sodelb's and the thought gives her a moment of pain. She rises, brushes the tears from her eyes and heads for the door.

It doesn't take long, the path is so familiar, trodden so many times at night and in early morning. She enters the oratory, suddenly hesitant, uncertain what to expect or feel. So much of this place is Sodelb. She can find the beauty in every detail; the altar, the cross marks on the rafters, even the wooden benches that often grew hard in the early morning worship.

She sits on a bench now, at the back, away from the altar and the mound that is Sodelb's grave. Her eyes adjust to the dim light. The altar and the cross that stands upon it become clearer. She sees then the beaten earth floor, now smooth and even. Her breath catches. What sign is left of the grave? She rises and moves closer, for a moment wondering if she'd mistaken its place. She kneels down, lays her hand on the ground and searches for tell-tale signs. The tears come again.

'She is still in our hearts.'

Cuimne looks up at Máthair Gobnait standing over her. 'But there's no sign of her grave.'

'That doesn't mean she's forgotten.' She places a hand on Cuimne's shoulder. 'I've asked Findbar to carve a marker. When it's finished we'll set it in.'

Cuimne puts her hand over Máthair Gobnait's, unable to speak.

'I know you miss her, but her spirit remains. In the music she left us and the joy she found in this community. I hope that you'll see that as well.'

'I will,' Cuimne whispers. 'At least I promise to try.'

Máthair Gobnait lifts her up and puts her arm around her. 'If you are willing you can begin by leading us in the canticles now. I've been looking forward to hearing your voice again.'

Later, to her mind, when she does sing, her voice isn't at its best as she begins the canticle, but it gains strength soon enough, and in the comfort and support of the other women she finds the notes, and the joy of singing them. When she finishes, her breath released, she feels somehow different, whole, yet not whole. Sodelb is there, closer in some ways than before, but something once again has shifted and realigned. She only wishes she knew what it meant.

CHAPTER TWENTY-FIVE

The thought is in her mind even before she wakes at the sound of the *Matins* bell. It is ever the time for stray minds and unguarded emotions. And she thinks of Maél. His sweet face, his tiny fingers curled around her thumb. How much he would have grown, even now. And soon, he and his brother would become too large for the little wooden box that provided a bed for them both.

These thoughts distract her as she pulls her woollen gown over her *léine,* fastens the leather belt around her waist and slips on the sandals. She makes her way to the oratory, falling in behind Siúr Ethne and Máthair Gobnait as they file through the door. She takes a place on the bench next to Siúr Mugain's comforting bulk and tries to focus on the opening prayers. It is only when they begin to sing that she feels drawn into the moment, the perfect blend of sounds echoing in her head and filling her spirit. Afterwards, she returns to bed and falls back into a deep sleep, her calm restored.

The calm lasts until the bell sounds for the next office at daybreak. This time there is no particular thought that causes her restlessness of mind and she looks to the singing once again to provide some relief. This time it is only the *Beati* that helps; its opening phrases so dear and beautiful, it can do nothing but soothe. She tells herself to be patient, to allow time to adjust to the life here, whose pace is so different to the one she'd been used to at home.

Later, she follows Máthair Gobnait to the hive in the hope that in the company of Máthair Gobnait and the bees her mind might find more permanent rest. The bees have come to life, thriving in the lushness of a warm spring. They surround each hive with constant activity, flying out to any likely location that might have nectar for the growing brood and then returning with their harvest.

At this moment, though, the bees are quiet, the early morning still a little cool. Máthair Gobnait, her veil and gloves in place, begins to check the hives to ensure there is plenty of food and a king bee is present. There is no wind. She wafts a smoking rush and lifts the hive carefully and completes the inspection.

'When we're finished here, while it's still cool, you could finish clearing the leaves from under the platform and spread some ashes there to keep the weeds away.' Even through the veil Cuimne can see Máthair Gobnait's smile. 'I suspect you, like the bees, find such a warm spring stimulating.'

'I am restless, Máthair Ab. I think it's that I've had little time for any contemplation and stillness these past few months and I need some time to adjust.'

'Stillness. It doesn't always come easily. Whether it's stillness of mind, spirit or body.' She moves on to the next hive and pauses. 'The bees are driven by God-given natural instincts. They know when it's time to be still and when they should be active. At the moment, the air is cool. The sun hasn't reached the flowers and warmed us all with its heat, so they remain in the hive. When the hive is heated by the sun, they know the time for stillness is finished and they must fly off and collect the dew. Their timing is faultless in that regard. We could learn much from listening to our instincts, as they do.'

The words echo in her mind and linger there. She hears them still when she clears the leaves from under the wooden platforms, the bees still quiet in their hives. She waits for the stillness to come, the stillness of mind that seems elusive whether her body is active or sitting in prayer.

~

She thinks of the bees at the next office and all the following ones, even singing the praise song she'd written to honour them. The effort she makes to harmonize her stillness with the bees becomes a daily practice. Sitting in the oratory, intoning the prayers, singing the canticles and the psalms and making countless genuflections, she cultivates the stillness of body and hopes the mind will follow. In between the offices she labours at tasks, whether it is the weaving, the spinning, the sewing, or assisting Máthair Gobnait at the hives and she tries to put her whole heart in it.

Nearly a month passes when Siúr Ethne comes to her when she is working at the loom, weaving some linen cloth. She tells Cuimne she has a visitor.

'A visitor? But who would be coming to see me?' She thinks of Ailill and Sárnat. Perhaps they had brought the twins with them. And then she thinks of Óengus. She licks her lips nervously. After all this time she had hoped the matter was considered closed. She rises up from her seat reluctantly.

'It's Bruinech, Colmán's wife.'

'Bruinech?'

'She's come here in the past, when she can, to hear mass when Epscop Ábán or one of the other priests is here. And recently she was baptized. But today she asks for you. She's waiting for you in the oratory.'

At first Cuimne is stunned to think that Bruinech would have come here, but realizes the comfort and security she found here for herself, Bruinech has found, too. She thanks Siúr Ethne and gives a moment to smoothing her gown and the veil on her head. Máthair Gobnait has allowed her to resume wearing the veil, but said that the time for her vows would come later.

She finds Bruinech sitting on the front bench, before the altar, her head bowed in prayer. Cuimne pauses at the doorway, notes the plain gown, the dark brat draped along one shoulder and the hair wrapped in a linen cloth that reveals only a simple braid hanging along her back. She moves forward as silently as she can in respect for Bruinech's prayer. She genuflects, takes the bench behind her and offers her own short prayer.

It is at this moment that a stillness of body and mind come together. It is a peculiar stillness, a calm that leaves her cold and heavy, like the air before a rare snowstorm. Bruinech turns to her and greets her softly.

'Thank you for meeting with me.'

'Of course I would meet with you. How did you know that I was here?'

Bruinech gives a wan smile. 'I have many friends here now and some of the labourers are kin to those who work at Raithlinn.'

'And how are you? How are Colmán and the family?'

'They are all well. Well enough.'

'Rónnat? She is finding it difficult losing her son.'

'We've all found it difficult since Domnall died.'

Cuimne pats her arm. 'Of course you have. I'm sorry.'

'That is, in part, why I came.'

'Your difficulties? Are there some herbs you would like to calm nerves or help you sleep? Siúr Feidelm or Máthair Ab would be better at that, though.'

'No, no, it's nothing like that. What I need only you can provide.'

Cuimne cannot imagine what else she can do, but she offers assurances. 'Of course, I will help in whatever way you wish.'

Bruinech looks away. 'It's Colmán. He has no heir, no child that will carry on the family line, no one to take on the farm and the household. No matter how much he might protest and spin out hope, a child is something I will never be able to give to him.'

'I'm so sorry, Bruinech. But are you certain that it's you who is barren?'

Bruinech, purses her mouth and nods. 'Before we were married, Colmán had a child with a woman, a distant cousin. They both died of fever soon after the child was born.'

'Are you looking for something to help you conceive?'

Bruinech waves her hand. 'I've tried all that. Brews, prayers, offerings. I see now that God has chosen otherwise for me. Colmán is reluctant to agree, though, and that's where I need your help.'

'My help?'

'Colmán won't divorce me and I wouldn't bring shame on him by saying falsely that he is impotent, or that he refuses to support me, or the other causes I'm limited to. He won't scar my face. It's nothing to do with the return of my *coibche*. The bride price finds no place in his mind. There is only one path I know he would take, if it was the truth.'

'One path?' Cuimne's mind searches frantically to identify the link she provides in this tangle. It is in the back of her mind but she refuses to accept it.

'I would have him repudiate me for another woman. You. I know he loves you, Cuimne, and for that I'm glad.'

'Me? No, no. You have it wrong, Bruinech. If you want Colmán to have children, why not allow him to take on an *adaltrach*? A second wife would surely give you both the children you desire.'

Bruinech smiles sadly. 'I'm sorry, I've explained this poorly. I want a divorce so that I might join this community.' She looked around her, her face taking on a glow. 'This is where I feel at home. This is where I feel a closeness to God and the beauty and joy of His creation and all that's in it. I never felt this joy at Raithlinn.' She looks at Cuimne intently. 'But to come here, I must divorce Colmán. And he must have a new wife. You. You're the one he has grown to love. I've seen that since you first entered our home. He followed you with his eyes, he lit up when you spoke. And when you left, something of him left, as well.'

'I'm sure that you misunderstood what you saw.'

'What I saw is the truth. And I come here now to ask you to please go to him. Say you will be his wife so that he can release me to come here and join Máthair Gobnait's community.'

'I-I don't know that I can. You're asking much of me.'

'Am I? I wonder about that. But will you at least think about what I've said?'

'I will, of course. But I can promise nothing.'

Bruinech nods. 'I understand. But I will hope and pray that you come to the decision that can benefit all of us.'

She rises then, leaves Cuimne sitting on the bench and all the deadened calm she'd felt before vanishes, her mind stirred up like a swarm of bees.

~

She stands among the hives, watching the bees fly in and out in the heat of the midday sun. They have moved onto different areas now for the collection, the early spring flowers gone now. One of them buzzes near her ear for a moment and she listens in the hope he might pass on some secret, but he hardly pauses and when he leaves she is no wiser.

'Cuimne.'

She freezes at the voice, her breath caught in her throat. She stiffens her back, puts a smile on her face, turns around and moves to greet Óengus. He meets her and catches her to him in a tight embrace, pulls back and then presses a kiss on her mouth.

She puts a hand to his mouth to stop a second effort. 'No, you mustn't. I am a *cailech* now.'

He releases her, confused. 'No. No, I cannot believe that.'

'It's true,' she says. 'I am living here now and I am happy.'

'No. I can understand that you would come here to escape Ailill and Lassar while I made the arrangements. They took longer than I thought.' His face crumbles. 'It was only that my father died shortly after I arrived home.'

Impulsively, she grasps his arms. 'Oh, Óengus, I am so sorry. That must have been so difficult.'

He gathers himself and nods. He takes a ragged breath. 'There is no doubt, it was a difficult time. It became worse when they assembled to elect the next king. I was certain they would see that I would make the best choice. But they didn't choose me.'

'But I thought you weren't *Tánaiste*.'

Anger flashes across his eyes. 'No, I wasn't. But I was the natural choice. I'm a skilled warrior. And I was his son.'

He states the last few words with loud force and it makes Cuimne jump. She makes calming noises and studies his face. It is drawn and tired and she can tell he has not slept for some time.

'Come, sit down over there with me.' She points to the bench near the *Tech Mor*. She can see there are only three men that have come with him and they stand uncertainly by their horses. Siúr Feidelm emerges from the *Tech Mor* then and ushers them inside while Aed leads the horses to the shed. Something about the second horse strikes her as familiar and after a moment she realizes it is her old horse. The one she rode when she was attacked. She looks over at Óengus, who has followed her gaze and now stares at her, his face full of alarm. His hand reaches instinctively for the sword in its leather scabbard that hangs from his chest and her eyes are drawn to his arm. The muscles tighten and she can see clearly the faint scar that marks his wrist and it is that scar that suddenly leaps out from her memory. Even if she could find the words to form the questions, she needs no other confirmation. The realization frightens her so much that her legs give way and Óengus catches her and holds her firmly.

'It was never meant to be this way,' he says. She tries to pull away, but his grasp is firm. He looks at her with pleading eyes, but she cannot bear it and turns her head away. 'You must believe me. All I ever wanted was to wed you. It was perfect. Your father and mine were kings and with you at my side I would be made *Tánaiste*. Diarmait knew that. He promised.'

She can hear the tears in his voice that has now become a near wail. She tries to still the trembling in her body and takes a deep breath. 'I had no knowledge of this promise,' she says.

'But I knew you loved me as you loved your brother and you would never object.'

'I loved you as I loved Diarmait, like a brother.' She tries to keep her tone quiet and calm, but the effort it takes is great. She looks beyond him, in the hope that Máthair Gobnait or someone might come and join them.

'There is no reason why we cannot still be married,' he says. He acts as though he hasn't heard her. He smiles strangely. 'I still love you and though I am not to be king, I have lands and will be able to give you a good home.'

She pats his hand and tries to be reassuring. 'Thank you. Your offer is very flattering, and if I had not already pledged myself here, I would.'

He grips her shoulders firmly. 'This place doesn't matter, nor any pledge you might have given these people.'

'But it matters to me.' Her voice is quiet but she can't control the quiver any longer.

His eyes darken and he gives her a little shake. 'No. You're the only thing I have left and I won't let you go. ' His grip tightens. 'If I cannot have you, no one else can. I nearly made certain of that before, but I will finish it this time.'

The fear rushes in and grips her, but still she fights it. The little ridge of scar at her side burns. 'I-I will say nothing of your deeds, if only you will let me live here, in peace.'

He stares at her, his face awash with various emotions, but his hands still hold her firmly. Her eyes cannot leave his and her chest heaves. She opens her mouth to utter a scream but nothing comes. He looks around him and she follows his eyes. She can see Máthair Gobnait standing near the *Tech Mor*. He throws her aside and strides off. She falls to her knees and watches him go.

~

She finds Máthair Gobnait up on the ridge, seated in her stone chair, gazing towards the valley. She listens as Máthair Gobnait seeks, counts and blesses all that is her view. Cuimne kneels on the grass beside Máthair Gobnait, puts her head on her lap and waits for the warm comforting hand to rest on top of it. For a while, she lets the silence between them wash over her, calm her enough so that she might find the right words and speak them. And when the words come, they are still a jumble.

'I'm so confused, Máthair Ab. I know things now compel me to take action, but I have also now promised not to, for reasons that are not honourable at all. And others ask me to take actions I'm uncertain I can.'

'A lot of different promises and actions seem to be demanded of you.'

Silence falls again and she lets it linger around her for a few moments. 'I am a coward,' she says finally.

'A coward, no. A woman who has been given many paths to choose, yes.'

'I'm afraid, so I am a coward.'

'What are you afraid of?'

She thinks a moment. Óengus left her without any further word, his anger evident. He'd retrieved the men from the *Tech Mor* with little apology and rode off as quickly as he could manage. But the threat of what he might do, and was well in his power to do, against her, lingered and haunted her at her tasks, at meals and during the offices. Days had passed and she'd seen no sign that he would come back for her, but she still feels uneasy. And her unease has led her in directions she had forced herself to turn from before.

'I've tried so hard to become as the bees and work at my tasks and remain still while at prayer, but I am failing miserably. Even the singing can no longer hold my spirit still.'

'The instincts bees follow are given by God to them and not to humans, Daughter. We have our own.' Máthair Gobnait strokes her head a moment. 'What do your instincts say now? What is God calling you to do?'

She gives it thought and the moments stretch. 'I'm not sure. There is much to be said for duty and obligation, but I am not brave enough for them.'

'Where does duty and obligation call you?'

Cuimne grimaces. 'Some would view it my obligation to return to my cousin and help bring evidence against my brother's killer.'

'But you would rather not do that?'

She considers this seriously, laying aside her promise to Óengus. Her brother's death still causes her pain, but now she can imagine the argument that led to the deadly exchange between the hot-headed men. Would she be any less fearful of Óengus if he was forced to pay *smachta* for Diarmait's death?

'I would rather not do that,' she says.

Máthair Gobnait nods. 'And the other paths people would have you take?'

'I-I guess there is the path I'm now on. And the part I have in supporting the settlement between Epscop Ábán and Fiacra that Ailill has so thoughtfully made for me. I will help the bishop's plan to expand the Church and Fiacra to link into a network of increasingly influential people.'

'You are happy about that path, of course.'

Cuimne nods and murmurs her agreement.

'But there are other paths?'

Cuimne pauses a moment and wonders if she should speak. Her eyes fill and then the words tumble out in a low voice. 'It is Bruinech. She would have me ask Colmán to divorce her in favour of me so that I can give him sons and she can join this community.'

The words hang in the air and Cuimne closes her eyes. They cannot be retracted but she wishes it was possible.

Máthair Gobnait finally speaks. 'I see. I guessed Bruinech might have asked you something of the sort when I heard she'd spoken to you.'

'You guessed?'

'She'd talked to me recently about hoping to join the community. She expressed a genuine calling in her search for a closer link to God and a love of prayer and meditation. But she has a true concern for her husband and his welfare. It would be natural to think of you as a way for her to join us. His care and love for you is obvious.'

'Is it?' She knows the answer before she poses the question.

Máthair Gobnait doesn't repeat the affirmation and asks another question instead. 'Does Colmán know of her request?'

'I don't know. She didn't say.'

'And your vocation here? Do you still desire the life Siúr Áine would lead or has Cuimne's the stronger draw?'

'I-I don't know.' She realizes now that she has never been certain of this path. Óengus's visit has only confused her more.

'Epscop Ábán would never tie you here out of obligation, you know. You can still practice your faith outside our community.'

Cuimne says nothing, but tears run silently down her face.

Máthair Gobnait lifts Cuimne up to face her. 'The woman I see before me now is strong, possessing a wonderful voice, a loving heart and a gentle soul. She is not the quiet, fearful Áine that graced our community and shadowed Siúr Sodelb. But neither is she the fierce, spirited and impulsive Cuimne that grew up motherless. Now she is something in between, but most assuredly a good woman.'

'She is a woman torn and a little bit afraid, that much I know.'

'She is a woman who now has great sympathy for others.'

'Please tell me what I should do.'

Máthair Gobnait shakes her head. 'You must make the decision yourself.'

~

She shifts her position on the bench so that she doesn't cast her needlework in shadow. The work is delicate, a piece of embroidery too special to risk any knots or stray stitches. It is an altar cloth, a gift of her work for Máthair Gobnait that she's been working on for some time now.

'Cuimne.'

She looks up and shields her eyes. 'Colmán.' The surprise of his appearance gives her a jolt, one made sharper by the fact he'd just been in her thoughts. She'd asked Máthair Gobnait to send word to him that she wished to see him, but she'd not expected him this soon. She feels unprepared and only hopes that she can see this conversation through with some dignity and little distress to either of them.

'You are well?' she asks. 'And your family, too?'

He takes a seat beside her, his manner stiff. 'We are all well.' He gestures to the needlework that lies untouched in her lap. 'And you? You seem to be thriving here.'

She looks down at the embroidery with its intricate cross design and fingers it. 'I've enjoyed working on this piece. It's for Máthair Ab, a cloth for the altar here.'

'I'm sure she'll appreciate it and everyone will admire the fine work of the *cailecha* who made it.'

'I'm not a *cailech*.'

'But soon will be.' His eyes flicker for a moment. 'Máthair Gobnait said you wanted to see me.'

'Yes, yes, I did.' She falls silent, searching for the words. 'I'm not certain you know, but Bruinech came here to speak with me not so long ago. She wanted ask something of both you and me. Something we might find difficult to give her.'

'I see. And what is that thing or things she would ask of us?'

She opens her mouth to speak the words but fails. She sighs. 'I'm sure you know how unhappy Bruinech has been. There is no one to blame for this and it appears the children she'd hoped for so long will never come to pass.'

'Yes, I know,' he says in a low voice. 'What would you have me do?'

'Her situation caused her to look for a different path than the one originally chosen for her.' She looks over at him. 'She would like to come here and join the community. Become a Christian and pledge herself to God.'

'Become a *cailech*, like yourself?'

'Not like me.' She speaks the words without thinking, but realizes they are truer than she first thought. 'No,' she says more slowly. 'Not like me at all. She is certain that she has a real calling, a real place here among the other women.'

'And you are not certain?'

'No. I am a Christian, but am I to practice my faith here, as a *cailech*?'

'No, you aren't going to be a *cailech,* or no. you're not certain about it?'

She gives a weak smile. Colmán was ever the legal representative, clarifying statements and words. 'She would have you grant her a divorce so that she can leave you and come here.'

'A divorce? We spoke about that some time ago and I told her my answer then.'

'She wants you to divorce her in favour of me.'

'You.'

Cuimne nods. 'She won't leave you and become a *cailech* unless you are content and have children in your future. She feels that by marrying me you will have that.'

'And what have you to say to that?' He turns away from her, his expression unreadable.

'She says you love me. Is this true?'

'You haven't answered my question.'

Suddenly she is nervous. 'I-I would need to explain some things. I am a Christian, Colmán, and nothing will change that now. I don't know if I'm able to bear children, so Bruinech may be wrong in that. I would also like to know if there are any other alternatives you would consider.'

'That's an answer I would expect from a legal representative.'

'I would say the same for you. You haven't answered my question, either.'

'But I am a legal representative.'

'Not at this moment. At this moment I would have you be Colmán, son, brother and someone who might want to woo a woman.'

'I'm not my brother.'

'I've never doubted that. And should there be any doubt, I'm not Áine.'

'Well praise the gods for that.'

'Is this your idea of wooing?'

'You might ask Bruinech about that.' He blushes a moment. 'No, don't ask her, please. I was worse then.'

'You mean you behaved worse than this and she still married you?'

He nods. 'But then I made no objection to the ridiculous bride price.'

'There's no bride price for me.'

'I'd pay it, anyway.'

She smiles at him. 'I have no fine gowns either. I left them with Sárnat.'

'You'd seldom find the time to wear them, I would see to that.' He blushes again.

She laughs. 'It is settled then. We will make a match.'

She is glad now they have found ease in each other's company and for the moment she can see herself content in this arrangement. This man makes her feel safe. And there is much to be said for safety. He will support her, but she no longer has to hide behind his strength. She will contribute her own. She looks down along at the row of *beachair* and hears the distant hum of the bees. They have collected their dew and are making the honey and wax. The king bee is busy with his work, ensuring the continuation of the community. Cuimne knows now that these bees work together. They support each other. Each one works hard to ensure the hive remains safe and survives.

GLOSSARY

adaltracht – second wife

aigne –type of lawyer, fulfils some functions of modern judge

aire déso – lord of vassalry

anam cara – soul friend, a confessor

a stor – treasure (form of endearment)

Aon scéal agat – have you any news

ban sídh – woman spirit who foretells death

banóircindeach –formal term for abbess

banríon – queen

bastún – lout

beacha – bees

beachair- hive

Bealtaine – May 1/ month of May

bóaire - prosperous rank of farmer

bothach - cottier

bratacha

brithen –trained lawyer, judge, arbitrator appointed by king for tuath

Buíochas le Dia – thanks be to God

cailech – nun (literally wearing a veil)

cailín – girl

cáin –set of laws

capall –pony/common horse

cern - millstone

cétmuinter – primary wife

coibche – dowry

craic – fun

cráthur -creature (as in 'poor thing')

cumal – highest unit of value in commerce, originally a female slave

derbfine – immediate family including 3 generations

dún – fort
Eóganacht –tribe/race of people
Episcopus Vagans – travelling bishop
Epscop –bishop (ancient form)
Érainn – tribe/race of people
Fáilte arais –welcome back
faithche –sacred surround in monastery
fidchell- board game similar to chess
Fidgenti – tribe/racial group
file- high level of druid/poet
fingal- kin slaying
fuidir – semi-freeman, tenant at will
goba- smiths
léine – shift/under dress
loég- calf (old)
lorica – protection prayer
lubhghorteoir – gardener
Lus na gCnámh mBriste - comfrey
manach – monks
manaigh – monks (pl)or people working on monastery land
Máthair- mother
medcuisec –soured milk drink
mo storín – my treasure
muimme – foster mother
nemed- academy for learning law, poetry, history
ócaire –rank of farmer less prosperous than bóaire
oenach- fair
ráth –fort, earthen rampart
rectaire – steward
seanachaí –story teller
Siúr –sister (nun)
smachta – fine/penalty/recompense

Táinaiste – successor (usually for kings or leaders)
Tech Mor- main house of religious community
termann –sacred area of religious community
Tir na n'óg – mythical land of youth
torc – necklace –gold ring with opening
tuath – people, kingdom
úan- lamb

HISTORICAL NOTE

There are many legends and traditions surrounding St Gobnait who came to Ballyvourney, probably around the late 6th or early 7th century and established a community of women. One legend says that she was descended from Conaire, High King of Ireland. In Kerry it is said that her father was a pirate and that she came ashore in Fionntráigh. An angel came to her and told her to travel until she saw 'nine white deer grazing together,' and that would be the place of her resurrection. Her travels took her many places in Munster and eventually she made her way to Borneach (Ballyvourney) and saw nine white deer grazing at Gort na Tiobratan. There she built her community and installed her bee hives. The bishop, St Abán, was her contemporary and some legends have it that he set aside the land for her to begin her community.

During the course of her life in Gort na Tiobratan, St Gobnait became known for her healing, using the honey the bees produced. She also performed many miracles, including sending a swarm of bees after cattle rustlers, throwing a bulla or heavy ball to raze a stone structure built by intruders, and catching the *gadai dubh,* the dark robber who tried to steal her horse and the stone mason's tools (his image is inscribed on a stone in the church ruins at St Gobnait's shrine).

Many of the religious communities of women in Ireland disappeared after the death of the founder, because the founder usually established the community on her own land which would revert to her kin at her death. St Gobnait's community was established independently of any kinship ties and the community continued after her death, but it is uncertain how long. The Synod of Kells, which met in 1152 and ratified the various bishopric sees and reorganised parishes, records a Romanesque church being built there at this time. The present ruin was built in the late Medieval period. During the Reformation the area was left undisturbed. Pope Clement VIII, in 1601, granted a 'special indulgence' of ten years and quarantines to the faithful who would visit the church on her feast day, February 11th. Later, a Protestant Church was built next to it.

St Gobnait's shrine is still a place many come to say prayers for healing and complete the 'pattern' or 'rounds', a series of prayers said at specific places. The rounds are also said on her feast day and on Whitsunday. The area includes the church, the well, and her burial site. There is also a twenty-seven inch 13th century wooden statue kept in the Sacristy of the Ballyvourney Parish Church which is brought out on her feast day and on Whitsunday.

In telling this story I tried to keep faithful to the legends surrounding St Gobnait, but also to keep faithful to the time period in which she lived. I researched and talked to many historians. I also read and discussed the oral history with many of the local people and historians. The time period was one of great change where the old power structures of the pre-Christian faith were being supplanted by the Christian faith. There was some tension between the two groups and also some accommodation. The Brehon laws were being written down slowly at this time period and some of the Christian elements challenged age old custom. But it is through these written laws that some of the peculiar aspects of the ancient customs can be seen and life of the early medieval communities can be discovered.

ACKNOWLEDGEMENTS

I owe a great debt to many people who helped me make this book a better reflection of the time period and a clearer picture of St Gobnait. Thanks go to Lisa Bitel, scholar and woman's historian for her great recommendations, Dáibhi Ó Chróinín, for his gracious help and recommendations, Áine Uí Chuíll for her help with the Irish, Peadar Ó Ríada, for his insights on bees and loan of the *Bechbretha,* Peadar and Eibhlín Ó Cheallaigh for the historical assistance, and Donal Healy for his lecture on St Gobnait.

I also want to thank my group of readers including Tim, Julia, Jean, Jane and Fan and also my editor, Jessica Knauss, and Jane Dixon-Smith for her wonderful cover design. Thanks also go to The Corning Museum of Glass for giving permission to use for the book's cover the image of Harry Clarke's goache design of St Gobnait for the stained glass window of Honan Chapel.

.

AUTHOR'S NOTE

Originally from Philadelphia, Kristin Gleeson lives in Ireland, in the West Cork Gaeltacht, where she teaches art classes, plays harp, sings in a choir and runs two book clubs for the village library. She holds a Masters in Library Science and a Ph.D. in history and for a time was an administrator of a national denominational archives, library and museum in America. She also served as a public librarian in America and in Ireland.

If you have enjoyed this book please post a review on Amazon. It helps so much towards getting the book noticed.

If you go to the author website and join the mailing list to receive news of forthcoming releases, special offers and events you'll receive A Treasure Beyond Worth, a FREE prequel novella to Along the Far Shores. .

www.kristingleeson.com

Printed in Great Britain
by Amazon